CHANGE   M LINE

Change and the Bottom Line

Alan Warner

Gower

Published 1995 in hardback by Gower Publishing

Paperback edition published 1997 by
Gower Publishing Limited
Gower House
Croft Road
Aldershot
Hampshire GU11 3HR
England

Gower
Old Post Road
Brookfield
Vermont 05036
USA

Alan Warner has asserted his right under the Copyright, Designs and Patents Act 1988 to be identified as the author of this work.

British Library Cataloguing in Publication Data
Warner, Alan
  Change and the Bottom Line
  I. Title
  658.1511
  ISBN 0–566–07560–1 Hbk
      0–566–08010–9 Pbk

Library of Congress Cataloging-in-Publication Data
Warner, Alan, 1942–
  Change and the bottom line / Alan Warner.
    p. cm.
    ISBN 0–566–07560–1
    1. Organizational change–Management–Case studies. I. Title.
  HD58.8.W374 1995   94–46134
  658.4′06—dc20   CIP

Typeset in Great Britain by Bournemouth Colour Graphics, Parkstone, Dorset and printed in Great Britain by Biddles Ltd, Guildford.

Preface

This book is a sequel, in storyline terms, to my previous two books on financial topics – *The Bottom Line* and *Beyond the Bottom Line*.

Colleagues suggest that it is driven by two factors. Firstly my desire to complete a 'Philip Moorley Trilogy', secondly my obsession with the romantic encounters of the two leading characters!

Whether or not these are my subconscious drivers, my conscious reason is a strong belief in the novel as a vehicle for achieving user-friendly management learning. I saw no reason to restrict the benefits to financial topics and all it needed was the willingness of colleagues to support me in the development of the 'technical' content. And, of course, a publisher who believed that a book of this kind on managing change would meet a market need. I hope that all of us are right and that the book will help readers to learn more about a highly topical subject in an enjoyable and practical way.

Guidance for the reader

This book is not intended to stand on its own as a novel, nor as a text book. It is intended more as a case study in change management from which readers can draw out learning and consider its relevance to their own situations.

As the 'novel' format does not always allow for full discussion of issues or the balanced presentation of alternative viewpoints, the Commentary at the back of the book (pages 197 to 219) is designed to fill these gaps and also to reinforce key learning points. I recommend readers to refer to the Commentary after reading each chapter.

Alan Warner

Summary of Content

about the dominance of the family members, both in terms of their personal influence and their place in the organisation structure. Some information about the company's business situation. PM tries to avoid being controlled by the family members and has difficulty in achieving this while still keeping good relationships with them.

9   After three weeks in the job PM returns home   50
and, over the weekend, meets the non-executive Director and Alan Angus. He reveals his frustration with the attitude of the family directors who are not being supportive and are restricting the potential contributions of their managers.

His discussions with Angus cover the following topics:
- more on the different ways of changing culture;
- the change cycle as a framework for managing change as a total process;
- the need to analyse the current situation before rushing into premature action;
- the importance of creating and communicating the vision;
- anticipating the consequences for the key players;
- identifying the winners and the losers and anticipating their attitude to change;
- the need to educate and involve the key influencers;
- how to remove barriers to change;
- defining outputs and setting targets;
- overcoming resistance;
- reinforcing new behaviours;
- evaluating and reassessing the achievement of the vision.

This chapter provides a framework for the remainder of the story by setting out the complete change cycle. It ends with PM being

reminded to look at strengths as well as
weaknesses when dealing with the family
members.
Alan Angus also suggests the requirements of a
good vision statement for PM to work on.

10 PM attends his first Board meeting and is not   67
impressed by the way the meeting is managed.
Afterwards he meets the family members on a
one-to-one basis and finds out more about their
fears and motivations. Key learning points are:
- how much more effective communication
  can be if people are in a private one-to-one
  situation;
- how you need to understand the personal
  situation of the key influencers if you are to
  understand resistance;
- how showing interest and concern will help
  to gain commitment to change.

PM also produces his first draft vision
statement after getting some further advice.

11 Alan Angus visits PM and encourages him to   81
review the organisation structure according to
business processes in order to remove some of
the barriers to change.
Key learning points are:
- how focus on processes can help you to see
  the organisation in a different way;
- the arguments for changing the structure to
  match the processes;
- further discussion of the arguments for and
  against changing people and their positions
  as part of the change process.

12 PM comes up against an unexpected barrier to   94
change in the resistance of the Chairman to
reduction of his power. This is because of
failure to consider his needs and the initial
response does not solve the problem. Key
learning points are:
- the need to consider the motivations of all
  the key influencers, however senior;

and he sets out to apply the principles he heard on the course, ie:
- the importance of listening and empathising;
- the need to understand the aspirations and motivations of all key players, not just those who are easy to deal with;
- the need to tailor the approach to each individual and to give maximum possible reassurance and certainty.

PM also decides to visit the factory in order to assess how far others are suffering from similar uncertainty. He finds out that not everyone is as fully informed as he would have hoped. The key learning point is the need to provide checks that communications are going down through the organisation in a consistent way and to fill any gaps if necessary.

19 There is a review of the effectiveness of the training at which the following points are highlighted: 169
- the need to link training programmes to the change process by the establishment of clear and related objectives;
- the difficulty of measuring outcomes but the importance of trying to do so as much as possible;
- linking training to the various stages of the change cycle;
- the use of training to overcome resistance and reinforce new behaviours; also the benefits of having training early on in the change process:
- the need for reinforcement after training has taken place,
- planning a structure of communications to pass the messages down, and
- the Chief Executive's involvement in this process.

20 Nine months later the change process is well 181

under way. This chapter illustrates the completion of the change cycle by a review process and a reassessment of the vision. The change process has been held back to some extent by the inability of family members to adapt to the required empowering style of management and this remains a challenge for the future.

PM hears of a new change process which is soon to begin – the flotation of Weetflakes as a public company – and wonders if this is feasible from both a personal and company point of view.

Chapter 1

I'm sitting behind my desk, the large desk which symbolised my power as President of Chapman Foods, one of New Jersey's biggest food producers and part of the powerful ABT group. But twenty minutes ago everything changed. All the power disappeared with these fateful words.

"I'm sorry Phil, but we're going to have to let you go."

The words came from Matt Talbot, Director of ABT and my boss for these last five wonderful years of success at Chapmans. Five minutes later I was still shaking, still sweating, still finding it hard to do anything but listen to Matt's explanation of why my American dream is over. He sat opposite me, on the other side of the desk, leaning forward awkwardly. I got the impression that he was not enjoying this either because, after a difficult start, we've been pretty close these last five years and we've come a long way together.

At last I managed to find a few words which began to express my hurt, my surprise, my indignation.

"But Matt," I said, "Chapmans have done so well, we've turned them round completely and, even by ABT's standards, we're making great returns. Sales and profits have been up every year."

"I know pal," replied Matt, his eyes unable to meet mine, "but that's not the point. It's ABT's personnel policy. They've decided they've got to make openings for the younger managers to come through. You'll get a good package, Phil – we treat our redundant managers very well."

Redundant! Somehow it's a word I associate with other people, not with me. It never even crossed my mind that it would ever apply to me with my track record of success but now, at the age of 52, it has. And here I am, in America during the worst recession of modern times, out of a job with a wife and three children to support.

Twenty minutes after Matt left, I sit staring at my office wall and the main thing on my mind is – how do I tell Jean and the children? They all love it out here in the States – Angela and Mark, now 17 and 15, are just like American teenagers and little Susie was born out here only three years ago. How can I tell them that their father, their symbol of status and reliability, is going to be unemployed? How will they take to the idea of returning to the UK where prospects for middle-aged unemployed executives are hardly more favourable? Though why am I assuming I'll go back to the UK? After all, I've been headhunted by other food companies enough times these last few years – if only I'd listened to them.

I'm brought back to present day problems by Karen, my secretary, who brings me an iced tea and enquires routinely about my meeting with Matt.

"Just fine," I say, realising that this lie is only delaying the inevitable, but also thinking that I must plan carefully how I'm going to break the news. Matt and I agreed that I would go at the end of the month, in ten days' time. The offer of two years' salary free of tax is conditional on a friendly and supportive handover to my nominated successor, Bob Palmer. I know Palmer well from when he was part of the internal audit team which started Chapmans on the road to profit improvement, soon after we became part of ABT and I became President.

I also remember his partner in the audit – Steve O'Rourke – who was destined to play a significant part in my life, by taking away and marrying the woman who was my VP Finance and also my mistress. Despite the success of my re-built relationship with Jean and the joy of having Susie – the late surprise arrival to our family – I still haven't been able to shake off the feeling of emptiness which Christine's return to the UK left me with. In my business and my personal life, there just hasn't been the same spark and excitement. I haven't seen her since – only an exchange of Christmas cards and a telephone conversation a couple of years ago. I confess that I was selfishly disappointed to hear how successfully her management training venture was going at the time and it was with unforgiveable pleasure that I recently heard a rumour that her business partnership had split up amid much acrimony. I also heard that her marriage was going through rough times too.

As I start to make notes about whom I will tell and when, I speculate about how she is and whether this traumatic change in my life might propel to me to see Christine Goodhart – Christine O'Rourke – yet again.

Chapter 2

I'm sitting in the opulent reception area of Woodall, Tennent, Executive Placement Consultants – the firm who "headhunted" me several times during the five years I was President of Chapmans. I look across at three guys who are also waiting on the other side of the smoked glass tables which are the centrepiece of the waiting area. I'm struck by their youth – they all seem about twenty years younger than me – and this reinforces my growing concern about my predicament.

I think back over these last two weeks and the sadness of my last days at Chapmans. I remember how many times I had to break the news to people who were close to me. How carefully I had to choose those fateful first words and how I had to organise the order, timing and method of communication to people inside and outside the business.

I also remember how much I was able to tell about people from the way they responded to the news and how this was often surprising. There were two main categories – those who thought about the impact it would have on me and those who thought about the impact on themselves.

After desperately agonising about the right way of breaking it to Jean that first evening after my meeting with Talbot, I found it surprisingly easy. She knew something was wrong as soon as she saw me and I asked her to come into my study, so I could tell her without the children being around. Before she'd even sat down she knew and, of course, she was in the first category – one of those who thought about me rather than herself. While I had been worrying about her having less money to spend on herself and the house, she could only think about the injustice of ABT's treatment of me and the blow to my pride.

When we told the older children later that evening, they were rather less altruistic, wanting to know if it meant we'd have to move, even return to the UK – a nightmare prospect for both of them. Little Susie didn't really understand, of course, and seemed encouraged by the idea of seeing a little more of Daddy. Though I love my little girl, this thought still fills me with dread – being at home with nothing to do but play with the kids. Quality time is what they call it over here, but it's not the same quality if it's all the time.

As I stop thinking back for a moment, I notice that the three young men have all been called for their interviews. Are they like me – unemployed – or are they being headhunted? I know that Woodall, Tennent normally only undertake headhunting for companies and do not take individuals like me as clients. But Gerard Woodall, their Senior Partner, agreed to see me in view of my past seniority and my previous contact with him when filling senior positions at Chapmans.

Again my mind drifts back to the last two weeks and the way the news was received by my management team. Perhaps the most gratifying response of all was from Al Morton, my VP Sales, whom I picked for that job, even though all his previous experience had been in Personnel. He didn't think of the impact on him personally, but he did think of the impact on the business.

"Phil, they can't do this," he said, "you're the one who's made Chapmans what it is. They must be crazy – giving someone like you away to one of our competitors."

Comments like this were quite common – everyone seemed to assume that I would walk into another Board position with one of the competition. Jane, my Marketing Director at Chapmans and another protégé whom I promoted when I became President, even asked me to take her with me. Much as I valued Jane and felt touched by her loyalty, I also suspected that this was more to do with her own insecurity. How would she get on with the new man? Would he be as willing to accept Jane's lack of strategic insight which, I believed, was more than made up for by her amazing energy?

As I continue to wait for my interview – over 20 minutes now – I think about my financial position. Half a million dollars after tax would seem a fortune to most people and it certainly means I don't have to take hasty action. But living off the interest wouldn't fund our current lifestyle and I want to be sure of what I'm going to do before I start to dip into the capital.

The receptionist answers the phone on her desk and then asks me to go through to see Gerard Woodall. I walk in to find him sitting by another smoked glass table, at one side of his enormous office. His secretary is there and she pours me iced tea.

I sense that Woodall is uneasy and I get none of the social chat with which he has always started meetings before. But then, of course, I was the client. He was providing the service. Now I'm not sure what the relationship is and, I suspect, neither is he.

"Phil," he says, "I hope you don't mind my coming straight to the point, I've only got half an hour."

I think to myself that this is because he's kept me waiting 20 minutes but, of course, I don't say so. I look at him expectantly, feeling like an office boy looking for his first job. I notice that Woodall, a neat little man usually full of confidence and charm, is sweating a little. I realise that this is as awkward for him as it is for me.

"That's fine Gerard," I say, "I only expected half an hour and only as a personal favour. I realise you don't normally deal with individuals but I would like your advice please – I know there's no one better placed to give it."

Gerard pauses, as if bracing himself to give me unpleasant news, and then proceeds to confirm my worst fears.

"Phil," he says, "I've known you for some time now and I've a great respect for you so I'll give it to you straight. I can't be optimistic about your finding something at the level or the status which you've been used to. Or even at a lower level, come to that. Companies are very reluctant to take on someone who has to come down in status."

I shuffle in my seat, beginning to feel uncomfortable, wishing I could be out of this room, out of New York, out of the USA. I think that maybe I'm like a little child who wants to go home because things are going wrong. I feel sweat rolling down my own forehead now and hope that Gerard doesn't notice. He doesn't seem to because he carries on painting his dismal picture.

"I've never known the job market in a worse state, Phil. This recession is having a far bigger impact than the ones in the seventies and eighties. And there are many more in your position. Companies like ABT are coping with the lack of growth and the reduced mobility of staff by retiring anyone over 50. So it's no disgrace to be in your position but that doesn't help you to get another post. I'll be frank Phil, I think you'd be better off back in the UK."

"What makes you think it would be any better there, Gerard? They've got a recession too you know."

"I know Phil, but they're coming out of it earlier. I spoke to one of our associates over there and he says that US experience is something that could give you an edge. Though obviously there'd be no guarantees."

I know in my heart that he's right and that he's doing me a favour by being so frank, but something inside makes me want to argue, however fruitless it may be. Somehow I find it hard to accept that I won't be able to find a job out here, being aware of the competitiveness of the food business and the experience I have to offer.

"OK Gerard," I say, "you understand the market better than anyone and I'm grateful to you for being so frank. But I find this hard to reconcile with the fact that your guys have approached me at least four times during the last three years about CEO positions with other food companies. And of course, like a fool, I turned them down."

Gerard turns to face me with a look which sums up his sadness and his embarrassment.

"That was before the worst of the recession Phil, and that was when you were still employed. I know it's unfair but the perception of your worth goes down when another company has let you go – I'm sure you used to feel the same when you were recruiting. And there's another thing which people tend to forget, Phil."

He gets up and walks to the window, preparing to shatter another of my illusions. He looks out at the skyline of Manhattan and then turns to face me again.

"It's great for the ego when a headhunter approaches you Phil, and we tend to use the weapon of flattery to get people to see us. But people assume that an approach from us means that they're going to be offered the job. We usually headhunt to arrive at a shortlist, just like we have done for you. You might have got one of those jobs but you'd have been one of several in contention. And, as I said, there are very few jobs at that level around now anyway."

I leave as soon as I can respectably do so, feeling humiliated and disillusioned. As I walk down Madison Avenue, I look up at the skyscrapers bearing down on me and suddenly I want to be back in England. I decide at that moment that I'm going home for good.

Chapter 3

It's four months later, in the middle of the British winter which seems to be much longer, colder and more miserable than it was when I lived here before. I'm sitting in the living room of the house we're renting in Wimbledon, conveniently close to London for the job interviews I thought I would be going to.

Though the house, a three-storey Victorian semi-detached, is far more comfortable than anything I would have had before I went to the States, it now seems poky and claustrophobic compared to what we became used to over there. I didn't expect a swimming pool but I thought that my limit of £1,500 per month might have been enough for something more spacious.

Life has not been easy since we arrived back. Jean has been fine – supportive and loving, enjoying being back with her family and friends. It's me and the children who are suffering. My job hunting has been even more depressing than I feared – the only interviews I am offered are with recruitment consultants and I can't help feeling an awful indignity as smooth young men, twenty years my junior, tell me time after time how tough the job market is.

The children have found it very hard to settle down. Angela has gone into the sixth form at the local comprehensive but is finding the transition from US to UK methods very tough. Already we're wondering whether to put her into private school or abandon any idea of her taking

A levels next year.

Mark is at the same school and is finding the work much easier, so we think he'll have no problems with his GCSEs. But his problem is a teenage rebelliousness which has become much worse since he left the USA. He loved it out there and was bitter about having to leave. I can understand and forgive that, but his surly manner makes both Jean and me increasingly short of patience. He also seems to be having problems relating to others of his age and is teased about his American way of speaking and thinking.

Life's a bitch, I think. 52 years old, no qualifications, on the scrapheap. I should have seen it coming. I've achieved far more than I ever dreamed of through being in the right place at the right time, working hard and being helped by others. But now it all counts for nothing.

Suddenly the phone rings and I answer it quickly. I know it's probably Jean's mother ringing yet again but I cling to the hope that, just for once, it might be about a job.

"Mr Moorley?" says a smooth voice, "this is Andrew Kent of Selection International. We met last week if you remember."

I do vaguely remember but it could have been any one of about seven who all looked much the same and all had names like Andrew Kent.

"I'm ringing about a really good opportunity which I think could be just what you're looking for. It's a Chief Executive position for a food manufacturer."

"Tell me more," I say. I try not to be too excited because I remember what Gerard Woodall said when I saw him in New York. People are headhunted for shortlists, not for jobs.

"Well it's Weetflakes, the breakfast cereals manufacturer. The present Chief Executive suddenly resigned last week and they need someone quickly. The Board thought that your CV was most impressive and they want to see you as soon as possible."

I think about Weetflakes. They're a household name but I can't remember where they're based. A vague memory tells me that it's somewhere a long way off. I ask Andrew Kent where I need to go for the interview.

"It's halfway between Scunthorpe and Grimsby," he says.

"In a village called Claydon. Is that a problem?"

"Of course not," I say, though I feel less confident about this than I sound. How would Jean and the children face being so far away? Scunthorpe and Grimsby! Couldn't be much more in the sticks. And even colder, I'm quite sure.

But I betray no sign of this as I agree to meet Kent early in the morning in two days' time. He says that he will drive me up to Weetflakes and will brief me further on the way. I find this a bit surprising but I guess I'm not very aware of normal practice among headhunters these days.

When Jean arrives home I try not to sound too optimistic – I don't want to build up hopes. But I test her about the prospects of moving so far away from family and friends. I'm surprised to find that she's attracted by the idea; already she's finding the proximity of her parents rather stifling after the freedom of the USA. She also points out something which had not occurred to me – the likelihood of much lower property prices and the chance to buy something larger.

As I expected, the children are less enthusiastic. Jean tells them before I can stop her and, when I stress that things are at an early stage, she says: "I know darling, but I have one of my feelings that you're going to get this job."

Sometimes it would be better if Jean had less faith in me, but her instinct gives me confidence. She usually is right when she has this kind of intuition and I feel the same way.

Mark gives me a look of contempt and mutters something rude about Scunthorpe as he stalks away from the dinner table and seeks refuge in the heavy metal music which soon starts to resound from his room. I wish he didn't make me feel so guilty about losing my job.

Angela is much more mature about things and seems quite pleased, but I notice that it's only after Jean speaks to her in the kitchen that she comes to me and says:

"I do hope this one works out, Dad. I don't mind where we go, honestly." The 'honestly' doesn't sound too sincere but I'm grateful that she's trying to be supportive.

"Thanks love," I say, "but it's very likely that nothing will come of it. There'll almost certainly be a short list. I'm just sorry there's so much uncertainty for you – you'll just be settled into one school and you'll probably have to move."

Jean then tries to look on the bright side by suggesting that country areas are likely to have good, traditional education systems. Mark is just passing through the room on his way out.

"There'll be even bigger bozos than the ones we've got here," he says, "country hicks – that's what they'll be."

He walks out and slams the door. I try on occasions like this to remember what it was like when I was separated from Jean and had to live away from my children. But, at this moment, I find it hard to do anything but long for the peace and quiet it gave me, particularly as heavy metal and door slamming has now awakened little Susie. She begins to cry in that persistent way which you know is not going to stop quickly.

Jean stands up to go to her and I'm reminded that being away from the children also meant being away from her. After all the troubled times we've been through because of my workaholism and womanising, I now need her as never before. I tell myself that I must never, ever, forget how good she's been to me these last few months.

Chapter 4

"I wanted to drive you up here Phil, so I can brief you on the way. I didn't want you to go in there without knowing what you could be walking into."

It's two days later and we're just joining the North Circular Road on our way to pick up the A1 North. I note the time so I can have some idea of the journey time.

It's Andrew Kent who is doing all the talking and the driving too. He puts the fear of God into me as he turns out to be one of those people who keeps looking at you while driving. Also I still find the high speeds rather dangerous after all those years of sedate 55/65 mph in the States.

"I'll be honest. One reason I thought of you for this job is because you need it very badly as well as being more than qualified for it. But it's not an easy situation and, if you take the job, you'll be their fourth Managing Director in three years. And the other three resigned because they found it impossible to achieve the change that is necessary."

I ought to be put off, but it's amazing what unemployment can do for one's selectivity. Instead I'm relieved and delighted that there doesn't seem to be a short list. I ask him about this and he says:

"No, Phil. Word has got around among likely candidates in other food companies and not everyone wants to live between Scunthorpe and Grimsby. And you are more than qualified – your Universal and ABT experience puts you head and shoulders above anyone else we could find. And though it may surprise you, your age is on your side. The three previous MDs were in their thirties and, frankly, I think it needs experience to cope with the Stocks family."

I ask him to tell me more and, as he puts his foot down and I feel the BMW 535 surge forward, he gives me the full story. It continues for about 50 miles, until we stop for a coffee at a Little Chef just before Peterborough.

Apparently Weetflakes was founded by the late Wilfred Stocks between the two world wars. Wilfred hit upon a new idea in breakfast food – large round balls of cereal with a unique taste and very good health-giving properties. I knew already of its well known brand – one which truly could be called a household name. I used to have them for breakfast as a child and my mother used to insist that we ate them with warm milk in the winter. They were always being advertised on television, though I cannot recall seeing them since I came back from the USA.

Andrew pulls no punches as he tells me about their present situation:

"The problem is, Phil, that they're being run in exactly the same way as they were in their heyday after the war. The Stocks family, and the various people who have married into it, control nearly all the top positions and it was only after pressure from their merchant bank that they agreed to appoint an outside MD. And it's quite clear that most of them don't want anyone from outside in that role. That's what's driven the other MDs to resign in frustration."

"Is it a plc?" I ask, thinking as I say it that I ought to have found that out before.

"No Phil, it's family owned, but four years ago Hill Benson, their merchant bank, took a 30 per cent stake so that some of the family could realise cash. That's why they were able to influence the MD appointment, though it's changed nothing at all so far."

"So who are the key players?" I ask.

"Well, there's Arthur the Chairman, by far the most influential and the biggest backwoodsman of them all, so I hear. Arthur is Wilfred's only son so naturally he has a special place in the business. He was both Chairman and MD before the new appointment was made.

"Then there's Arthur's son Willis who is Marketing Director, and his nephew Freddie who is Production. There's also two of Arthur's sons-in-law who are in charge of Research and Sales. Have I missed any of the functions?"

"Finance? Personnel?" I enquire.

"Oh yes, of course. They don't have a Finance Director, just a Chief Accountant and he works very closely with Arthur. Arthur has always taken a very close interest in the financial side, I think he may even have been an accountant himself at one time. Personnel? I don't know. I was approached by Arthur direct. I think I recall seeing a Personnel Officer but she was fairly junior – dealing with non-management recruitment and personnel records, that sort of thing."

"OK Andrew, so the mission impossible is to change an organisation controlled by people who don't want to change. But surely, if there are obvious problems, don't the family see the need to change?"

"They certainly see the financial results declining. They realise that it is becoming increasingly difficult to compete with Kelloggs and the other big boys, particularly when they are so dependent on one product. But they are a very strange lot – amazingly negative. They can't think of what to do but they are superb at finding reasons why ideas will not work. 'We've tried it before' or 'that would never be acceptable' are typical comments. They even do it to each other as well as to ideas from outside. So you get total paralysis in decision making."

"So the previous MDs just got fed up with the inertia?"

"Well, they tried to break it. They were pretty dynamic and assertive characters. But when they tried to push change through the system – like new distribution methods or product development – it got blocked at the implementation stage."

After our stop for coffee, there's now a period of silence as the A1 runs into the M18 and we are soon on the M180 to Humberside. I begin to warm to the challenge while not underestimating the extent of it. I also realise that it's likely to be impossible on my own – in the midst of all the Stocks family – and it could be a good idea to insist on authority to recruit new people if necessary. From what Andrew was saying, I should be in a strong position to dictate terms. I'm over-qualified for the job and they are desperate to find someone who has not been put off by the casualty list of previous appointments.

"Your fax said that I'll be seeing Arthur and the Director representing Hill Benson, Andrew," I say. "Will I see them together or separately?"

"It's been together for the other interviews so I would imagine that will continue," he replies.

"What about the relationship between them?" I ask.

"Chalk and cheese best describes it," says Andrew. "Martin Egerton is quite young, a typical high flying merchant banker – public school, Oxbridge, straight into the City. Arthur Stocks left grammar school at 16 to work in the family business and became a professional north-countryman. Loves to call a spade a spade and to tell you he's doing it."

"Is he bright?" I ask.

"Oh yes. That's one thing they have in common, Phil. People can underestimate Arthur – he is very shrewd and you must remember that."

"But what about the balance of power between Egerton and Arthur?" I ask.

"I think Egerton is at least as influential in the decision. Hill Benson hold 30 per cent and they're getting pretty impatient about what has happened. So are some of the family who don't work in the business. It's in both their interests to appoint someone who will stay and Arthur will find it hard to say no if Egerton thinks you're the right person."

"Will he agree to my bringing more outsiders in?" I ask. "Maybe that was the mistake the others made. Were they on their own?"

"Yes. Or at least certainly the last one was. There have been very few outsiders appointed as far as I know. Why do you think that's so important Phil?"

"Because I don't overestimate my own abilities, Andrew. I'm no management genius or magic turnaround man. Where I've had success, it's been because I've had some good people around me who shared the same values and the same vision. Now maybe I could find people like that at Weetflakes but I'd like to have the option to bring in one or two from outside. And, from what you've told me, finance and personnel sound like the obvious gaps. I'm not naive enough to think I could easily shift the Stocks family from their present positions."

As we continue on the M180 and I see a sign saying Claydon 10 miles, I think back to my career, in particular to the way I've been helped by the flair of those I've been lucky enough to have working for me. First and by far the most important was Christine Goodhart, a beautiful and talented accountant who changed my life in many ways and who, in my two Chief Executive jobs, gave me the financial knowledge and confidence which revived my flagging career.

More recently two young men whom I promoted, Al Morton and Mike McDivett, have been the real reasons for my success in the USA after Christine left to return to England. Al was a personnel man turned Sales Manager; Mike a brilliant marketeer whom I appointed Product Development Manager and who revolutionised Chapman's product range. I feel vulnerable at the thought of this kind of challenge without the support of people I trust, and I feel I need to insist on bringing in my own people. I fantasise about bringing Christine, Al and Mike in as my management team, but realise that my influencing skills would be unlikely to persuade them all to move to a village between Grimsby and Scunthorpe.

Nevertheless this does not stop me continuing to daydream as Andrew Kent drives along in silence. I am awakened from my fantasies as we enter the village of Claydon and, almost immediately, we see the enormous sign that signifies the entrance to the Weetflakes factory.

The Weetflakes logo covers the whole of the roof of the factory building and it brings back memories of the packet on our family breakfast table forty years ago. Perhaps the unchanging logo is a symbol of how things have failed to move with the times. I guess I'm going to find out pretty soon.

Chapter 5

Ten minutes later I am shown into Arthur Stocks' office by a very pleasant north country lady who appears to be his secretary. Andrew Kent is apparently not going to be present so I am seeing Arthur and Martin Egerton on my own.

I'm rather surprised to find only one person in the room when I enter and I immediately realise that this can only be Arthur Stocks. He is tall, overweight, exuding confidence and presence. It it wasn't for the cheap cut of his clothes and his northern accent, you might take him for the Chairman of any large plc. He has a ruddy, weatherbeaten complexion, crinkly white hair and, I'm surprised to find, a very friendly manner.

"Welcome Philip," he says walking towards me from the back of his spacious office. "I'm Arthur Stocks, the Chairman of Weetflakes. I'm pleased to get to know you."

We shake hands and I say something appropriate in return. I decide I'll take the initiative by asking where Martin Egerton is.

"He's on his way, Philip. We had a message that he'll be here shortly. But it's a good chance for us to talk privately. I was really impressed with your record, lad, and pleased that you're interested."

I want to interrupt and say that, at 52, I may be a few years younger than him but I'm hardly a lad. But Arthur doesn't want to be interrupted, he wants to talk – at length. About his late father, about the history of Weetflakes, about his family, about the pride he has in what has been built. I find it quite endearing and amusing as I sit nodding from time to time, realising that this is probably all I have to do to be offered the job.

After about ten minutes he seems to realise that he should do more than talk at me and suddenly says, "Well Philip, what would you like to know?"

I know I should probably ask something about the company which will start him on another monologue, but I don't. He's irritated me and I can't help wanting to stop him in his tracks.

"Why have three Managing Directors left in three years?" I say.

I expect him to prevaricate or to go into some rambling self-justification, but he doesn't.

"You're very direct Philip. I like that. We're going to get on well, I can see. Why did they leave?" He walks round from behind his desk and sits on a chair beside me. He looks me straight in the eye.

"Because they tried to change too much too quickly, Philip. They would probably tell you that it was me and the others who wouldn't change. That's not true. We accepted that change was necessary but they didn't manage it well."

"Where did they go wrong then?"

"It happened differently for all three but the underlying problem was the same in each case. They had plans, pretty good plans some of them and they consulted me about what they wanted to do – that was fine. But they never asked me about the way it should be done and the time it should take. They thought they knew it all but they didn't know about Weetflakes, about what makes the people who work here tick . . ."

Just as I'm getting interested and beginning to wonder if I'd been misled by Andrew Kent's description and my initial impression of Arthur Stocks, the door opens and Martin Egerton enters, breathless and apologetic.

"Arthur," he says, "I'm sorry I'm late. You must be Philip Moorley. Martin Egerton."

Martin is tall, handsome, elegantly dressed, well spoken – an example of the husband which most middle class mothers want their daughters to find. I like him immediately – he has a friendly look and an open demeanour which makes you want to trust him.

Arthur suggests we adjourn to the boardroom down the corridor. As we enter, I see Arthur's portrait on the wall next to one which has to be Wilfred, the founder. The same aggressive look and piercing eyes are enough to tell me that he is Arthur's father.

The balance of power between Martin and Arthur is interesting to observe as the interview progresses. They are polite to each other in an exaggerated way and they each ask me questions, but there is no doubt in my mind where the power lies. To the superficial observer it might seem to be with Arthur. To anyone who understands subtle undertones, it is clearly with Martin Egerton. He is the one who changes the orientation of the interview on several occasions and thus controls the agenda. Several times he qualifies what Arthur says and then adds "Isn't that right Arthur?" Each time Arthur meekly acquiesces. I begin to realise that Arthur Stocks may be as shrewd as Andrew Kent says, but he seems to be a paper tiger. I even begin to feel sorry for him. Also a certain amount of puzzlement – with people like Arthur around, why couldn't the three previous MDs bring about the change they wanted?

After about half an hour, the interview seems to be going my way and they are both beginning to talk as if I already have the job. Martin asks me if I have any questions and, with my confidence rising, I reply.

"Yes gentlemen, I have two."

"The first?"

"If I decide I would like to appoint one or two people of my own choice at top level, will this be a problem?"

I see Arthur shifting uncomfortably in his seat and I notice that Martin makes no attempt to reply. He merely says, "And the second question?"

"It's really a continuation of the conversation I was having with you Arthur, before Martin arrived. Why did three able Managing Directors with track records at least as good as mine, leave in frustration at being unable to bring about change. What was the real problem?"

Martin Egerton looks at Arthur Stocks, sitting by his side at the boardroom table. "You answer the first question Arthur, I'll answer the second."

Arthur looks across the table at me and asks, "How important is it to you, this request to bring outsiders in?"

"I don't know until I've met the management team whether it will be necessary, but I won't take the job if you say it's not possible. So that makes it pretty important, I guess."

I notice how Arthur loses his superficial confidence at this challenge and I realise how easy he is going to be to handle. He will always be ready to back off from anyone who is prepared to challenge him. I suspect it doesn't happen very often at present.

"Philip," he says, "I like you very much and I want you to have this job. You're open and you're tough – I like that in a man. You can bring in some managers from outside if you want to, but remember one thing."

I wait for him to carry on. I can see that he is emotional and is having some difficulty in saying what he thinks.

"The people here are family to me. Some are real family and some have married into the Stocks family, but that's not what I mean. Everyone who works here feels like my family. You will be authorised to do what you think is right for the business but you must remember what I've said. You must treat people fairly, otherwise we won't get on as I would like us to."

I think for a moment about what he's said. I decide to repeat it back to him so I can be sure that he and Martin have no doubt.

"What's right for the business and treat people fairly, as you would your own family. I'm happy to go along with those guiding principles when deciding whether new appointments are necessary and for any other decision, come to that."

There's an awkward silence. I decide to exert my growing control over the interview by breaking it.

"My second question, Martin. You were going to tell me why the three previous MDs couldn't bring about the change that was required."

"Yes." I can see that he's a little uncertain. "You said you'd spoken to Arthur about this. He's much closer to it than me. Tell me what you already know and I'll expand on it."

I once again admire Martin's adept handling of the interview. I look at Arthur and say, "Correct me if I'm wrong please Arthur, but I understand that they all tried to change things too quickly, without understanding the culture, without thinking about the inbuilt resistance to change that is there in a business with a history like this one."

"I think that sums it up well, Philip," says Martin. "Don't think that the support from the Board wasn't there. We had firms of consultants to produce strategic plans that made a lot of sense and still do. You must take the most recent one with you when you leave. But every attempt to do the things that are necessary seems to have become bogged down at the implementation stage. No one person seems to have been responsible – just a general resistance to change which no one could put a finger on."

"If you want my opinion, Philip," adds Arthur, "it's that the MDs we had were young business school types, full of jargon which no one could understand. They didn't really understand people, particularly people north of the Trent. They thought they only had to write memos and produce plans for things to happen. They didn't understand that, up here at Weetflakes, you have to persuade people to want to do things. I could see why things had to change because I'd read the plans and been at the meetings, but no one passed it down to those at the sharp end."

I resist the temptation to say that, as Chairman, that was perhaps something he could have helped with, but there are limits to how far you can push your luck at a first interview. I notice that Egerton looks across at his fellow director and I think, from the irritated expression on his face, that he's wanting to say the same thing.

The interview drags on and, at times, I wonder where it's going. Arthur takes every opportunity to outline his homespun philosophies; Martin seems to be trying constantly to re-assure me that it is not a mission impossible. I find that I like Martin Egerton more and more but wish desperately that I could see him on his own. With both of them there, they are being guarded and talking to each other as much as to me. I feel a strong underlying tension between them.

Eventually Arthur's secretary comes in to tell us that lunch is ready and Arthur leads us down a corridor, past some rather dingy offices and into a foyer that leads to the Weetflakes canteen. There is a buzz of conversation and a lot of movement as people of all ages and all sizes, mostly in rather dated white overalls, make their way in and out.

We are led away from the main entrance and down a side corridor with some small rooms either side. We enter the last one on the left and find Andrew Kent inside. Arthur is immediately called out by a young man with a worried look and Martin, Andrew and I are left on our own.

"Well," says Andrew, "how did it go?"

"You'd better ask Martin," I say.

"In the unlikely event that you should still want the job Philip," says Martin, "all I can say is, when can you start?"

Chapter 6

I'm at home having my evening meal with the family six hours later. I've already told Jean about the interview, the lunch and the news that, if I decide to take this job, I'm no longer unemployed.

But, as I travelled back with Andrew Kent, I began to think about the implications. Uprooting the children again, trying to integrate Mark into a north country environment which will be even further from the American lifestyle he loved so much. Trying to find a school which will enable Angela to obtain some A levels and thus take her into a decent university. And making sure that I don't allow the challenge of this new job to make me forget about Jean and her needs – something which led to our splitting up once before.

The challenge of the job is daunting as well as exciting. I've had bigger jobs in the past but never one where others have failed so resoundingly before and where so much is expected. And it's not my marketing or business skills that they have chosen me for, but a belief that I can bring about the changes which others have failed to achieve.

On the way back in the car I was able to read the papers which Arthur gave me before I left – including the strategic plan which my immediate predecessor had tried and failed to implement. I found the content of the plan highly impressive.

It was based on identification of the distinctive

competencies of Weetflakes, which were surprising to me. The strength of the brand was what I had expected – but the other two areas of competitive advantage were surprising. One was, and presumably still is, the extremely good relationships with the big retailers – words like trust and partnership were mentioned. The other is their very good reputation as quality suppliers of 'own label' cereal products to one of the three top retailers in the UK. Weetflakes is regarded by this company as the only supplier who can match the quality of branded products.

The plan concentrated on the need to develop this area of business as a key strategic thrust rather than as the marginal activity which it has been before. This, the plan argued, would establish Weetflakes as the main supplier of breakfast cereals in the UK. The core business of branded products would stay and would be the classic 'cash cow' to fund future investment in other own label products.

Existing production would be continued in Claydon but, as more own label contracts are signed, the plan is to set up factories and warehouses in the South, West Midlands and Scotland.

I can see why there has been such resistance to change. The traditionalists are bound to question the idea of the branded products being a cow which can be milked to provide growth in own label – something which they have probably seen as a threat rather than an opportunity. This, combined with the plan to move the centre of gravity of production away from Claydon, is bound to have a negative impact on those who are emotionally committed to Weetflakes as it is now.

I find it difficult to play my part in the conversation over dinner with my family, with all these ideas swirling in my head. It has never been easy for me to push work thoughts aside when I get home. Not that dinner time conversation has been a feature of our family life since we returned from the USA. Mark usually sits there sulking and saying little, Angela is often tearful about her lack of progress at school, while Jean and I have tried to be as hopeful and positive about the future as possible.

Jean already knows about the job and that I'm going to

accept it. She seems genuinely delighted and is looking forward to the move – anything to restore certainty to our lives is what she said. We agreed that I would tell the children during the meal. I try the lighthearted approach.

"Well you two, where would you rather live, Scunthorpe or Grimsby?"

I'm pleased at Angela's response.

"Oh Dad, you got the job! Oh that's wonderful. I don't care where we go as long as you're working again. I couldn't do worse in school in Scunthorpe than I'm doing here anyway."

I'm so pleased at her response that I feel like crying – yet the cynic in me asks myself if she's been primed by Jean. Mark's response is to say "when are we moving?" in an aggressive tone and, after I say "as soon as we find a place to live," he stands up and makes for his room. Heavy metal music once again filters down from upstairs.

An hour later Jean's gone out to her aerobics class and I'm on my own. Ever since I knew I was taking this job I've had this vulnerable feeling of being alone. I guess it comes from being made redundant from a job where I was king of my castle, had a large number of people around me, could rely on others to share in my decisions and give me reassurance.

I think back to the person who always gave me the greatest support of that kind – Christine Goodhart. I haven't seen her in the four years since she left her job as my VP Finance at Chapmans and moved to England. She rang me up a couple of years ago about some research she wanted to do, but we didn't meet. I thought of ringing her when I first came back to the UK but I knew that Jean would not have liked it. My wife still finds it hard to trust me where women, and particularly Christine, are concerned, and I can't blame her. Even now, as I think about giving Christine a call, I'm not sure about my real motives. She is married now, of course, so any hopes of reviving our affair should be out of the question anyway. But then I remember the rumours about her marriage being in trouble.

What could be more natural than to call an old and trusted business colleague for advice and also to check if she might be interested in a change of job? When I last spoke to her, she said she was making a great deal of money in her management training venture but was not sure where the business was going. They had reached the size they originally wanted to be but the partners could not agree where to go next. Thus I was not too surprised to hear later that the partnership had split up.

I look at the telephone numbers in my diary and think – what the hell! What do I have to lose? Will the job of Financial Director of Weetflakes, halfway between Grimsby and Scunthorpe, be just the challenge she's looking for? Fat chance!

As I press the buttons on the telephone, I feel a few butterflies in my stomach, the sort you experience when you haven't spoken to someone for a long time, particularly someone who was once so close. The phone rings and her unmistakably soft and confident voice comes on the line – "Christine O'Rourke." I'm taken aback for a moment. I knew her married name but I'd never heard her say it before. It had just been Christine when she called me in the US.

"Christine?" I ask as if I didn't know, "Guess who!"

"Phil," she replies, sounding pleased. "How are you? How's Jean? Are you over in the UK – you sound pretty near?"

I try to answer three questions at once by telling her as quickly as possible about my recently changed situation. She cannot believe what ABT have done to me and sounds genuinely surprised.

"How could they do that Phil? I just can't believe it. Steve used to tell me how well Chapmans were doing in ABT."

I notice that she says "used to tell" and realise that there must be a problem between them, otherwise she'd have been sure to have heard about my leaving ABT. I ask about Steve.

"We split up about six months ago, Phil. We sort of drifted apart. I've been really tied up in this business and Steve took a job with ABT in the Far East. I guess I didn't care enough to go with him and that caused us to make the final split."

"I'm sorry Chris, I really am," I say, knowing that, in reality, the reverse is true. I think to myself, in a rather self-satified way, that I never thought it would last anyway.

I briefly tell her about my new job and the extent of the

challenge. Before I can even ask her, she saves me the trouble.

"I'm sorry Phil. I think I know what you're leading to but it's no use your even asking. My days of being a Financial Director have gone. I've got the taste for training and doing my own thing. You won't know this, but I've just left the partnership to start a new business with another guy who's been working with me on some really exciting projects. My new partner's really good, in fact you might benefit from meeting him. His name's Alan, Alan Angus."

The first thing that comes into my mind – is this the new man in her life and is this really why she and Steve split up? I have the same irrational feeling of jealousy, even after four years of not seeing her. Instead of enquiring about this I ask, "What's his speciality, finance training too?"

"No Phil, and that's why I'd like you to meet him. His speciality is managing change and he's absolutely brilliant at it. It's not only management training – it's also consultancy and advice to top management. And it sounds as if that's what you're going to need."

She says she'll arrange for this Alan guy to call me. I give her my number and say I'll look forward to hearing from him. I feel deflated when she rings off quite abruptly, saying, "I expect we might bump into each other if you do decide to work with Alan."

As I put down the phone, I hear Jean arriving home and I feel terribly guilty. I decide that I'd better not tell her who I've been speaking to.

But as she comes in and I see that smile which symbolises everything that is good about our present relationship, I decide to tell her. Because I know that, even if I do see Christine again, it won't make any difference. My future is now going to be settled, with Jean and my family, at a village between Scunthorpe and Grimsby, at a company called Weetflakes.

Chapter 7

I park my car in the pay and display and look for the offices of Angus O'Rourke. The address sounds quite impressive – Dearden Court, High Street, Amersham – and I find that it's a modern office building set back from the High Street, with a pleasant little garden courtyard as part of its L-shaped design. I wonder why they chose Amersham but then remember that it's close to the business school which Christine's original partners left to form their business.

It's 10 o'clock on Saturday morning and the office building looks deserted. I see the smart plaque with a rather amateurish AOR logo and the Angus O'Rourke name. I wonder if Chris is going to be there – it wasn't mentioned when Alan Angus rang me to fix this meeting. It's the Saturday before I start at Weetflakes on the Monday, only two weeks after my visit to Claydon and my phone call to Chris.

I knock on the door and a small, boyish looking man with a friendly face answers it. At first I think that this can't be Alan Angus because he looks much too young. But something about his confident smile makes me realise that he is older than he first looks and is a man to be reckoned with.

"Philip Moorley," he says, "do come in, I'm Alan Angus. Christine has told me such a lot about you – it's really good to meet you."

I walk inside and notice that they don't have a reception

as such, just an office where a secretary would normally sit. To the side there is a staircase and Alan leads me to it, telling me that their meeting room is up there.

On the first floor there is a small outer office with two desks and we go into the meeting room. I notice photographs of a young wife and family on one desk – obviously Alan's – but nothing on the other.

"Is this where Christine sits?" I say and he nods. "Doesn't she work Saturdays?"

"She works pretty well all hours, Phil, and I often find it hard to keep up with her. But she said it would be best if she kept a low profile on this project and said you would understand why. Am I right?"

He looks at me so directly and with such a friendly open smile that I'm not as offended by this as I otherwise might have been. I realise that Alan Angus has got some rather special powers of communication which I can't quite put my finger on. I begin to understand why Christine left her partnership to join him and want to ask him about the circumstances. But, before I can, he's straight down to business.

"Right Phil. Now I understand that our meeting is exploratory, with no commitment on either side. Christine briefly described your new challenge and thought that I might be able to help."

"Yes Alan. But I'm not sure how. As I understand it, you're in management training and I'm not yet sure what needs there will be at Weetflakes."

"Well, management training is a rather loose term to describe some of the things I'm involved in, Phil. Christine's previous partners are much more orthodox trainers who run business school type courses and are very good at it. One of the reasons why Christine left is because she enjoys and believes in the type of work which I do and which she is moving into as well."

"And that is?"

"It's difficult to give it a label without sounding pretentious, Phil. But I guess you could call it change consultancy, usually involving some kind of training activity at some point but that is not the driving force."

"And you think I need that kind of help?"

"Don't you?"

"I'm not sure, to be quite honest. I know I need some kind of help, that's why I rang Christine. But I was thinking of recruiting one or two permanent people I could trust, who would help me to counter the resistance to change which seems to have defeated the others who've tried."

"I think that was why Christine asked me to see you, Phil. She was worried that you might be rushing into easy solutions like that. When it might be the wrong thing to do."

My initial reaction to this is something along the lines of "who does this young whipper-snapper think he is?" He must be twenty years younger than me and he's trying to tell me how to manage a business, when all he does is run training courses. We all know the old saying that those who can't do, go into teaching.

Yet I say none of this and his friendly manner and lack of pretentiousness stop me even thinking it for long.

Particularly when he goes on to say, "It may well be a good move, Phil, and I can understand why you may, at some point, want to do it. But I thought it might be helpful for us to talk about the change process first. To give you some kind of framework within which you can start to make these decisions once you get involved."

"The change process?"

"Yes Phil. My specialism is managing change. I know you may think it's a bit of a cliché – just a fancy way of describing the management of people in an organisation. But looking at your desired changes as a total process does help you to see your decisions in a broader context and stops you making a number of separate judgements which may not be right when seen together."

"Like appointing new Personnel and Financial Directors?"

"Right Phil, right. I thought we could start by examining the different ways you can bring about change, to give you a framework for those decisions."

He picks up a pen and begins to write on the flipchart in the meeting room. I'm already finding that, in much the same way as it used to be with Christine when we discussed financial matters, there is something in this young man's manner which gives me confidence. I'm also beginning to be interested in what he has to say, despite my natural in-built cynicism towards any kind of behavioural jargon and theory. I've heard this phrase 'managing change' before but always thought it was indeed a cliché. What else is there to manage in a world which is changing all the time?

Yet Christine and now Alan were right to question my desire to bring new people in. It was a premature and easy, instant solution which I would have criticised if others had done it during my time at Chapmans. I realise how useful it is to talk these things through with someone who can challenge your reasoning and your motivation. I say all this to Alan.

"Thanks Phil. Christine said how willing you were to accept that you can learn, despite your immense experience. I think that is probably the most important quality of really successful top managers."

Like anyone else I love a bit of flattery, but I feel that he does mean this and that he's right. I don't admit that my main reason for being so willing to learn is that I'm desperately unsure and insecure, something which was not helped by being made redundant at the age of 52.

Alan turns round from the flipchart and says, "Philip. I'd like us to think about culture – organisational culture. What does that mean to you?"

"I'm not sure I've ever seen a definition. I guess it's the things which are accepted as normal?"

"Yes, that's one way of expressing it. My favourite definition is the quote 'the way we do things around here' – the combination of all the norms, values, beliefs, accepted practices which an organisation develops over time."

"And which it is very hard to change."

"Right Phil, very hard. Christine tells me that you did it very successfully at both the places you worked together but that it took you a long time to achieve."

"And she was very instrumental in the change, as were several others whom I brought in or promoted. That's why I instinctively wanted to do the same at Weetflakes."

"And it might well be necessary. I was only warning you

against doing it too quickly and thinking of it as the only solution. I'd like us to think about all the ways in which you can change a culture. One is to change the people as you've suggested."

He writes up on the flipchart:

HOW ORGANISATIONAL CULTURES CAN BE CHANGED

1) By changing people

"It's interesting," he says, "that in one of the most successful and high profile changes of culture in recent times – British Airways – they identified that, in addition to everything else they did, certain people had to go and new faces had to come in to key positions. They felt that the militaristic culture they had – going back to the days of government ownership – was too strong to be changed without some change of people. And that's a decision you will have to make once you've analysed the position more deeply."

"BA's change in culture was to put customers first, am I right?"

"Eventually, Phil, and if we'd got time I could go into great lengths about the change programme which eventually achieved that. But interestingly the first stage of the culture change they identified as necessary was to put people first. To establish a culture where people mattered, where employees cared about relationships with each other, was regarded as the first stage towards the eventual transformation."

I say that I would like to hear much more about that story some time in the future and he agrees. I find myself being sucked into the assumption that my relationship with him is going to be a long-term one and I don't mind. The idea of having someone outside the organisation to talk about these matters seems very attractive, though I guess I will have to think about cost at some point too.

"So how else can we change cultures, Phil? We can change the people, what else can we change?"

"Their positions, I suppose. I once managed to change attitudes by moving a personnel man into a sales management role. He was brilliantly successful and it made everyone stop thinking in narrow, functional terms."

"Right Phil. Very important and very effective too. When Abbey National brought about their culture change, they deliberately looked to change the positions of managers who had been in the same job for more than seven years. And that suited both the organisation and the individuals."

I like the way that Alan relates his ideas and frameworks to real life examples. So many management trainers and gurus I've heard talk in jargon and theory. But if I can relate to my own experiences and feel that they are supported by those of other companies, I can have much more faith in the ideas.

I see that Alan has walked to the flipchart again.

"I'd like to add a third way of changing culture Phil, one which is much more difficult to achieve and to measure."

The flipchart soon reads:

HOW ORGANISATIONAL CULTURE CAN BE CHANGED

1) By changing people
2) By changing positions
3) By changing beliefs and attitudes

"It might be useful to think back to your own experiences, both as a Chief Executive and when you were below that level. How far were beliefs and attitudes changed and how was it achieved?"

I think back to Chapmans. Not to when I was Chief Executive (or President as they called me in the US) but to when I was Vice President, Sales and Marketing. Then the President was Richard Watts – a genius of a man who was dynamic, hyperactive, always looking for improvement. I still remember the impact he had and the feelings of respect and admiration I had for him. Feelings which haven't been forgotten, despite his sudden decision to leave Chapmans once the take-over battle started and despite the affair he had with my wife whom I thought was ever faithful.

Alan resists the temptation to break the silence and waits for my reflections to produce an answer.

"I guess it's the example of the people at the top, Alan."

"Right – something which we often refer to as role models. People will emulate the behaviours they see at the top."

"Will they necessarily, Alan? Doesn't it depend on the respect they have for those at the top?"

"To some extent. Respect certainly helps. But I would say an even more important factor is whether the behaviours are seen to lead to success. And, of course, the culture change which this brings may not always be positive."

"What do you mean?"

"Well, I used to do some management training work within companies owned by Robert Maxwell before he fell off his boat. And I can assure you that, whatever respect people had or didn't have for Maxwell, he did tend to be copied. And most of the people who copied him hadn't got the force of personality to bring off the same management style."

"So, if I can provide people with some new role models at Weetflakes, it could be a factor in bringing about change. So surely that strengthens the case for bringing in new people?"

Alan Angus looks me straight in the eye and then moves across the room to help himself to a fresh cup of coffee and to fill up mine.

"Phil," he says, "I hope you won't mind me saying this – I feel rather humble after all the success you've had and after all the good things Christine told me about you. But I do think you need my help or, at least, the help of someone like me."

I can see that he's embarrassed or, at least, he's making a pretty good show of pretending to be. Either way he's prepared me very effectively for a hard hit.

"Okay Alan," I say, "say what you think. It's the only way we're going to work together and I think I can take it."

He sits down again and those clear, sincere eyes fix mine.

"Phil. I can see already that you have a tendency to grasp things and see them as instant solutions. That is tempting and a lot of people have made a lot of money thinking that way. You've heard of Tom Peters?"

I nod.

"He decided that there were eight instant solutions to excellence and success and even he now admits that this was over-simplifying the complexities of culture change. What I want us to do is look at all the factors involved in change; look at the complex and unique culture which you're going to find at Weetflakes on Monday and then . . ."

He pauses and looks at me, saying, "And then Phil, what do we do?"

"We manage change?" I suggest.

"Yes, eventually. But first of all we produce a plan for change which will pick out the best of the ideas and frameworks which are available and apply a unique mix to Weetflakes."

I can see his point but can't resist finding a reason to challenge him. I have always loved an argument.

"That's all very well, Alan, and very helpful. But I can't avoid providing a role model the day I start on Monday. I have to make some assumptions about the style required, haven't I?"

He looks at me with an almost resigned smile which I can't quite understand.

"Chris was right about you," he says, "she said that you would always challenge everything and that you would do it in a very pragmatic, practical way. Yest Phil, of course you're right. To some extent the planning has to begin now. You – we if you'll let me help – have to make a decision about how you're going to play it on Monday and in your first few weeks. Because this will be vital to your eventual success."

Four hours later we adjourn to a pub down the road and I have to call Jean to tell her that I won't be back until about 4 pm. In those four hours we had been through the other ways in which culture can be changed and the flipchart ended up looking like this:

HOW ORGANISATIONAL CULTURE CAN BE CHANGED

1) By changing people
2) By changing positions

3) By changing beliefs and attitudes
   - role models
   - communications – videos, magazines, etc.
   - group discussions/team briefings
   - one-to-one counselling
   - training courses
4) By changing (improving) skills and knowledge
5) By changing structures and systems

Time seemed to fly as we debated the extent to which devices like videos, magazines and posters can in fact change beliefs and attitudes and the relative merits of each. We were very much in agreement that those mechanisms which encourage participation and discussion are likely to be most effective in bringing about attitudes which will cause real and lasting changes in culture.

At one stage we began a fascinating debate about the difference between management training which changes beliefs and management training which changes behavioural skills. In the end we agreed that it was a false dichotomy because nearly all training has elements of both. Again Alan quoted British Airways, telling me that, of all the things that changed the culture during the courses they ran to improve people and customer skills, the mere fact that the Chief Executive, Colin Marshall, took time to visit staff during the course was by far the most powerful.

Alan also warned against the simplistic distinction which trainers often make between knowledge and skills. He said that the work he does with Christine often combines financial knowledge with behavioural skills and they both make a contribution to culture change. I didn't need too much reminding of this because, at an early stage, Christine reminded me of the links between management accounting and behavioural skills. Training people to produce realistic budgets is an example of such a combination which can contribute to culture change.

We also discussed budgets as an example of the type of system which can be changed to move the culture in certain ways – for example, budgeting can be moved further down the line to encourage more involvement in plans and more awareness of financial issues. We discussed reward and appraisal systems as agents of culture change and I began to produce a list of questions about present systems in Weetflakes to work on next week. We later extended the list of questions to the other areas of change we'd discussed, before realising what the time was.

As Alan brings the drinks and sandwiches to the table in the pub, I say, "But we still haven't decided what style I should assume on Monday, Alan. What do you think?"

"My role is not to make your decisions for you, Phil. I can only help you to ask the right questions and make all the plans you can before you go."

"But, from our discussion about role models earlier, I have to be very careful and not act too quickly, am I right? I need to have a feel for what's required once I get up there."

"Yes Phil, that's right. Far too many top managers jump in too quickly and try to impose styles and solutions which have worked elsewhere. That is maybe what those other guys did wrong at Weetflakes. I think you should talk to a number of people in the first few weeks and have an open mind about what's required."

"And then meet with you again?"

"If that's what you want, Philip, but I'm afraid that next time you'll have to pay."

As we walk out of the pub and into the car park, I've already made up my mind that I will see this young man again. He is so easy to talk to and I'm pretty sure I'm going to need someone to talk to at Weetflakes, someone with no axe to grind, someone who won't tell me what I want to hear.

Before we shake hands and go our separate cars, he says, "But there is one thing I'd like you to think about in your first few weeks, Phil. Something which almost everyone who's written meaningfully about change agrees upon. To bring about culture change you are going to need a **Vision** of what you want Weetflakes to be and you'll have to persuade others to share it and buy into it. So regard that as the starting point for your plan to change the culture."

"And how soon should we meet again?"

"Maybe I could come up to see you there in about three weeks?" We fix a date which I say I will confirm later.

"Remember me to Christine," I say as he walks away to his car. The time I've spent with Alan Angus makes me think that he's going to make just as significant a contribution to my career as his partner once did.

Chapter 8

"I'd like you all to know that I'm delighted to be joining Weetflakes and to be working with you. Please let's make this very informal – I'm just here to listen at this stage. I'd very much like to hear about anything you want to tell me about our company."

I say this as we are gathered in the Weetflakes senior management dining room, just before starting lunch on my first day. It's not the way I would have liked to meet my new management team, but it was difficult for me to change the arrangements which Arthur Stocks had made. I worry about the very idea of a senior management dining room and resolve to put this on my shopping list of things which I want to change. But, I keep reminding myself, I mustn't act too hastily, just watch, listen and learn, a style which is alien to my normal action oriented nature.

I think back to the weekend, or what was left of it after I got back to Wimbledon late Saturday afternoon. Mark was out on Saturday evening with some of the similarly way-out friends he has recently taken up with, so the atmosphere was that much more pleasant. Angela and Jean have a good relationship these days and Angela bathed little Susie and put her to bed before the three of us had a pleasant dinner together.

Angela seems to have warmed more and more to the idea of moving up North and it was she who suggested that, as it's the first week of the Easter school holidays, all five of us should go up on the Sunday. Her idea was for the four of them to look at houses during my first few days at Weetflakes.

So while I'm at Weetflakes, Jean is with the rest of the family at Grimsby's best hotel. Mark was, to say the least, unhappy about coming and sulked all the way up the motorway. I don't know what has happened to the happy and likeable teenager I knew when we were in the USA, and I keep asking myself how far it is the move which has caused the problem. Or would he have reached this rebellious phase anyway? I guess I'll never know but I can't help worrying about how little patience I have with him and whether the father/son relationship we once had has now gone for ever.

I try to put all this out of my mind as we help ourselves to the sumptuous buffet which seems to be normal fare for Weetflakes senior managers. I try to establish who's who at this early stage and relate this back to the descriptions given me by Andrew Kent on that first car journey.

I notice that they all grab their food rather quickly and return to the tables, each of which has four seats. I realise too late that I'm likely to be marooned on my own with Arthur at the last table. I decide that, as I'm supposed to be running this place, I'll be assertive and set the right tone early on. I walk up to a table of four and say, "I hope you don't mind if I suggest that I take one of these seats. I'd like to rotate round several tables over lunch and thus have a chance to chat to you all."

Four pairs of eyes look at each other uncertainly and then three of them all focus on a fourth. As if by an unwritten signal, that fourth person gets up.

"I'll move," says a late middle aged man, small and tidy looking, with a thin face and half-moon glasses. "I'm Ernie Taylor, Chief Accountant," he says, "Good to get to know you, Mr Moorley."

I ask him to call me Phil and thank him as he moves to the table with Arthur and two empty chairs. The other three introduce themselves and I realise why Ernie was the one to move. The rest are 'family'.

Freddie Stocks tells me that he is the Production Director – he is friendly on the surface though there's just a trace of irony in his voice as he welcomes me to Weetflakes. He's clearly trying to demonstrate his role as the most senior person present as he tells me more about the other two at the table. They are the sons-in-law which Andrew Kent told me about – Julian Weatherall, Research and Development Director, and Martin Moss, Sales. Weatherall has a rather supercilious air about him, emphasised by a strong public school accent. In contrast Martin Moss comes over as a very friendly person, an easy smile coming to his face as he talks. I recognise this likeable manner as the sort which helps sales directors to be successful.

I'm struck ˌby the way that Freddie dominates the conversation as I ask them questions about Weetflakes. It's only when I direct questions at Julian and Martin personally that they say anything and even then, I feel that their replies are being affected by Freddie's presence.

Freddie is small, dark, chubby and round-faced, with piercing blue eyes which give a strong impression of power and determination. He talks loudly, almost embarrassingly so, and with a confident tone which does not leave much scope for doubt or challenge. I remember that he's Arthur's nephew and I suspect that he will be a formidable ally if I can persuade him to support me, but a formidable enemy if I can't. I don't know whether he was part of the problem with the previous MDs, though to judge by the content of his replies he is very much in favour of change. Then I remember what Alan Angus also told me in the pub on Saturday – never mistake talk *about* change for action *to* change. He quoted a term used in one of his other client companies – the TAGG manager who 'Talks a Good Game' but does anything to delay action.

I'm soon impatient to meet some of the others present at the lunch, in particular Arthur's son Willis. After seeing the impact which Freddie had on the other two at this table, I speculate about whether it will be the same with his cousin. If I am right about Arthur being a paper tiger, surely the main resistance to change must come from the next generation, holding the key positions of Production and Marketing Directors.

Just before I leave this first table, I look around to see if I can locate Willis. I look and listen for the one who's doing the most talking and soon find him. I can see the facial resemblance to Arthur and hear from quite a distance away a similar northern accent, laying down the law with the same certainty and dominance as Freddie.

I excuse myself and walk up to the table where Willis is holding forth. I stand by his side waiting for him to finish his sentence and the other three turn nervously to look at me, obviously uncertain who to give their attention to.

"I wonder if I might take a seat at your table and ask one of you to go over there," I say. "It's such a good chance to meet you all on my first day."

"No way lad," says Willis, "we're all enjoying ourselves much too much."

My heart pounds at the thought of a public confrontation on my first day but Willis gets up, shakes hands with me forcefully and says, "Only joking Mr Moorley, of course you can – you're the boss after all. George, you go over to sit with Freddie – you can lobby him about the new lorry purchases, now you've had a go at me."

A young, fair-haired man, for once without a northern accent, introduces himself as George Plant, Distribution Manager, and leaves to join Freddie. I resolve to chat to him before long because I know how crucial distribution costs and supply chain efficiency are likely to be to the implementation of the new strategy.

I find it hard to take a liking to Willis. His 'joke' was carefully calculated to show his lack of respect yet make it difficult for me to confront him without appearing to lack a sense of humour. It was his way of saying to the others at the table – he doesn't frighten me.

I ask them all to call me Phil and direct the conversation in a way which makes it very difficult for Willis to dominate. I find out that the other two are Peter Thackray, who is Chief Buyer, and Gavin Simmonds, Marketing Manager, who, he tells me, handles day to day marketing issues, leaving Willis free to deal with strategy.

"Aye," Willis butts in, "and I've been known to get involved in some day-to-day issues too, haven't I lad?"

I deliberately ignore Willis by directing a question about

new product development to Gavin Simmonds. I can tell
that he and Peter, as at the previous table, are severely
restricted in what they can say, purely by the force of Willis's
presence. He is very much a young version of Arthur, except
that you feel Willis would not back away from confrontation
in the same way as his father.

After half an hour of fascinating discussion, both in terms
of the information I obtain and the games I see being played
between the three of them, I move on to another table,
obviously populated by the small fry. I meet Amanda Slade
who tells me she is Arthur's PA, as well as being Personnel
Officer. After chatting to her for only a few minutes and
noting her only too obvious sex appeal, I form an
uncharitably quick and prejudiced view about her likely role
as Arthur's PA. I tell myself not to judge too quickly, but her
lack of knowledge of personnel matters does nothing to stop
me doubting her value to Weetflakes.

I am much more impressed by Stephen Young, the
Management Accountant. I am amazed to find that he
reports to Ernie Taylor the Chief Accountant whom I
dispatched to sit with Arthur on the other table where, I
notice, they are sitting in silence. Stephen is articulate,
mature for his years (he looks late twenties but behaves mid
thirties) and knowledgeable about the business, something I
always look for in financial managers.

The other one on this table is Joe McEvoy, Factory
Manager on the Claydon site, a dour Scotsman who says
little and appears to weigh the few words he uses very
carefully. Before long I seem to be in a dialogue with
Stephen, with the other two looking on but saying little.

I notice Stephen looking up to my left and then see Arthur
and Willis standing by my side.

"We thought we'd take you back to Willis's office and
show you the numbers, Philip," says Arthur. "The latest
sales figures are particularly encouraging, following Willis's
new marketing initiatives."

I'm amused that 'the numbers' means sales levels to
Arthur and Willis and, because I know how poor the current
level of profitability is, I can't resist saying, "To me the most
important number is the bottom line, Arthur, so I'll be

wanting to know about profit as well as sales levels. What I've seen at the bottom line so far hasn't impressed me at all."

I'm pleased to see them lose that superior air which seems to be a feature of the Stocks' manner and I decide to continue my assertive approach on this important first day. I say, "Anyway, I'd rather spend an hour or so alone in my office right now, Arthur. I've met a lot of your colleagues over lunch and I've received a lot of information. I want a little time to think about it and digest it. I'll let you know if I want to see anyone."

I notice that Stephen Young and Peter Thackray, who are now standing together, are smiling at each other as I put Arthur and Willis down in this rather obvious way. I wonder if I'm going too far but I'm determined not to let them dictate my agenda.

Ten minutes later I'm back in my office. I decide to write down the organisation as I understand it and make some notes about the key players. I draw an organisation chart:

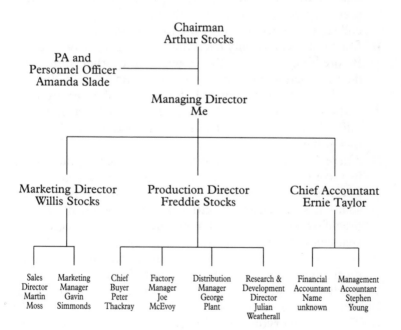

I realise how much power this structure gives to the Stocks family. I remember hearing from Andrew Kent how Arthur is very close to Ernie Taylor and keeps a special eye on financial matters – thus Willis, Freddie and Arthur control all the key functions. I notice that, even though the sons-in-law have the title of director and presumably attend Board meetings, they report through Willis and Freddie.

I start to make notes about the people I've met but soon become unhappy with this. I'm making prejudiced judgements, based on an artical social situation which should never have been organised on my first day. I decide instead to write down the information and impressions I obtained during the lunchtime discussions.

1) Freddie and Willis seem to be the ones with the power and influence.

2) The two sons-in-law, Martin Moss and Julian Weatherall, do not seem to have much more power than other managers. Indeed, one or two comments indicated that they were shown a certain lack of respect by their colleagues, particularly by the Stocks brothers.

3) Martin Moss has only been Sales Director for two years. Before that it was Arthur's younger brother Jim, who died suddenly. From the comments made about Jim, it was he who was responsible for the excellent reputation and relationships with the retail trade. Yet Martin, with a difficult act to follow, has make a good job of keeping this going.

4) There have been few significant successes in marketing in recent years and, despite numerous efforts at theme advertising and almost continuous promotions, market share has declined. Weetflakes has 7 per cent of the breakfast cereals market compared to 8 per cent five years ago and 10 per cent ten years ago.

5) New product successes have been confined to variants on the basic product. All attempts to launch other cereal products or move into different markets (e.g. snacks a couple of years ago) have failed.

6) Though everyone (including the Stocks brothers)

accepts that own label could be developed further, the tone and language used in discussion indicate that they do not like producing supermarket brands. I was also concerned that it wasn't until I asked Stephen Young, the management accountant, that I discovered that profitability levels of own label are surprisingly good. No one else had any idea.

7) There was a similar reluctance to accept the problem of the main production site being so far away from the centre of gravity in the UK. The lack of informed replies to my questions indicated that either they don't understand the importance of distribution times and costs in the modern business environment, or they don't want to.

8) The finance function seems to lack clout and is seen as 'bean counting'. Arthur is supposed to be Ernie Taylor's mentor but neither of them seems to have any concept of modern management accounting. This explains the poor quality of information I saw when I glanced through the Board reports this morning. All the emphasis is on production and sales statistics, little on profit and cash generation. Yet Stephen Young is obviously producing information which is not reaching top management.

9) Personnel (or Human Resources as I knew it in the USA) does not seem to be a high priority. "Amanda deals with the canteen and that sort of thing" was a typical comment from Julian Weatherall, also pretty typical of his patronising manner. There appears to be no grading structure, no general system of appraisal – "it's up to each manager," said Freddie – and no succession planning. I'm all in favour of managers handling their own personnel management to some extent but there must be an HR strategy and some structure to guide it.

I put down my pencil and look out of the window, considering what to do next. I recall what Alan Angus said to me as we parted only two days ago, "Don't rush into judgement or action. Collect the facts, assess the people, keep all your options open, be assertive but don't do anything to damage relationships."

Just as I'm about to ring and ask George Plant to come and see me, the phone rings.

I pick it up, asking myself whom I will need to be assertive with now – I guess it must be Arthur, Willis or Freddie trying to plan my day for me. But it's not, it's Jean.

"Darling," she says, "we've found the most wonderful house – you'll love it. We all do, even Mark. Can you come and see it, before it gets dark?" From my knowledge of her and her excited tone I know for certain that this house is the one we'll buy.

I look at my watch and it's 3.30 pm. My initial reaction is to say no but, on reflection, I think that maybe it's a good idea, another way of displaying my determination to control my time and priorities in these first few weeks. I'll have half an hour or so with George Plant and then leave before 4.30.

I ask Jean for directions to get to the house she seems to like so much.

"Turn left out of the factory gates and it's about five minutes, a road called Fairfield Drive. The house is called Fairfield Farm House."

"Five minutes?" I say. "How many miles?"

"Phil, don't be silly," she says. "It's five minutes walk, not drive. The house is here in Claydon."

At that moment I see yet another difference between living in the USA and in the North of England. I wonder what it will be like living so close to the job. Yet another change I'm going to have to accustom myself to.

I ring George Plant, only to find that he's in conference with Freddie. I ask for a message to be sent in, requesting a meeting as soon as he's free. Five minutes later I'm surprised to see him enter with Freddie at his side and they both move towards the chairs opposite my desk.

"Freddie," I say, "I would prefer to see George on my own please, just to help my familiarisation. I'm sure you have many other things to do."

The look he gives me as he goes out of my office leaves no room for doubt about the animosity he feels towards me. I've certainly achieved my goal of asserting my authority on my first day, but already I seem to be in conflict with at least one of those whom I need to influence to bring about change.

And only two days ago Alan Angus told me that a key factor in managing change is to persuade the key influencers on to your side.

Forty five minutes later, after a meeting with George Plant which confirmed my worst fears, I walk towards my new home on Fairfield Drive, wondering what the hell I've got myself into.

Chapter 9

I'm back in Wimbledon, relaxing with the papers over breakfast. I'm down south for the first time after three weeks at Weetflakes, it's Saturday morning and, though I could do with a rest, I have a busy day ahead.

Martin Egerton of Hill Benson rang me at my hotel earlier in the week and asked if he could see me confidentially, some time over the weekend. He's coming to Wimbledon at 10 am, in about an hour's time. I'm not sure why he's coming. Is it just to monitor my progress or is there something specific he wants to tell me? I wonder what Arthur would say if he knew. I certainly can't wait to tell Martin about Weetflakes – I've been bursting to talk things over with somebody ever since the first day. I'll also have a second opportunity when I see Alan Angus who is coming here at 2 pm to help me review my progress.

I've grown to like living here in Wimbledon and it was with mixed feelings that I agreed for Jean to give notice of termination of the lease, to be confirmed when we exchange contracts for our new house within the next two weeks. I knew I was wasting my time trying to argue when I first entered Fairfield Farm House and saw Jean's face. But it was the enthusiasm of both the children which convinced me. They love the idea of a long, rambling farmhouse with its six acres for Angela to have her horses and outbuildings for Mark to play his music. All my questions about running costs and repairs were dismissed as irrelevant and even I had to admit that the price was amazingly low by New Jersey and Wimbledon standards.

Before Egerton arrives, I try to collect my thoughts about the situation at Weetflakes. I am convinced that we have the makings of a good management team who can carry through the new strategy, but they are restricted by the presence and the history of the Stocks family. This is not always an intentionally malevolent influence – Arthur, and to a lesser extent Willis, are careful to be supportive – but there is a paralysis of action without their express consent.

Stephen Young, the management accountant, is a good example. He has several ideas to improve management information but reports to Ernie Taylor. Ernie assumes, rightly or wrongly, that Arthur would not be interested and neither Stephen nor Ernie has the influence or the confidence to break outside the silos of the organisation structure and sell their ideas direct to management. Gavin Simmonds has similar problems with his ideas for marketing innovation which never seem to get past his boss, Willis.

With the people reporting to Freddie, it's even worse because Freddie is more open in his determination to resist change. Whether it was my assertive stance on my first day, or whether it was inevitable, I have a clear opponent here. And, despite the fact that he is Arthur's nephew and not his son, he seems to have even more influence just by the force of his personality. People are undoubtedly afraid of him.

I need to discuss this with Martin Egerton. First to find out if Freddie has been an obvious obstacle before, secondly to see how possible it might be to remove him if there is no other way.

The meeting with George Plant on that first day demonstrated the problem very well. Here is a man, with a good track record with Unilever and United Biscuits, apparently incapable of expressing a view about anything. Two years of working for Freddie seem to have taken the confidence away from him. "You'll have to ask Mr Freddie" – *Mr* Freddie, can you believe? – was his stock response to my questions about the costs and feasibility of regional distribution centres. I felt that I might as well have let Freddie stay in the meeting, because every answer was given with a look over the shoulder.

The rest of the management team, apart from Ernie Taylor and the lovely but hopeless Amanda, seem to have the potential to deliver the results I want.

Egerton arrives early and Jean makes us some coffee. He tells me he lives in Richmond, just down the road. He seems reluctant to move on to business and I decide to leave it to him to set the pace. Eventually he begins to talk about Weetflakes.

"I don't like this cloak and dagger stuff really, Philip, but two of the three who resigned told me that it would have been different if I'd been available to talk things through, off the record, early on. So I'm giving you that chance. Hill Benson is determined not to lose a fourth MD and we're not bothered about going through formal channels."

I tell him how much I appreciate that and how much I need someone to talk to after three weeks of involvement with Weetflakes. I also tell him about Alan Angus and he seems to approve. He says that an external consultant could well have helped my predecessors to cope.

We seem to be getting on well as I tell him about my experiences, but I do not feel it is doing any more than giving me a chance to unburden myself. I decide to raise what I now regard as the key question, "Martin, I'm not one to jump to conclusions too early or to go for the easy solution, but I believe that I might have to say that one of the Stocks family – probably Freddie – has to go if we are to get where we need to be. Where will you stand if that is the case?"

"It's not the first time I've been asked that question, Philip, and your predecessor didn't like my answer. He resigned a week later. So I'm going to give a different answer this time, though I fear it might not be the one you're looking for."

I have an unpleasant feeling in the pit of my stomach as he says this. I sense that he's not going to back me but I'm pleasantly surprised.

"If you want to sack Freddie or Willis, that's bound to be a Board decision. You must understand that. And I only have one vote, which will certainly be yours if you make your case convincingly. But there are three of them and the two sons-in-law. You might feel you could influence Moss and Weatherall to vote with you, but I doubt it and it would be terribly messy."

"So, I'm stuck with them, whatever they do and whatever impact they have?"

"Not necessarily. There is also the question of shareholding. I represent 30 per cent and – please treat this as totally between you and me – I know I could get over 20 per cent of the shareholders to back me, if it really came to the crunch."

"Stocks family shares?"

"Yes Phil, that's all there is apart from our 30 per cent. Arthur was not the only child of Wilfred and the shares are well spread – please don't ask me any more questions about who holds them."

"So you would use this voting power if it came to the crunch?"

"Yes. And the threat of it would probably be enough. If not, there would probably have to be a public flotation of shares – that's the price the other 20 per cent would need for their support."

The more I think about this the more I like what I hear. A flotation, independence from the Stocks family, being Managing Director of a plc.

As if anticipating my thinking, Martin follows up by saying, "But please Phil, however much you may like the idea of booting out the Stockses, you must treat it as a last resort. I've told you because I want you to stay with Weetflakes and because I trust you to do all you can to bring about change without the trauma of ousting the family."

I realise the implications of what he's saying only too well and test my understanding by adding, "And you wouldn't back me unless you believed I'd tried everything else beforehand?"

"You're as open as you are perceptive Philip," is Martin's reply and he lightens the atmosphere by a brilliant impersonation of Arthur Stocks' professional north-countryman accent, saying, "I like a man who calls a spade a spade, ee lad, that I do!"

Martin Egerton leaves about noon and, as I have lunch

with Jean and the children, I have difficulty in keeping my thoughts away from Weetflakes. Jean is busy telling me about the wonderful traditional virtues of the children's new school and how kind the headmistress was to Angela. She also tells me about the potential problem for Mark because the same kind headmistress hinted that his hair will need to be cut before he starts. I make some fatuous comment about being willing to use the scissors myself and, as both Angela and Jean give me looks that could kill, Mark rushes from the table to the usual refuge of his room and his music. I'm grateful when the door bell rings – Alan Angus arriving – because it means that the deserved dressing down I'm going to get from Jean will at least be delayed.

I'd confirmed the location with Alan Angus earlier in the week and also agreed a fee. He seemed to think I might baulk at £750 for half a day, but my American experience taught me never to be surprised at consultants' fees. Or, indeed, never to doubt their value if you find the right person. As I open the door and see the young boyish face again I have my doubts, but after only a few minutes I'm reminded of his confidence and his perceptiveness. In particular I recall how good he is at allowing me to see my own weaknesses, without offending me.

I run through the events of the first three weeks, telling him about the hostile attitudes of the Stocks brothers, particularly Freddie ever since I put him down on the first day. How I find Arthur anxious only to avoid confrontation and Willis paying lip-service to new ideas but generally behaving as if I wasn't around. Yet, in response to Alan's penetrating questions, I have to admit that it would be very difficult to produce a case against any of them for lack of co-operation – indeed they are studiously careful to give a superficial appearance of support.

I go on to tell him that underneath the Stocks family you have this potentially high calibre management team who have been cowed into lack of initiative and confidence. But yet again I have to admit, in response to more questions, that it is difficult to blame this directly on the Stockses. Indeed, in conversation they complain about the lack of proactivity – "if you want something doing you have to do it yourself here," was one comment from Freddie – yet I know it's because of the attitudes and culture which the Stockses have developed over the years.

I then tell Alan about my conversation with Martin Egerton, in particular about the problem, but the ultimate possibility, of replacing Freddie.

"Phil," says Alan, looking concerned and even a little despairing, "can you recall what we agreed at our last meeting, regarding your first few weeks?"

I think back and it hits me. It's my usual failing. I've opted for the instant solution, when I'd promised that I would watch, listen and analyse the situation before preparing an action plan.

"I think Martin Egerton was very shrewd in giving you the reply he did, Phil," says Alan. "He's not ruled out supporting you if you want to take drastic action, but he wants it to be the last resort. Probably because, like me, he's concerned that you may be rushing in too quickly."

I feel like becoming defensive. Like saying that all I wanted to do was check my position with Martin, just in case. But I know I'm kidding myself. I just wanted Freddie out, to show the Stockses who's boss, to clear the way for me to make the changes I want with unchallenged authority. Yet, after my discussions with Martin earlier and now with Alan, I realise that such an action would probably be counter-productive, particularly at this early stage. The trauma of sacking Freddie, particularly where his 'crime' would be hard to pinpoint, would probably do more harm than good, particularly to my relationship with Arthur and Willis.

"You remember the framework I gave you last time, Phil – the five ways of changing culture?"

I think back to three weeks ago and realise that I haven't even thought about what he told me then, despite my interest at the time. I resolve to do better from now on.

He erects the portable flipchart stand he's brought with him and shows me the page we used last time. It all comes back to me. You can change people, positions, beliefs and attitudes, skills and knowledge, structures and systems. I was hell bent on rushing into trying to change the people, without giving the other options a chance.

"Okay Phil," says Alan, "let's learn from this. Today I thought we might look at another framework which will, I think, remind you again not to rush into things and give some structure for your thoughts and actions over the next few months."

"With the emphasis on thought coming before action this time?"

"Yes Phil, and it's my role to help you do this. You must avoid damaging your position by acting too hastily."

I ask myself whether I've done that already with Martin Egerton, probably one of the most important people I need to influence. Will he have been impressed by my request, so soon after my appointment? I doubt it. How long did my predecessors take to make a similar approach?

While I'm worrying about this, Alan has begun to write on a new page of the flipchart.

"Phil," he says, "I'm going to show you a framework which is often called the change cycle. It's a composite version of the ideas of quite a few writers in this area. I've leaned quite heavily on the work of Rosbeth Moss Kanter, have you heard of her?"

"Yes, I saw her on TV while I was in the USA. Something about giants learning to dance?"

"Right Phil, that's her. And that's what you have to get Weetflakes to do. It may not be a giant by IBM's and General Motors' standards, but you have to teach the key players some new dance steps if you're going to get them moving. And that's tricky when they've been dancing the same way for so long."

I remember also that Kanter's book is somewhere in the attic and decide that I'll dig it out to read while I've got time on my hands in the evenings, until we finally move house. I realise how, in the past, I've heard people like Tom Peters and Kanter talk about management and change, without realising that this is stuff I can and should be applying. What Alan seems to be giving me, and which I have not had before, is the vital bridge between management theory and practical application, which so often fails to be crossed.

While I'm thinking this, I see that three boxes have appeared on the new page of the flipchart:

A FRAMEWORK FOR CHANGE

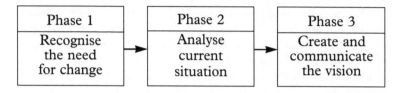

Phase 1	Phase 2	Phase 3
Recognise the need for change	Analyse current situation	Create and communicate the vision

"Okay Phil," says Alan, turning round to face me, "there are 13 phases in my composite change cycle and you're only at Phase 2. Or at least that's where I would like you to be."

"But I've jumped ahead a bit, is that what you're saying?"

"You certainly were in danger of doing that and perhaps that's partly my fault in not offering you this full framework before."

"No Alan, don't blame yourself. You were pretty clear that I should only observe in my first few weeks. And you also mentioned the need for a vision before I move into action."

"Right. That's the next step. You've recognised the need for change and so have the Weetflakes Board, otherwise you wouldn't have been brought in. There may be some individuals, like Freddie and Willis, who do not recognise the need and are potential obstacles to change, but we will address that issue in later phases. You're now carrying out Phase 2 – analysing the present position – and I'd like you to spend some time with me later, sharing more of the information you've gained. I can then help you to assess what is missing, what you still need to find out, before we move on to further phases."

"And then I need this vision. I've given it some thought but, before going any further, I wanted to check if you recommend any particular structure."

I find it surprising how I'm so readily deferring to this young man who has had far less experience than me. I've had my share of mission statements and corporate objectives at ABT and this idea of a vision seems, at first, to be yet another variation on the same theme. Yet such is the confidence I have in Alan, and in his knowledge of change, that I find myself putting aside my normal cynicism. My faith comes more from personal chemistry than anything else

– we seem to have developed a remarkable rapport in a very short time.

"We'll come back to the vision later, Phil, if that's okay. And I will suggest a structure for you to work to. Before that I'd just like to take you through the rest of my change cycle, then it will be a lasting framework for all our work together."

He writes on the flipchart again – coming down the right-hand side. As he's writing he adds, "And don't forget, you don't just have to create the vision, you also have to communicate it. The business world has been littered with cases of CEOs who had brilliant visions but failed because they couldn't communicate. And this will be vital in your case, probably the single most important part of the cycle."

As he draws more boxes on the flipchart, I think about this. How do you sell a vision of Weetflakes as a main supplier of own label cereal products, with its centre of gravity moving away from Claydon, to people whose whole working life has been spent believing that the strengths of the company are its brand and its Claydon factory?

Then I look at the boxes Alan has drawn and realise that the next phases of his change cycle will, to some extent, enable me to address this issue. The new phases are (see figure opposite).

"First of all Phil, I should say that I don't believe that life, and therefore managing change, is as simple or as sequential as this. In practice we will have to be flexible, but at least this framework helps us to know when we are slipping outside the ideal, logical change process."

"As I was doing by wanting to remove Freddie? Because that would be Phase 7 – removing a barrier?"

"Yes Phil, that's right. But don't think that Phase 7 merely concerns removing people, though that may be one way. As we discussed last time there are other ways which may be less painful in the long run."

"I know you're right, Alan, and it's good that you keep reminding me of this. But sometimes you consultants overestimate how much you can change people. To some extent, people are what they are and managers like me, who've had a great deal of experience, often know intuitively how far change is likely to be achievable."

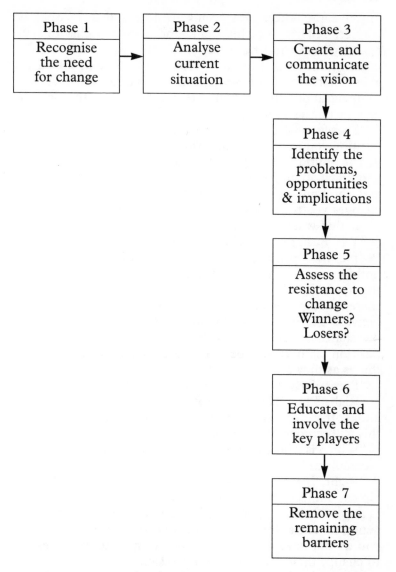

Phase 1	Phase 2	Phase 3
Recognise the need for change	Analyse current situation	Create and communicate the vision

Phase 4

Identify the problems, opportunities & implications

Phase 5

Assess the resistance to change
Winners?
Losers?

Phase 6

Educate and involve the key players

Phase 7

Remove the remaining barriers

"So it's important that they have someone like me to be devil's advocate, just in case they might make that judgement too early."

This exchange amuses and satifies us both. I'm impressed by how he achieves a good balance when coping with my intuitive prejudices. He seems to accept that I could be correct, but reserves his right, and sees it as his role, to challenge me. And he seems to be able to do this without irritating me in the way that others have done in the past. I guess that's why I'm paying him such a large fee. As I'm thinking about this, I notice that he's talking through the various phases of his cycle.

"Phases 4 and 5 are particularly important. I will be wanting you to tell me about the company, the people, what you've found out in your first three weeks. You've said a good deal about Freddie but much less about Arthur, Willis and the sons-in-law. We'll need to think about how the changes you're proposing will affect everyone."

"Is that what you mean by winners and losers?"

"Yes. Because it could be critical to the action we take. People who resist change usually believe that they have nothing to gain from it and that they will be better off with the status quo. Do we know what the Stocks family's relative shareholdings are and could that explain, say, the difference between the attitudes of Freddie and Arthur? If Freddie has few shares and relies on the status and income of his present position, it may not be surprising that he wants to keep things as they are."

"Particularly if he thinks he might get my job if I fail?"

"Right Phil. That's the sort of thing we need to think about. If we can get them all to see themselves as winners, this will remove most of the barriers."

"Which is where Phase 6 – the education and involvement – comes in?"

"Right. If you do this phase well, it can make Phase 7 almost unnecessary because that is where you win their hearts and minds. Though it's likely that there will be some action to take at this stage. For instance, even if you find that you do not have to remove people, it may still be necessary to change their places in the organisation."

"Such as giving someone like Freddie a different job, maybe?"

"Maybe Phil, maybe."

His pained expression indicates that he's still unimpressed by my desire to convert everything into action at much too early a stage. But he refrains from saying so – it isn't necessary now that he's made me so aware of this weakness.

I'm impressed with the logic and the practical nature of these phases of the change cycle and I'm surprised to find myself being curious to see the rest of it. Alan's getting short of space on the flipchart so we move on to a pre-printed paper which contains the total framework.

I look at this and, as is my tendency with such frameworks, I can't resist trying to find weaknesses. I decide to share them with Alan – after all, he's being well paid and he might as well earn it.

"I can see Phase 8 clearly in my mind, Alan – I guess I would define outputs in some kind of business plan." He nods approvingly. "But I have some problems with 'start change activities' because I'm not sure that we haven't already done this at Phase 7. Surely Phase 7 – removing the barriers – *is* the start of the change process?"

"I see your problem, Phil, and there may, in practice, be grey areas between them and loops back at that and many other stages. My suggestion is that we define the change activities in your case as the things which need to be done to achieve your business objectives – own brand, move centre of gravity, etc. – and Phase 7 as those things which need to be put in place before the change activities are attempted. They remove the barriers and create the right conditions to move the business to where you want it to be."

"Like what?"

"Like changing the organisation structure, getting the key players on your side, maybe even removing people or bringing in new ones. The idea is to create organisational processes which are compatible with the change you want to bring about. At a later stage I'll talk to you more about processes, when we get on to the organisation structure you want to work with."

Words like 'processes' would normally turn me off as being too academic, but I heard a lot about this kind of thinking at ABT, during my last year at Chapmans. And I realise that the new strategy at Weetflakes will require a rethink of all existing structures and processes. Marketing and sales in particular will require very different ways of

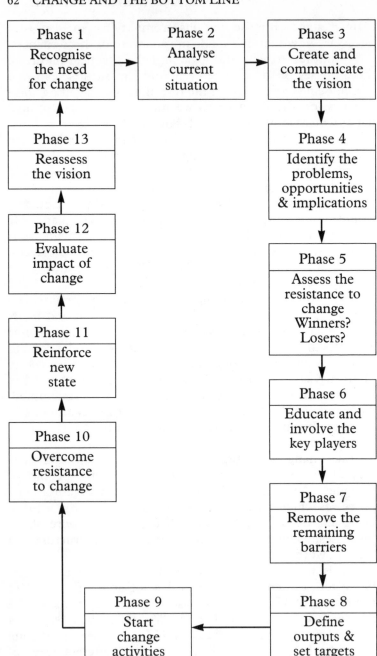

operating when own brand is more dominant, and the relationship between them is likely to be totally different.

I decide to continue being devil's advocate.

"Okay Alan. I'll buy that, but Phase 10 worries me a bit. How come you meet resistance if you've removed the barriers at Phase 7?"

"Christine was so right about you," says Alan, "you're making me work for my fee. Yes, of course that would be the case in an ideal world. But my experience, and I'm sure yours if you think about it, is that, however well you plan for change, there will always be some resistance you don't expect, and you have to be prepared to deal with it. I'll offer you some concepts and frameworks when the time comes."

His mention of Christine reminds me of his business relationship with her. It says something about him, and the interest he's created in his ideas, that I had almost forgotten. I decide that I will ask him for a bit more information about their work together before he goes, partly to satisfy my own curiosity about her present personal life.

Time is moving on now – it's nearly 5 pm – and I ask if we can have a quick break for me to hear the football results. That part of British life was one of the things I missed most while in the USA and I don't like to miss out. We agree to finish by 7 pm and I nip out to pass this on to Jean so she can plan our evening meal accordingly. The atmosphere in the lounge, where Jean and Angela are watching TV, is still frosty.

Alan quickly takes me through Phases 11, 12 and 13, emphasising particularly the importance of Phase 11, reinforcing the new state. He says that new behaviours have to be given positive reinforcement, otherwise there will be a tendency to slip back. He mentions how often some early success at implementing change can cause those at the top to relax and thus allow previous practices to drift back.

"I guess that's why you also need Phase 12 as the evaluation stage," I say, becoming more comfortable with this framework every minute. Alan nods in agreement. "But I'm rather surprised that Phase 13 requires you to reassess the vision. I thought the very idea of visions and mission statements is that they are permanent, otherwise people have no consistent sense of direction."

"That may be the case with a corporate mission statement, Phil, though even there I believe it needs to be reviewed from time to time. But the vision in this context relates to the particular series of changes that you want to bring about. There must come a time when you've implemented your business plan to change the way Weetflakes operates. Then, depending on what further changes are needed, you'll need another vision to start off that process."

"Or maybe not, if we are where we want to be."

"Maybe not, but the rate of change taking place in the outside world usually makes it necessary to make change a continuous process."

I feel suitably put down by this obvious point because I know he's right. The likely rate of change in manufacturing technology, distribution methods and retailer bargaining power in the food sector is such that, even if we position Weetflakes where it needs to be, another change process will have to be planned, though with luck not as fundamental as this one.

We spend the time until 7 pm doing further work on Phase 2, having agreed for me to look at the vision next week. Alan's incisive style of questioning means that I examine more critically the information and perceptions I've brought back with me, in particular my assumptions about the attitudes and behaviour of the key players.

He makes me realise even more clearly that, if I tried to confront Freddie or Willis about their resistance to change, it would be very difficult to point to actual behaviours. Indeed, he even makes me realise that I have avoided communication with Freddie after that awkward first day and have not yet had a meaningful discussion with him. I resolve to do so early next week.

When I describe some of the discussions I've had with Willis and Julian Weatherall, particularly about new product development, Alan makes me think about whether that could be an even more serious potential problem. Gavin Simmonds is obviously frustrated about his inability to have his marketing ideas listened to and it seems to be a lot to do with poor communications between Willis as Marketing

Director and Julian as Research Director. As I know that our ability to make new own brand products available quickly will be a vital part of our new strategy, I agree to explore this one further.

Alan also gives me new insight by persuading me to use adjectives which describe the strengths (not the weaknesses) of the directors, including the Stockses. I'm surprised to find that both Willis and Freddie come out of this rather well and it makes me realise how much I would be losing if either of them went. The flipchart looks like this.

Freddie	**Willis**
● Experienced	● Popular
● Determined	● Gregarious
● Strong willed	● Creative
● Respected	● Persuasive
● Powerful	● Influential
● Deep knowledge of manufacturing technology	● Deep knowledge of marketing

Admittedly these qualities relate to the business as it is, rather than as it needs to be, but there is no doubt that these are qualities which should not be cast aside lightly. I see it as a significant achievement by Alan to convince me of this and it makes me look forward to seeing Freddie and Willis again on Monday with more positive intentions.

Before Alan leaves (which I realise with guilt and foreboding is well after 7 pm) he briefs me on the way to approach the creation of the vision. He stresses that I must adapt it to words and style with which I'm comfortable. He leaves me a briefing on a page of the flipchart which looks like this:

Requirements of a Vision Statement

● A clear statement of what the business will be like if change is achieved.
● It should appear to be both achieveable and desirable.
● Based on values which everyone can buy into.
● Quantitative and qualitative elements.

- Something which energises people and gives them an incentive to let go of the past.
- Also challenges people to commit to the future.
- Has real substance, not just rousing words.

I agree that I will work on this and that we will meet in a couple of weeks, probably up in Claydon this time, so that he can get a feel for the environment. We will then make progress on Phases 4 and 5, using the further information I will have collected by then.

I walk him to the front door and we see Jean in the hall. I introduce her to Alan and she puts on a very charming manner, which I know will be reversed when she gets me on her own. Tactlessness with Mark over lunch and being nearly an hour late for dinner is likely to be an unfortunate combination.

I walk outside with Alan, towards his car parked on the narrow road outside our house.

"How's Christine, by the way?" I say, hoping this will lead on to some news about her personal life.

"She's fine Phil, just fine." He hesitates before he opens the car door. Then he turns to me.

"I suppose you ought to know, Phil, and I hope it doesn't affect our work together. I left my family last week to go to live with Christine. I guess you can understand how these things happen, more than most. And you know what sort of person she is."

Yes, I know. I know too well. Though I reassure him as he gets into his car that it will make no difference, I know it will. Because he has done what I never had the guts to do. And, however helpful he has been, I don't really want to spend more time with him.

Chapter 10

It's Friday of the following week and I'm at a Board meeting, the first since I've been at Weetflakes. Apparently they take place monthly. The meeting is entering its third hour and I'm puzzled about what has been achieved. As I look down the table, I see Martin Egerton, trying hard to conceal his impatience, and I strongly suspect that he's wondering the same thing.

Arthur is in the chair and, to put it kindly, he is not the most effective chairman of a meeting I've ever met. He lets the discussion go off at tangents, never seems to seize the opportunity to move on and can't resist embellishing every agenda item with his own philosophy of business.

The bigger problem, however, is the agenda. It's full of items which really shouldn't be dealt with at a Board meeting – Christmas card, staff outing, for instance – and those that are important, such as the financial position, would have been passed over without discussion had it not been for my intervention.

I've been trying hard to keep a low profile, but I couldn't resist saying something in response to their complacent attitudes. I heard Ernie Taylor, who attends as Company Secretary, tell us that sales were "over budget" and profits were "on budget". I intervened to say that, whether or not it's on budget, 4 per cent return on sales and 7 per cent return on capital are nothing to write home about. I was not sure what to make of the silence that followed, broken by

Martin Egerton's sensible suggestion that we review the required profit levels when we start the next budget preparation process which will begin quite soon.

At the moment George Plant has come into the meeting to present his capital proposal for replacement vans and lorries. I'm grateful that, at last, we're going to discuss something which makes an impact on the business. Yet I'm concerned about this purchase going ahead because it may close options for future reorganisation of distribution.

Fortunately, it's not difficult for me to raise enough questions for the proposal to be delayed. I wonder if it would have gone through without my intervention because it was very poorly presented. There was no financial justification at all – just a statement that the fleet is getting old, bigger and better vehicles are on the market and we need to replace about half of them. I ask about repair costs, about the possibility of leasing rather than buying and also whether we have considered subcontracting all or part of the distribution operation.

The answers clearly indicate that a decision needs to be delayed and, in order to ensure this as well as put down a marker about my likely future intentions, I say to Arthur, "I'd like to defer this one in any case, Mr Chairman, because, when we review our future strategy, I would like to have as many options as possible and maximum capital availability."

Arthur looks across to Freddie and I expect some opposition. But I'm pleasantly surprised.

"No Chairman, I agree with Mr Moorley. It's a large amount of money and it's best not to rush into it."

My surprise is tempered by the knowledge that Freddie and Willis are always careful to be supportive in public, and with Martin Egerton and Arthur there it was perhaps predictable. Nevertheless, I decide that this will be a good time to have that one-to-one discussion with Freddie.

I approach him as the meeting breaks up just before lunch. I suggest that we go out for a drink and a sandwich at a local pub, then have a chat afterwards. He agrees, a little grudgingly maybe, but it would have been easy for him to find an excuse not to come.

I suggest that we drive a little way out to a pub I've seen in the next village about three miles away. I think that we might not be sufficiently relaxed in one of the Claydon pubs, with other Weetflakes personnel around.

I deliberately keep the conversation away from Weetflakes while we're driving there and as we get our drinks. I try to adopt Alan Angus's suggestion of asking open, not closed, questions, not allowing Freddie to escape with easy, yes or no answers.

I'm surprised to find that, although he's 45, he married only recently a woman much younger than him, who used to work in the sales office. They have two children under three and another on the way. He tells me that his all-consuming passion is cricket, but that the demands of his young family have impeded his activities for the Claydon first eleven. I notice that his voice softens, and the piercing blue eyes seem less agressive, when the conversation moves away from Weetflakes.

As I start to eat my tuna sandwich and Freddie tackles his sausage and chips, we begin to talk about Weetflakes. I find it hard to persuade him to open up about my predecessors' problems but, in response to my question about job security, he says, "I just felt, well all of us felt, that they didn't see us as part of their plans. That was the problem, Mr Moorley."

For about the fourth time I ask him to call me Phil and he responds by calling me nothing at all. Why is it that they find it so difficult to be informal up here? I ask him whom he means by all of us.

"Well us Stockses I guess, and Julian and Martin. We all felt insecure and we still do, to be perfectly honest. People assume that, just because we're family, we have lots of brass and don't need to worry. But we've got young families and, in my case, my mother's holding all the shares from our side of the family."

So, without my having to probe very far at all, I've found out that Alan was right about Freddie's needs and motivations. He's got a young family, he needs a regular income and he saw the previous MDs as coming to take it away. And I was in danger of falling into the same trap.

As our meeting moves from the pub to his office (at my

suggestion, to try to continue the more relaxed atmosphere) I find some good reasons for wanting to keep Freddie at Weetflakes. I discover that his knowledge of manufacturing is complemented by a surprisingly up to date view of distribution costs and logistics. I'm also staggered to find that he doesn't disagree with the conclusion that regional manufacturing and distribution centres are needed. Indeed, he claims to have suggested it years ago but to have been overruled by Arthur and Willis.

Unfortunately I'm unable, at this stage, to stop Freddie going into a long catalogue of management failings, in everyone else but himself. He gives many more examples of Arthur and Willis resisting change and keeping Weetflakes back in the 1960s. He is particularly scathing about his own team – Julian Weatherall is "a public school twit", George Plant is "frightened of his own shadow", Joe McEvoy "can't communicate with anyone", Peter Thackray "has no initiative". He reserves the worst criticism for Amanda Slade – "Lord knows what she's paid for".

I feel sad that the conversation has turned this way, but can't resist allowing him to go on because he seems to be enjoying it and I'm picking up useful, if rather biased, information.

In the end I turn the situation round by asking who is delivering good value. To my surprise he says, "Ernie Taylor does a sound job and so does Martin. Don't underestimate what Martin Moss has done for our relationships with the trade. Willis and Arthur will tell you that it was Jim Stocks who built them up and, good man though he was, it's Martin who's really gained us ground. And we've worked really well together to deliver some good deals for the top retailers."

I'm curious about his view of Ernie Taylor, who seems to me to be one of the worst performers of all. I ask him why he values Ernie so highly and his reply makes me realise that, for all his experience, Freddie has no idea what sort of support he should be getting.

"He's accurate, he gets the numbers out for Board meetings, he does what we tell him. For a bean counter, he's okay."

I try to persuade Freddie to talk about some of the work

Stephen Young, the management accountant, is doing, in particular some of the costings of distribution activities which I have seen. I'm amazed to find that Freddie doesn't know of this work and clearly regards Stephen as a clerk who works for Ernie.

Our meeting ends on a friendly but indeterminate note. I deliberately give no assurances but ask to see him the following week.

"I'm putting together a vision of what I want Weetflakes to be, Freddie, and I'd like to share it with you."

Encouraged by the improvement in understanding I've achieved by this one-to-one with Freddie, I decide to do the same with Willis later the same day. I say that I will go to his office and I notice that, unlike Freddie who asked me to sit in one of the easy chairs at the side of his room, Willis lets me sit across the desk from him.

Willis is as unlike Freddie in appearance as it is possible for a cousin to be. He is quite tall, around six feet, with greying hair and looking more than his 43 years. His face is long and angular and breaks into a smile easily, though you are not sure if the eyes are smiling as much as the mouth. And behind the eyes you suspect that there is a certain insecurity, because the mind does not quite match up to the superficially impressive manner.

I'm fascinated by the difference between the way Willis behaves compared to Freddie. Until today's meeting, Freddie has emanated non-verbal signals of suspicion and hostility, particularly in public. Yet at the pub and afterwards, he was friendly and open about personal and business matters, far more so than I could have expected.

Yet with Willis it's the other way round. In public he has been supportive, almost going out of his way to appear so, particularly when his father has been in earshot. Yet, when I try to persuade him to talk about himself and about his hopes and fears for Weetflakes, he just clams up. Maybe I should have started off with him in the pub too, but all the open questions I can think of don't persuade him to talk for more than a few words. It's almost as if being on our own is embarrassing for him. Maybe it requires him to reveal too much about himself, without the protection of his loud social manner and northern joviality. This reminds me how important it is to avoid judging people solely by their public face.

I find the whole situation difficult but decide not to give up. I tell him about my need to develop a vision and that I would like him to share it.

"Tell me what your vision of Weetflakes is Willis – what do you think it should be like in, say, five years' time?"

He pauses and is clearly uneasy.

"I'm not sure I can do that easily, Phil. I haven't thought about it for a long time. Your predecessors told us what we had to do and employed expensive consultants to justify their ideas."

"Forget that just for a minute, Willis. Give me *your* vision, assuming for the moment that we have a clean sheet."

He still looks uneasy but, after pausing for a while to make up his mind, he seems, at last, to come off the fence.

"My vision, Phil, is to bring the Weetflakes brand back to where it used to be – market leader, household name, part of children's growing up. And that means investment – in advertising, in-store promotions, product improvement. More variants on the basic products and some new innovations in different cereal types. That's my vision Phil, but no one ever listens to it. And that includes my dad."

I suddenly see Willis's problem and realise that he is going to be a far greater challenge than Freddie. He is living in a 1960s time warp. He doesn't understand that his vision has been overtaken by events. Events which have made the brands of supermarkets like Sainsbury and Tesco more powerful than many of the manufacturers. Events which have seen a polarisation between the international giants who can afford to invest in expensive global marketing and the regionally based pygmies who struggle to find a profitable niche where they can survive. Kelloggs can invest in the way that Willis suggests because the cost is only a small percentage of their massive turnover. But for Weetflakes to compete on equal terms it would require an investment which is totally unrealistic.

Yet how do I show Willis that these are the facts of life, and how do I get him committed to a different vision? I decide to probe further.

"I can see that you would be excited by this vision, Willis, and so would I. But let's just say that it proves to be unachievable after we've given it our best shot. How would you then feel about the vision of Weetflakes which the consultants put forward? Concentrating on own label and maybe moving some of the activities away from Claydon?"

He stands up from his desk and turns his back on me to look out of the window, at the vans lining up to load, all bearing the Weetflakes brand.

"If I'm honest, I think that I'd probably rather do something else and live off my dividends."

He's suddenly changed, in just a few minutes, from the reserved, closed person who started this meeting to a man who is full of visible emotion. I wonder if he'll regret this conversation later on and if maybe I will too. I have obviously hit an emotional button which triggered off some pent up feelings. I decide I'd better try to calm the atmosphere a little.

"I'm sure it won't come to that, Willis. I want you to stay whatever the strategy because you've got too much experience to throw away. I hope to convince you that we can work together to achieve a vision that we are all committed to."

I leave his office straight away because we both seem to feel a little awkward. I realise that these individual discussions are giving me greater value than a week of meetings and I decide to try to catch Arthur before he goes home. I'm now curious to know his feelings about his son and his nephew, and how far he believes that Willis is serious in his desire to leave if he can't re-create the past.

Arthur is alone in his office and, I suspect, ready to go home, even though it is before 5 o'clock. One of the mysteries of Weetflakes so far is what Arthur actually does, or at least what he will do once I'm fully settled in. I've always had doubts about splitting the chairman and managing director roles, particularly when both people are working full time. I know that this is something I'll have to confront before long, but today I'll concentrate on his views about the younger generation. I know that I'll have to be careful when encouraging him to talk about Willis – fathers inevitably find it hard to be objective about their own sons.

I start by telling him about my desire to create and communicate the vision which will help to start the process of change. And the need for me to hold discussions about the implications of the change for the people in the business. I lay it on pretty thick by saying, "I was struck by what you said at my interview about the people at Weetflakes being family to you. And I guess that applies to Willis and Freddie more than anyone else. I've therefore decided to pay special attention to them and to their needs, not just for them but because of all the skills they have to offer."

I wonder rather guiltily what Arthur would say if he knew what I'd been thinking over the previous weekend, in particular the conversation I had with Martin Egerton.

But he looks at me with an expression of total approval on his face. He says, "Now that's what I like to hear, Philip lad." I've given up trying to stop him calling me lad. "They have a great deal to offer if they're treated right. That's what didn't happen before. You say that you're wanting to meet their needs, perhaps I can help you there."

"I'd appreciate it Arthur," I say. "What do you think will make them committed to my – our vision of Weetflakes?"

He pauses for a while and looks me rather unnervingly in the eye, something he hasn't done much before. It's almost as if he's trying to test my sincerity.

"I'll deal with Freddie first, Philip. He just wants to be valued, to be involved, to be given a clear brief. He's no strategist, is Freddie, but he's a great doer and very loyal, once he's on your side."

"And maybe disloyal if he's not on your side? Isn't that what happened with the other MDs?"

He looks me in the eye again. "You're no fool, Philip. Yes, that sums Freddie up very well."

"And Willis?" I ask, hoping that he'll continue his open approach.

He looks away this time, obviously uncertain how much to tell me. There's at least thirty seconds of silence. He then comes back to me with a question.

"What do you think Willis's needs are Philip? You say

you've spoken to him. What did he say?"

I realise that I'm taking a risk by telling the truth, but I decide to do so.

"Basically he said that he wants Weetflakes to be like it was twenty years ago, otherwise he's rather be out of it."

This visibly shakes Arthur for a moment. I think that he might be going to erupt, either in anger or in tears. I see his knuckles go white as he grabs the arms of his chair.

"That lad's a great disappointment to me, Philip. You see why Hill Benson wouldn't accept him as MD? No vision, you see. No ability to accept change. Yet he has tremendous talent at marketing and new product development, as long as he's given direction. I was able to do that once – I only hope that you can do it now."

"I rather think that depends on him too, Arthur. Whether he's prepared to accept my direction and, in particular, whether he's prepared to buy into the new vision and use his talents. I have to convince him that his marketing and product development skills are just as important in the new situation."

"But are they, Philip?"

"Oh yes Arthur, absolutely. That's the mistake people make about supplying supermarket brands. They think that you just have to be the manufacturing arm of a top retailer, who tells you what to produce. But the retailers are looking for innovation in new products and promotions all the time and that's what can give us a competitive edge."

"Well, if you can convince Willis of that. . ."

I interrupt to say: "If *we* can convince Willis, Arthur – I need your help. I've a feeling that that was another mistake which my predecessors made."

"You know Philip," says Arthur, "that is absolutely right. You're very shrewd. I really do believe that you're the one who's going to save Weetflakes."

I don't respond to this rather extravagant comment. I decide that I'll take advantage of the positive relationship we're developing by asking him about another missing link in my knowledge of the motivation of the key players.

"What about you, Arthur?" I say. "What do you want from Weetflakes?"

"Me, Philip? I just want Weetflakes to survive. I'd like to keep involved, though I've no illusions about my future contribution. I realise that you're taking over now and that I'll be best to take a back seat. As long as. . ."

Here he pauses, unable to find the words, not because of emotion, more because he seems embarrassed.

"As long as?" I encourage him.

"I suppose as long as I'm confident that the business is in the right hands and, if I'm honest, that Willis is happy. I don't want him to do anything else, Philip. I'm worried that he'll go and start his own business somewhere and lose his shirt."

We chat for a little while longer, moving on to talk about some of the others. I find that Arthur shares the high opinion of Martin Moss and surprises me by not giving all the credit for the successful sales operation to the much lamented Jim. Arthur tells me that his late brother was 12 years younger than him and the heir apparent to the top job at Stocks. The business never recovered from his death, in Arthur's view.

I also find that Arthur shares the universally low opinion of Julian Weatherall. However, as this seems to be because of his constant conflict with Willis, I'm not sure how objective this information is.

I feel guilty as well when I discover that Arthur is equally concerned about Amanda Slade's contribution and that my unkind speculation about her role as Arthur's PA was wholly unjustified. Apparently she is Arthur's niece – his sister's daughter – but I am given the impression that they are all rather fed up with her lack of commitment.

I decide not to say anything when Arthur extols the virtues of Ernie Taylor as Chief Accountant. Like Freddie, he has no idea of what Stephen Young is doing or of the potential contribution which a good management accountant could make to the business.

As I leave Arthur's office, he comes up to me, shakes my hand and grabs my shoulder. I find it a bit embarrassing and instinctively pull back, worried that he's going to hug me. Instead he says, "Philip. You're the man for this job. I wasn't sure before but now I am."

As I get back to my office, relieved to be away from the

embarrassment of Arthur's touching, and apparently genuine, display of emotion, I decide to spend an hour or so reviewing my position before I go back to the loneliness of my hotel room.

I get out the paper which Alan Angus gave me on the change cycle. I focus on Phases 2, 3, 4, 5 and 6 and draw a new dotted line on the paper to complete a loop.

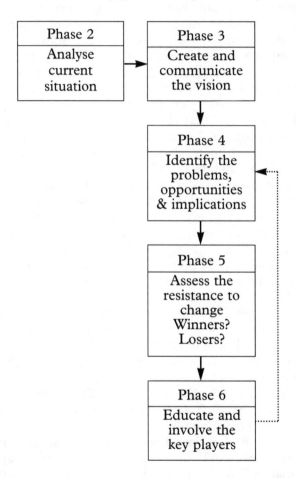

I decide to tell Alan Angus next week that life at Weetflakes is not as neat and tidy as his change cycle suggests. But then I remember that he made this point himself at our last meeting. It's a logical process and a checklist, but not an inflexible framework. In practice, the process of assessing the problems and implications of the vision and discovering who are the winners and losers requires you to begin involving the key players. And that can cause you to modify your view about the problems, as happened with Freddie this afternoon.

Looking at the paper reminds me that I may have created the vision in my own mind but I still have to communicate it more widely. I pull out of my locked office drawer the paper I wrote on Sunday when Jean went out for a couple of hours. After Saturday's tension, I didn't dare work again while she was there, though I could tell that she knew how much Weetflakes is occupying my thoughts at present. In the end I was ashamed to find that I was relieved to be back on the M1 on Sunday evening. I must be careful not to become too obsessed – I just hope relationships with the family will be better when we all move to Claydon.

My first vision statement, which I tried to prepare according to the brief which Alan gave me, did not take me long to draft. I've never had any doubt that the strategy suggested by the consultants is absolutely right – it reinforces all my views about the way smaller operations in the food business have to go if they are to survive. It also has strong similarities to my own plans for Chapmans in the USA, before I was booted out.

But, although the content was straightforward, it was still not easy to prepare a vision statement which met the criteria of Alan's brief. It had to energise people, to encourage them to let go of the past, to make them commit themselves. At the time Alan briefed me on this I thought it was rather cliché ridden, but I now see the benefit of trying to meet these criteria. My first draft stated what Weetflakes needed to do, but lacked inspiration.

I then phoned a friend who was a neighbour in the States and now works in AT & T's European operation. I knew that AT & T are keen on 'visioning', to use the phrase I'd heard in the USA. My friend told me of three principles which they work to in AT & T and which I found helpful:

- It should be short and strong enough to arouse emotional commitment.
- It must point out a strategy for achieving competitive advantage.
- It must align with the organisational culture and values.

After a great deal of trial and error, resulting in many alterations, my Sunday efforts resulted in the following:

A Vision for Weetflakes

- To retain and build on the current strengths of Weetflakes – its name, its brands, its people, its technology.
- To create a profitable business which is recognised by its largest customers – the top ten retailers – as the most innovative and flexible cereal supplier in the UK.
- To be regarded by customers as long-term partners, providing high value to them and to the ultimate consumer.

I read it again and decide that, five days later, it still looks good. I deliberately put the name and the brands first to reassure people that they still remain key assets. I believe that the vision will be seen to be desirable, achievable and, as my AT & T friend also mentioned, measurable. We can set targets for profitability and ask the top ten retailers how they see us. It stresses the need for partnership with these customers and the need to provide value for the consumer, without specifically mentioning own label products.

I look at my watch and see that it's gone 6.30. I decide that, before going to my hotel, I'll walk round the factory just to show a presence and see what's happening. There's just one light in the office block, along the corridor about 70 yards from my office. I decide to walk down that way, and go out through the side door to the factory.

It's unusual for anyone to be in as late as this so I assume that the light I saw has been left on. It's the training room. I walk in and find Amanda Slade lying on the floor with Julian

Weatherall on top of her, making noises which suggest that he's in the middle of an orgasm. I see Amanda's terrified eyes staring at me and make a hasty exit.

Chapter 11

It's Thursday morning of the following week and I'm waiting for Alan Angus to come and see me at Weetflakes for the first time. I've been on the point of cancelling his visit several times, but each time I've stopped myself. How stupid it would be to allow the progress I've been making to be held back because I'm jealous of his relationship with Chris. Because he did what I could never bring myself to do until it was too late – leave my wife and family to live with her. I guess the strength of my feeling indicates that, deep down, I wish I'd done so.

Yesterday I decided that I'd end the uncertainty by telling Freddie and Willis that Alan was coming and how he was helping me. I suggested that they might join our discussions at subsequent meetings.

I seem to be building good relationships with both of them now, particularly Freddie, and as part of the process of 'educating and involving the key players' I shared my vision statement with them. I was satisfied, but not elated, at their response. Willis in particular was quite guarded, as if to say 'it's up to you'. But at least there was no outright rejection and I plan to present it to the rest of the management team later today, at about 3 o'clock.

As I'm now getting on so well with Freddie, I decided to confide in him about Julian and Amanda. He was first incredulous, then intrigued and ended up in helpless laughter as I described the brilliant timing of my entry. He said that he had had no idea of any relationship and that, from a family point of view, it was 'dynamite', because Julian's wife is Amanda's cousin. I'm dreading having to talk to either of them and they've kept well out of my way so far.

Alan arrives around 11 am and I update him on what's happened since our meeting, in particular the more positive contact with Freddie, Willis and Arthur. There's something about Alan's manner which makes me seek his approval and I find myself slightly disappointed that he is not effusive in his praise. As I look at his young face and his slight, tiny frame, I can't stop myself wondering what Chris sees in him. But then I recall how she used to tell me off for assuming that women were only attracted to young, Adonis type males. The husband she preferred to me was also small and, I thought, a bit of a wimp.

But Alan Angus is no wimp. He asks me a large number of questions, in particular he seems keen to become aware of how the company operates – the business processes as he calls them. I show him the vision and this time I'm not disappointed by his reaction. He tells me it's excellent and I revel in his approval.

He's not sure about my presenting it at today's meeting and he asks if we can review that decision later. I'm concerned about the idea of cancelling the meeting at this late stage, but say nothing for the time being.

As my secretary Julie brings in some coffee, I ask Alan what's next.

"You're moving round the change cycle fairly well, Philip, and we're at the stage where we can start to consider the barriers to change – Phase 7, if you remember. You're obviously progressing with educating the key players, which is fine."

"Do you want me to suggest the barriers which I think might be in the way?" I ask.

"No Phil, not yet, I want us first to look at the organisation and how far it is likely to impede change as presently structured. I mentioned at our last meeting that it's useful to match your organisation to the key business processes. I'd like us to brainstorm these for a few minutes."

I've always been sceptical of jargon so I ask him just what

he means by key processes.

"A series of activities which people in the business have to carry out to meet its objectives," he says, rather as if he's learnt it from a text book.

"Like manufacturing?"

"Yes, but isn't manufacturing just one activity which is part of a larger process?"

"You mean the supply chain?"

"Right Phil, let's put that up as the main central process which is our starting point."

He writes up 'Supply chain' as the first entry under the heading of 'KEY BUSINESS PROCESSES'.

"So what would you add to the list, Phil? Think of fundamental processes which are necessary to achieve your new vision."

"Managing customers would be my first priority. We'll need good, lasting relationships."

He writes up 'Managing customer relationships' as the second entry.

I think more about the implications of our strategy. We'll need to have an efficient supply chain, work in partnership with our customers and, as I tried to convince Willis last week, innovate with new product development even more than before.

"Innovation is also critical," I say and 'Innovation' goes up on the flipchart.

"These are your fundamental business processes, Philip," Alan says. "I'm sure of that from what you've told me before. But let's also think about the support processes, what else you need to do well to support your supply chain, your customer relationships and your innovation."

I begin to realise what he's talking about, something which is clearly lacking at Weetflakes. "Financial information?" I say and he pauses a little before writing it up.

"Just financial?" he asks.

"No, of course not," I say. "Certainly we need better management accounting but it's also information on sales forecasts, production efficiency. Although, in fairness, Weetflakes are quite good at non-financial information already. It's the financials where they're so weak."

Alan nods and adds 'Information management' to the list.

"I'm going to chart these in a moment, Phil, but there is one more to add, one which you might expect me to include. One which supports all the processes."

"One which I'd expect you to include? It must be around the people, I guess."

"Right Phil. The process of managing the people will be fundamental to your vision and it's one which you, as MD, will have to drive. In fact, once the strategy has been launched, it may be the main process which you ought to manage."

"Supported by a Personnel Director?"

"Maybe, Phil. Let's discuss that later, once we've linked the processes to your organisation. Now have we left anything out?"

I look at his list for a moment. It shows the following:

Key business processes

- Supply chain
- Managing customer relationships
- Innovation
- Information management
- Human resource management

I pick up his pen and write up one more entry which has just occurred to me.

- Quality management

"I'd like to think it wasn't necessary, Alan, but, having looked at Weetflakes' present control systems, I'm afraid it's going to be. We're going to need a big quality management initiative to achieve the standards necessary for the vision."

"OK Phil, that's good. Anything else?"

"Well yes, I guess there must be but I'm not sure how it fits in."

"Where what fits in?"

"Marketing. That's rather fundamental, isn't it?"

"Yes, but you're still thinking in functional rather than

process terms. Isn't marketing part of managing your customer relationships? And your innovation process?"

I nod in agreement but feel that there's still something missing. Of course! "Brand management, maintaining the value of the branded products. Not so important as it was under the previous strategy, but still something which must not be neglected."

"OK Phil, let's put all the processes on your white board here and we'll see how it fits."

He picks up a duster and, with my agreement, clears off some notes I put on the board earlier. I wander out to ask Julie for more coffee while he begins to draw his process framework.

When I come back, I see this on the board:

Weetflakes' Key Business Processes

"How do you like it, Phil?" he asks, looking rather pleased with himself.

I decide to wipe the smile off his face. In reality I do like it, but he's missed off what is probably the most important process of all.

"Where's the innovation process, Alan? Didn't we agree that was fundamental?"

His face drops. "How stupid," he says, "it should be alongside the top two."

"No Alan, just a moment. I've had an idea which puts innovation where it should be and covers the brand management problem too." I take his pen and put innovation in its rightful place at the top of the tree, with brand management coming down as a new branch, linking to consumers.

I stand back and look at the finished framework. I realise that there's still one missing link which needs to be put into place: the accounting process. Information management is essential but so are the statutory needs for reporting. And separating the two processes in this way makes it clearer than ever that Stephen Young needs to be Information Manager, freed from the stackles of Ernie Taylor and the traditional accounting function.

The whiteboard now looks like this:

Weetflakes' Key Business Processes

I like what I see but then the cynic in me – never far away – takes over again.

"This is all very interesting, Alan, and I found the exercise useful, but what do I do with it?"

"It will remain with you as a model and I'm sure we'll improve on it as we think further about the business. It should help you in many ways – for instance, for setting performance measures or looking at competitive advantage in terms of the cost and quality of each process. Michael Porter's done some interesting work in that area. But its first purpose is to help you to structure your organisation. If you are to manage change effectively, you want an organisation which, as far as possible, is geared to the key processes, even if this cuts across conventional functional structures."

I feel the need to challenge what he's saying because so much hangs on this. An organisation's structure should be complementary to its business strategy – I learnt that much on the various management courses I've attended over the years – but Alan is approaching this in a way which is new to me. I ask him to justify this emphasis on processes by giving me examples of companies which have benefited from it.

"That's difficult, Phil, because this is a very new area. But I can quote you examples of companies such as AT & T, Rank Xerox, Hewlett Packard, which have saved money and improved efficiency by analysing and then improving their key processes. But the best example is a company in a business similar to yours – the Personal Products Division of Unilever – which reorganised to great effect after analysing their processes. And, interestingly, their model is very similar to yours."

"I guess it would be," I say. "They're FMCG and have a similar customer base to ours. But are the business schools advocating this process approach?"

"Some are, Phil, and the rest will follow. Like many senior managers you have the touching belief that new ideas come from the academic world. My view is that they tend to follow what top companies are doing several years later. Then they package it for those who have not caught on."

My instinct is to argue with this. Everyone knows that business schools do research and I've always assumed that companies follow their ideas. But when you think about it, what do they research? It must be what companies are doing. I'm now so confident in Alan's judgement that I decide to go along with him, at least for the time being. But I'm still worried about this meeting later in the day when I'm to present my vision. It's now noon, only three hours before the arranged time, and I ought to let everyone know if I'm going to cancel it. I'm curious, even slightly irritated, that Alan questioned my having the meeting today. I ask him why.

"I just wanted to see how you were doing, Phil, and how much progress we would make today. You do have. . ." he hesitates, apparently uncertain how far he can go. I've noticed that he does this when he's going to give me some negative feedback. His technique is to have me ask him to carry on, thus taking the sting out of the criticism and making me seem to ask for it. I'm tempted not to co-operate but we're getting on so well, it seems a shame not to go along.

"Go on, Alan. We know each other well enough for you to tell me straight."

"You do have a tendency to rush into things and I wanted to be sure that you're ready to communicate it in a way which will win them over."

I fight back the temptation to be defensive, to tell him that my 'rushing into things' brought me continuous success at Universal and ABT, two of the world's top companies. I fight it back because I know that this situation at Weetflakes is different, in many ways more challenging than anything I've come across before. It is therefore right that I should be challenged and restrained by someone like Alan.

We decide to have a working lunch and spend a couple of hours looking at the way we need to structure the organisation. Then we will have a run through what I am to say about the vision and the detailed strategies which will support it, with Alan throwing a few likely questions to check that I am fully prepared.

When we start to discuss the organisation, I go to the flipchart and draw up my own job title at the top in the conventional way.

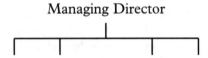

Managing Director

Alan looks at what I've done and says, "Before we move on Phil, there are two matters I'd like to raise. First of all, you've left out Arthur as Chairman, which is perhaps an indication that you have to address that issue."

I nod in agreement, relieved in a way that Alan shares my concern about the current situation and certain that I must grasp the nettle quite soon. I then say, "and your second point?"

"Just the fact that you've drawn the chart in conventional hierarchial terms. You could have designed your structure in process terms, just adding names to the chart we did earlier."

I pause, uncertain how to proceed, rather uncomfortable with this suggestion.

"It's all right, Phil," he reassures me with good humour, "Please go ahead as you planned if that's how you're most comfortable. I just wanted to make the point. But try, as far as possible, to link processes to responsibilities."

For an hour we go through the difficult exercise of trying to fit the business processes to an organisation structure with which I can feel comfortable and which will accommodate people who are now at Weetflakes. Once I became convinced that it was undesirable to get rid of Freddie or Willis, but instead that we should capitalise on their strengths, I knew I had to have an organisation structure which recognised that.

The final outcome, which in the end I am reasonably comfortable with, looks like this:

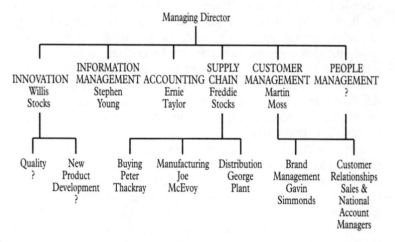

Inevitably the final structure is a compromise. I need to give Willis a key role which will capture his imagination, and the title 'Director of Innovation' will convey a vital message to him and to everyone else about its importance. I decide to take away day to day brand management from him and make it part of customer management. All promotion and marketing of brands has to be in close liaison with retail customers these days and I don't want any conflict within the organisation between the promotion of Weetflakes brands and own label. The strategies for the two will need to be closely related in the future and Martin Moss can ensure that this happens.

Giving Willis quality management is a compromise which I am able to rationalise quite easily. For the time being, until quality has been made an integral part of supply chaim management, quality control needs to be powerful and independent, something which Willis can provide. He can also, by being close to new product development, provide control at the vital stage when new products have their specifications fixed and monitor quality during the launch.

I put question marks next to quality management and new product development because I can't see how anyone at Weetflakes could fit in. It is difficult to know how much I am influenced by my own dislike of Julian Weatherall and my knowledge that he and Willis do not get on, but I just can't see him fitting into either role. Julian's present role as R & D Director, reporting to Freddie, seems to focus more on reducing the costs of existing products than anything else, and his record of new product innovation has been poor. And he doesn't have the right personality to deal with the difficult process of quality management, requiring the ability to influence and educate Freddie and his colleagues to get things right first time.

The question mark against people management is less difficult to justify, because Amanda Slade is clearly not capable of the crucial task of helping me to manage the culture change, or of eventually making me less reliant on Alan Angus. It increases my respect for Alan when he agrees on this point, reaffirming his view that I must have a high calibre personnel director as an urgent priority.

I realise only too well that the consequence of this structure is that Julian and Amanda may have to go, and I ask myself whether some subconscious Freudian influence has moved me that way, after that embarrassing encounter in the training room. I decide to tell Alan about this and I follow up by asking him how he now feels about my sacking people, after being so critical of my premature attempts to ditch Freddie.

"I've never had a problem with you asking people to leave, Phil. It's your decision. I was concerned that you were thinking of it as the easy option, before we'd looked at the impact on key players, before we'd considered the organisation structure. I can see your problem about finding Julian and Amanda in the training room because, whatever you think or say, they will see a connection. But, looking at the situation logically, they do not appear to have a role in the future of Weetflakes and there is probably some merit in a few changes in people taking place. As I said at our first meeting, some new faces can help and good new people looking after quality, new product development and personnel should help to balance the fact that the Stocks family have been retained."

"Though Julian and Amanda are family, if you remember," I remind him.

"Oh yes, of course. I suppose that's an issue you'll need to discuss with Arthur, Willis and Freddie. But before we leave this, there is something about your structure which worries me."

"What's that?" I ask.

"It's customer management reporting directly to you. Customers are within the supply chain process and I'd rather see Martin Moss reporting to Freddie."

"Well I'm sorry, Alan," I reply, for the first time today feeling irritated with him and his slavish emphasis on processes. "I just don't agree. We both said that the handling of customer relationships is one of the key business processes and I'd prefer to give that dominance. I personally want to drive the development of relationships with customers over the next few years and that means much more than managing the supply chain with them in mind. It means developing new products for them, keeping our Weetflakes brands listed and helping them with special promotions. And, apart from anything else, Martin Moss is one of our biggest assets and I want to improve his status. Reporting to Freddie, rather than Willis as he is at present, will not achieve that, whatever your precious process chart might say."

"Okay Phil, Okay," says Alan, "you've made your point very powerfully. I just wanted to test you out. I've never pretended that the process chart should dominate your final decision, it just plays a part. But the chart does show you how important it is for there to be good communications between Freddie as Supply Chain Director and Martin as Customer Management Director, or whatever you plan to call him. Do they get on well?"

"Yes Alan," I reply, "that's another reason why I'm confident that this structure will work."

"Fine Phil, but I hope you'll remember this discussion if you ever decide to change the people in either of those two jobs."

I can see his point. If you structure an organisation on the assumption that people have good informal relationships, that decision must be reviewed when the people change. This is fairly typical of the advice which Alan gives – practical, possibly rather obvious common sense, but the sort which is often forgotten.

We have only a few minutes before the time we agreed to rehearse my presentation of the vision. Alan reminds me of the need to discuss the future of the Chairman's role with Arthur, and maybe later with Martin Egerton. We both agree that a part-time Chairman's role or a figurehead title such as President would be desirable, but this must only be done with Arthur's support. The impact on the culture of being seen to treat him badly would make the prospects for change that much more difficult. I mention to Alan that only last week Arthur told me he would be happy to take a back seat role, so I do not anticipate a great problem in persuading him to accept this.

"And I suppose I'd better phone Andrew Kent to ask him to headhunt me a Quality Manager, a New Product Development Manager and a Personnel Manager," I say.

"Personnel Director, Phil," says Alan, "or at least I would recommend so. Partly to send a message about the importance of the role but, even more crucial, so that you can appoint someone of high calibre who is able to give you real advice and support."

"Didn't you say you might be able to find someone and save me the headhunters' fee?" I ask.

"Yes Phil. I did and I have someone in mind. But I'm not sure if you'd want her."

"Her?"

"Yes. She's just what you need. Bright, assertive, down to earth. A great deal of experience. And just coming over to England from France after a broken relationship. So she's even available at short notice."

"So why do you think I wouldn't want her?" I ask, with rising curiosity.

"Because her name is Marie Goodhart, Christine's younger sister."

Chapter 12

I wake up in unfamiliar surroundings and, for a moment, can't think where I am. During these last six weeks I've been at Weetflakes I've become much too used to my pleasant but rather basic hotel room at the Grimsby Moat House, only managing two weekends back in Wimbledon.

Suddenly I realise where I am. Yesterday we moved into our new home and today I will, for the first time, be going into work from Fairfield Farm House, less than half a mile from the Weetflakes site. I look at the alarm clock by the side of the bed and see that it's 6.45 am. Jean is fast asleep by my side and the sun is streaming in through the curtainless window, straight into her face. It brings out the lines around her mouth which I have noticed more and more these last few years, but all they seem to do is to make her lovelier than ever. To me she never seems to grow old as other women of her age do.

I'm amazed that little Susie hasn't woken up yet, after all the excitement of the move. I expect it's because she was so late going to bed, staying up while the rest of us had a drink to celebrate our new home.

I'm looking forward to family life here in Claydon. Somehow we haven't been together as a family since the day I heard I was leaving Chapmans, and now we have the chance to make up all the lost ground. In particular I need to spend more time with Jean and to bring our relationship back to the heights of our time in the USA. Somehow with us two, there are no half measures. We're either as loving and romantic as a pair of teenagers or we're drifting apart. I've felt much too much of the latter during the last month or two.

I also need to build on the improvement in my relationship with Mark. Yesterday he was almost like the son I knew in the USA, his enthusiasm for the new house overcoming his usual tendency to object to everything. I promised to help him fix a basketball practice area behind one of the outhouses so that he can take up again the sport he loved so much in the States.

I get up and wander onto the landing, bending my head to avoid hitting the low doorway. It feels very cold as this is a big house and the rather antiquated heating system has only just come on. This is one of the many practical problems I foresee, but they have been pushed aside in the face of everyone's enthusiam for the house, including, I have to admit, my own. I suspect that I'll be putting my hand in my pocket for many years to come, but my pay-off from Chapmans and my generous salary from Weetflakes make this less of a problem than it might have been.

I go down the winding stairs and make my way across the hall which is still littered with packing cases. I feel quite relieved that it's Thursday and I have to go in to work, leaving the others to finish the clearing up. In the kitchen it is pleasantly warm because of the Aga cooker which Jean insisted on installing before we moved in. I help myself to a glass of orange juice from the fridge and sit down in the chair beside the Aga. I think about the next two days at Weetflakes which promise to be eventful, to say the least.

It's now three weeks since Alan Angus visited me and we had the management meeting at which I presented the new vision. That meeting went quite well and achieved as much as I could have hoped for. I was particularly gratified by the positive response of Willis, whom I deliberately tried to win over by emphasising the importance of innovation. I think I've finally convinced him that moving to retailer own brand products as the source of future growth, doesn't necessarily mean that the Weetflakes brand will be forgotten. Also that own brand products require more, not less, creative skill from the chosen suppliers. Our retail customers will be looking for us to take the lead in innovation and this is the way we can gain a competitive edge.

The following week I shared my ideas on organisation structure with Freddie, Willis and Martin. I saw them all individually – I still notice that the Stockses find it hard not to play games at meetings – and was again pleased at the response. All of them favoured the departure of Julian and Amanda, though not underestimating the family tensions which will result. Freddie suggested rather deviously, but not too seriously, that we should blackmail them both into resigning as Julian would do anything to avoid his wife's finding out about Amanda, particularly as the wife holds the purse strings in the Weatherall household.

But just as I felt that I was cruising smoothly around the change cycle, I began to realise why Phase 7 – removing the remaining barriers to change – is there. I hit an unexpected barrier in Arthur. I found that Freddie and Willis were fully in agreement with my view that there is no role for a full-time Executive Chairman. Willis, who I thought would know Arthur's hopes and expectations better than anyone, was confident that he would accept a part-time role with pleasure and relief.

But we were wrong. Apparently Arthur's idea of 'taking a back seat' does not mean anything less than full-time presence. He took it very badly and, for some reason, associated the suggestion with our plans to remove Julian and Amanda, which he also opposed. On Monday this week Willis, Freddie and I had a crisis meeting to decide what to do after both of them suffered family pressure over the weekend. I wonder if there are family matters which I don't fully understand behind Arthur's response.

We decided on Monday to offer Arthur the position of President for life, and suggest that he continue as Non-Executive Chairman for two days a week with a flexible consultancy contract for three years. It is a ridiculously generous offer by all that is rational, but a necessary price to buy Arthur's support. He is much loved and respected by many at Weetflakes and the change process would be set back immeasurably if he were seen to oppose it. My concern now is that the damage has already been done and that, whatever we offer him, he will not support me. Freddie's theory is that, deep down, Arthur hates the idea of the new strategy more than anyone else and this is his way of showing it.

Yesterday, in my absence, Willis was to see Arthur with the new offer, and it is a measure of the trust I now have in him that I was prepared to let him deal with this while I was away. I've noticed that both Freddie and Willis respond positively when I show confidence in them – I just hope I'm not doing this too much, too quickly.

Today Willis will let me know the outcome and we'll probably see Arthur together. Assuming that we are reasonably confident of Arthur's support, I will then see Julian Weatherall and Amanda Slade, before announcing their departure and the new organisation structure at a management meeting tomorrow. The timing of these events will be crucial.

My day is made even more hectic by the fact that Alan Angus is coming to see me first thing this morning. His visit was arranged a while ago and he was due to arrive around lunchtime, but I changed the arrangement so I could obtain his advice before the important meeting with Arthur. I also propose to introduce him to Willis and Freddie if there is time.

The final event to complete a very full day is the interview which Alan has arranged for me with Marie Goodhart late this afternoon. He will stay on to introduce me to her and then leave us together. He suggested that I take her to dinner, but I declined. To be working the first day after the move is bad enough. To tell Jean that I would be out for dinner with the sister of my former mistress would be likely to start divorce proceedings!

I'm really seeing Marie against my better judgement, but Alan's view is, if she is the right person and is too good to miss, why should I turn her down? The least I can do is see her and then consider the pros and cons. It was hard to argue with this so, in the end, I agreed for Alan to approach her.

Apparently she is Christine's half-sister. Their father left Christine's mother at an early age and married a

Frenchwoman, going to live with her in the suburbs of Paris. Marie was therefore brought up in France and went into personnel management after graduating in business studies. It was fascinating to hear more about Christine's personal life. I knew that her parents had split up but I hadn't heard any details before. She was always very reticent about the subject.

I'm unbelievably curious about Marie and how she will compare with Christine. Alan is reluctant to tell me anything more about her, saying that I should make up my own mind. I have this vision of a slightly younger version of Christine, with longer blonde hair and a slightly slimmer figure.

It's now 7.30 am and I realise with surprise that I've been sitting thinking about Weetflakes for 45 minutes. I hear Susie begin to shout for attention upstairs and, five minutes later, Jean comes into the kitchen with our lovely little daughter in her arms. The three of us have a pleasant breakfast together, leaving the two older kids upstairs to sleep in, something which they both like to do these days, often to my intense irritation. I tell Jean to be sure to wake them soon after I've gone so they can help her, and she makes a pointed comment about how it would have been useful to have me around too.

But generally the mood between us is not too bad. She obviously loves this house and is going to be happy here. We've spent so much time apart in the last few months that it's a pleasure just to be together. And though it is nearly thirty years since we married the first time, there is still some excitement from doing simple things like having breakfast together in a new home. I ask myself if the atmosphere would be quite so pleasant if Jean knew that, later on today, I will be interviewing Christine's sister for a job. I guess I know the answer to that, so I decide to say nothing for the time being.

I enjoy the walk to the office, feeling quite smug that I'm able to leave behind in the drive the new BMW 735 which was delivered only last week. It's a lovely morning although it's very cold for early May. There's a spring in my step as I enter the Weetflakes site. Somehow having a home base makes me feel that I'm really settled here.

Alan Angus is waiting for me in reception as I enter – I

agreed for him to stay overnight in Grimsby at our expense. I'm hoping that, before long, I won't need his advice to the same extent, though last time we met he was hinting that his firm might be able to help with some of the management training necessary to support the planned changes. I gave him some hopeful indications as I very much want to keep in touch, but much will depend on the views of the new Personnel Director.

Alan follows me to my office and I ask Julie to let me have urgent mail and messages from yesterday and to bring us coffee. As we sit down I tell Alan about the problem with Arthur and then spend a few minutes with Julie while he thinks over the implications.

As Julie leaves my office, I pour coffee and ask Alan for his views.

"I think we were both guilty of paying too much attention to Willis and Freddie," he tells me as he takes the seat opposite my desk. "We should have seen Arthur as another key influencer and should not have assumed that he would be happy to be shunted to one side."

"But how could we have known, Alan? He said he wanted a back seat."

"We'd have realised if we'd thought it through, Phil. Arthur's not likely to be affected by money or status like Freddie or Willis. He's had all that. Like many older people he just wants to feel that he's needed. And while MDs were coming and going, he *was* needed. While Willis wanted protecting, he was needed. But now he sees you coming in, taking over effectively and getting on well with Willis and Freddie, he's having to face the fact that he has no role."

"Okay, Alan, I accept that you could be right. But it doesn't really help, does it? Because what could we have done about it anyway? In a company of this size which is not a plc, there is no role for a full-time Executive Chairman. And the idea of giving him any other job in this new structure is unthinkable. And what worries me is that, if you're right about his motivation, offering him a meaningless title like President and paying him an over-generous consultancy fee are not going to help."

"That's right, Phil, and I might have counselled you against it if you had asked me, but it's done now. And there may be no perfect solution to this problem – if there really is no role for Arthur, no one can change that. But what you can do, and the more genuine you are about it the better, is to convince him that you really *do* need his advice, that he will actually have to earn his consultancy fee."

"But how can I? I find Arthur's homespun philosophies a bit of a joke, to be honest," I reply.

"I think you can, Phil. It strikes me that you benefitted from Arthur's advice before you brought Willis and Freddie over to your side. And it would probably have been better to have asked him first before you decided how to deal with Julian and Amanda."

I realise that Alan is right and, if I can only convince Arthur of my sincerity, it might just solve the problem. No one knows the Stocks family and the Weetflakes culture better than him and he must be the best sounding board for me to try out ideas for change even if, to some extent, I use him as devil's advocate.

Around 11 o'clock we seem to come to a bit of a halt, with nothing else that can usefully be done until I've found out what happened when Willis met Arthur the day before. For the first time I wonder if I'm obtaining full value from what Weetflakes is paying for Alan Angus's time, and it confirms my view that now may be the time to begin to phase out his involvement as personal consultant.

I suggest to Alan that he goes off to work in an empty office while I see Willis and we agree to meet at lunchtime to decide how to handle the rest of the day. I particularly want him to be around when Marie Goodhart arrives – I'm not sure why but I'm anxious about meeting Christine's sister on my own.

Willis comes to see me as soon as I call him and I'm pleased to see that he brings Freddie with him. These two seem to be getting on particularly well these days. I suspect it's because they now believe that I'm here to stay and therefore there's no longer any need for them to compete for the succession.

Willis describes his meeting with Arthur. It's good news, bad news. Arthur has now accepted that Julian and Amanda have to go, though I have some concern about why he's changed his mind. Apparently Willis slipped in the news about their affair and this turned Arthur right against them. He was full of indignation about the calibre of people who marry into the Stocks family.

Willis then moves on to describe the difficult discussion about his father's future. He had trouble reaching the root of the problem and found that Arthur clammed up completely when asked what he would like his future role to be. The meeting was inconclusive, apart from agreeing that Arthur should see me on his own later today. Apparently Willis did not even feel it appropriate to spell out the details of our offer.

I then mention my discussion with Alan Angus and put forward Alan's theory about Arthur's motivation – that he just wants to feel that he has a useful role and that money and titles will not help. Freddie still sticks to his view that Arthur doesn't want the strategy to happen and is, deep down, the firmest opponent of change.

Willis looks pensive and stands up from the chair opposite my desk.

"You know, Phil," he says, "your friend could be right. It's difficult to think of one's father wanting to be needed, but maybe I'm too close to him. You see, previously his main concern was for me – wanting to be sure that you'd keep me on and that I was to be part of the future of Weetflakes. Now he's sure of that, he's turning his attention back on himself. And yes, he needs a real role. He's not one to be fooled by phoney titles or bought off with a consultancy fee."

We agree that the best plan is for me to see him over lunch and set out the role I would like him to play – as my sounding board, adviser and change consultant. Willis and Freddie express an interest in meeting Alan Angus and they agree to take him to lunch. I warn them about his youthful appearance and his tendency to ask questions rather than offer instant solutions.

I introduce Alan to the two of them and then ring Arthur to see if he's available for lunch. His secretary answers and tells me that Arthur's walking round the factory – always one of his favourite occupations – but that he will be back any time. She tells me that he has no commitments over lunch so I ask her to arrange sandwiches and tell Arthur that I'll be along in half an hour.

When I arrive Arthur is sitting at the table by his desk, looking disapprovingly at the sandwiches.

"Trying to deprive me of my hot lunch, are you lad?"

I regard his attempt as humour as a hopeful sign. I decide to proceed very gently at first.

"Arthur," I say, "I've been here two months now. You've had more experience at Weetflakes than anyone else. How do you feel I'm doing?"

"You're not doing any good by beating about the bush, Philip. I told you I liked you when I first met you and I do. I thought you'd be good for Weetflakes and you seemed honest and open. But then I find that you want me out. After I supported you all along, you kick me in the teeth."

"Arthur," I say, "you say that you want me to be open and I will. We have to face facts. I was recruited to be MD of Weetflakes. I strongly believe that the company is not big enough to have a separate full-time Chairman as well as an MD. If we were a plc or if the strategy had to be developed from scratch, maybe there would be a separate role, but there isn't. And if I didn't face that fact we would get in each other's way and there would be conflict."

"So I'm on the scrapheap while you, Willis and Freddie run the show?"

"No Arthur, not necessarily. I've been thinking things over these last few days and I realise that I was overlooking one thing. The culture of Weetflakes, with all its history and family tensions, is far too complicated for an outsider like me to cope with on my own. I've made several mistakes already because I didn't understand the people or their motivations." I fail to mention that he is the prime example. "I want the best person to advise me before I implement the changes which are necessary and without question, Arthur, that's you."

He wants to know what this means and I tell him that I want us to hold monthly meetings for me to keep him in touch and for him to advise me. He will also meet the new Personnel Director on a regular basis. In addition he will continue as non-executive Chairman and be Head of the Board Audit Committee which I propose to set up shortly. I don't even mention money or whether he will also take the title of President. He asks if he can keep his office and I say no problem. As I leave him to rejoin Freddie, Willis and Alan, I think I may have cracked it. He asks for 24 hours to think it through, but I think I've won him over.

I'm pleased to find, as I return to my office, that Freddie, Willis and Alan are in animated discussion. All the indications are that they have got on well and I suspect that a few drinks at the local pub may well have helped. I sometimes worry at the tendency of Weetflakes' management to knock back several beers over lunch but, on this occasion, I'm quite grateful.

I decide that, even though they seem to have made a good start, it's too early and too much of a risk to let Alan be involved in discussion of the personal issues concerning Arthur, Julian and Amanda. I ask Alan to leave us for a while, to greet Marie Goodhart when she arrives and then to let me know.

Willis, Freddie and I then discuss how to manage the timing of our interviews with Julian and Amanda, followed by an announcement of their departure and the new organisation structure. We agree, with some reluctance, that as Julian will almost certainly take it badly, we should tell him mid-afternoon tomorrow and ask him to go immediately. Otherwise he's likely to spread dissension before we can explain the re-organisation and give assurances to other key players like Martin Moss and Stephen Young.

Willis and Freddie say that this will also be good timing from a family point of view, giving them time over the weekend to deal with the inevitable reactions. Freddie seems confident that the damage within the family and at Weetflakes will be limited because of Julian's unpopularity. He also suggests that Julian may not make trouble since he will be terrified that we will reveal his affair.

Freddie and Willis go back to their offices and I even have ten minutes to return a couple of phone calls before Alan Angus rings. One of the calls is from Jean to tell me that the central heating boiler has gone wrong and they are all freezing cold. I try to sound concerned and promise to ask one of Weetflakes' people to let her know of a good local heating engineer. I ring Joe McEvoy in the factory and he promises to contact Jean with a recommended name. I suspect that she was wanting me to go home to help, but I'm too involved here even to consider it.

As soon as I come off the phone, Julie pops in to ask if Alan can bring in Miss Goodhart. Julie is a very discreet, middle-aged lady who is proving to be one of the best secretaries I've ever had.

"What's she like, Julie?" I ask, hoping at least to be slightly prepared.

She pulls a face and says, "It's difficult to describe her, Mr Moorley, she's not what I expected from her CV. But you'd better make up your own mind."

A minute later Alan Angus walks into my office with the woman who, he's suggesting, should be my new Personnel Director. As she comes through the door, I can hardly believe what I see.

Chapter 13

Marie Goodhart is as unlike her half-sister as any woman could be. Instead of being slim, elegant, attractive and blonde haired like Christine, she is pleasantly plain with a short, stocky figure which completely fails to bring out the best in the expensive suit she is wearing. Her face is round and chubby with a small mouth and a snub nose, only her large brown eyes showing anything like the attractiveness of her sister. Her hair is mousy brown and looks as if it has been cut this morning, using the nearest basin.

I try to be composed as I take all this in. Alan introduces her and she moves forward to shake my hand. Suddenly my impression of her is changed as she says "Good to meet you, Philip", in a loud, confident voice which has a touch of French and American in the accent. Despite her unprepossessing appearance, this woman somehow seems to exude a dynamism that I wouldn't have dreamt of as she came through the door.

This impression is confirmed as the interview begins and soon I ask myself who is interviewing whom. I was rather arrogantly assuming that Marie needs to convince me that she is right for Weetflakes. Her questions make it clear that she also needs to be sure that Weetflakes is right for her.

She's been well briefed by Alan and already knows the names of the top people, the new strategy we're pursuing and the problems encountered by me and my predecessors in managing change. I ask her about her own experience at managing similar situations.

"I've worked in three French companies and two of them were family controlled, with some similar problems. And I can assure you that the problems of the Stocks family and Weetflakes pale into insignificance next to some French and Italian family businesses. But I think you're wrong if you look for experience of identical situations. Every situation of managing change is unique and it's dangerous to pretend that you can adopt a standard approach."

I decide to take advantage of Alan's continued presence by putting Marie on the spot. I'm quite keen to see how she responds to some of the concerns I used to have about frameworks like the change cycle.

"So you don't believe in what we are doing here then – managing change with a stage by stage approach. Presumably you know of Alan's change cycle?"

"I've seen it and other similar versions before. They're useful for management training and may be appropriate for some projects where there's a discrete set of variables which you can manage. And, from what Alan's told me, it was a useful way of warning you of the dangers of acting too quickly. But, in most situations, the world doesn't stay still long enough for you to work stage by stage. Even with your situation here, which is fairly unusual, you must already have found yourself looping back and around the change cycle."

"Which, to be fair, is what I've always advocated," interjects Alan, a shade defensively, I think.

"But why is my situation so unusual?" I ask, genuinely interested in her view and already appreciating the quality of her mind.

"Maybe not quite so unusual, perhaps it's better to say relatively uncluttered. You've come in as a new broom with a new strategy. Weetflakes' existing business seems to be proceeding relatively independently, with experienced people in place to keep things going. So you can spend time with Alan, planning how to re-organise and change things. In most of the companies I've come across, you're reacting to day to day events, trying to keep the business going, while planning for change with insufficient time to do it and with turbulence all around you. You may stay lucky, I hope you do, but I wouldn't bank on it if I were you."

I think about this and realise that to some extent she is right. I have been very fortunate in keeping away from day to day problems at Weetflakes and perhaps I haven't appreciated enough the management ability of Freddie, Willis and Martin which has enabled me to do this. As I'm thinking I notice Alan Angus, sitting at the end of the table, on my left and her right as we face each other. He looks quite amused at the encounter which is developing between Marie and me. I decide not to disappoint him.

"OK then, Marie," I say, "you're very sure about what I shouldn't be doing to manage change in Weetflakes. If I offered you the job as my Personnel Director, how would you help me?"

She asks me if she can have a glass of water and I ask Julie to bring one in. I guess she's giving herself time to think – quite an operator!

"I would be your eyes and ears, Philip, where people issues are concerned. And, I hope, your sixth sense too. I would expect you to consult me whenever there is a decision to be made which affects people, particularly where widespread change is involved. I hear that you're also going to use Arthur Stocks in this way which is, I think, very sensible. You can't spend enough time sounding out different opinions on the likely implications of change. I expect I will give you a different view from Arthur, an external view – at least for a while – and a professional personnel view. Because with me, Philip, you're getting a professional personnel person, through and through. And, judging by what I've heard from Alan, that's what you need."

Somehow, from this small dynamic woman, this statement doesn't sound conceited. Her voice rings out with a confidence which doesn't encourage you to challenge her. And her CV also confirms her solid experience as a personnel professional. I glance down at her CV and remember that she spent a year at McKinseys, as an HR consultant. I decide to ask her a question about it.

"I see that you spent some time with McKinseys, Marie. What would they offer in this area of managing change?"

"I think that would depend on the situation, Philip, whether you're talking about a small project or, as in your case, changing a total company culture. And the frameworks which McKinseys offer tend to change with time, as new ideas develop or as one fad wears off and another comes along. But there is one enduring framework which I used when I was there and which I still find helpful. I think it could be useful to you, as a sort of checklist for your culture change. It's called the Seven S framework. Have you heard of it?"

It rings a vague bell from past management courses I have attended, or was it a book I read? I seem to associate it with Tom Peters and I ask Marie if it came from him.

"It was used by Peters when he was at McKinseys and it's mentioned at the beginning of *In Search of Excellence*. To some extent Peters built on the Seven Ss when he did his research for that book."

I'm impressed by the extent of her knowledge and the confidence with which she expresses it. There seems nothing pre-prepared about this. I ask her to tell me more about the Seven Ss and she asks if she can use the flipchart. I feel like saying "this is just the way your sister used to help me," but, for some reason, I hold back. This is not someone to trifle with. Increasingly I'm feeling that I need Marie Goodhart in Weetflakes, very much.

She goes to the flipchart and begins to draw some lines. I notice yet again how small and squat she is, her head only reaching to the top of the flipchart stand. She could almost be a little child from the back view but, when she turns round, the power of her personality re-asserts itself and her physical appearance is forgotten.

I look at the flipchart and see what she's written. It looks like this (see opposite).

She explains it like this, "McKinseys developed this framework to ensure that top management who wanted to bring about change realised the need to have everything in place. If any one of the seven Ss is not considered, or if any one of them is not compatible with the other six, there will be problems in managing the required change."

Once again I find myself being sceptical about a

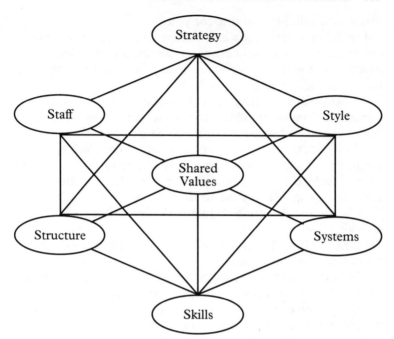

superficially attractive framework, one which is associated with perhaps the best known of all management consultancy firms. I decide to use this scepticism to test out Marie again and to see how she reacts to a tough challenge.

"I'm sorry, Marie," I say, "but I don't see why I should believe this. You were very sceptical about Alan's change cycle which I found useful and want to stick with. Another framework seems too much to me and is only going to confuse the issue. And really, Seven Ss! It makes me laugh. How come they all happen to begin with S? I suspect it's a fancy label and they've put in items beginning with S, just to make it sound good."

I watch her closely and she doesn't bat an eyelid. There's no swallowing, no sweating, no faltering of the voice. Instead she gives me a lovely friendly smile which disarms my aggressive manner.

"Well Philip, we're going to have some good times if you offer me this job and I take it. Christine told me that you loved to challenge what others accept and that was why it was so stimulating working for you."

I'm relieved that she's mentioned Christine so that now I can raise it later without embarrassment. I'm also impressed by the confident manner of her response. But I'm not going to let her escape yet.

"That's fine, Marie, and I'm flattered that you and Christine have been talking about me but, come on, answer the question. What do these Seven Ss do for me?"

"Well, let's take your present situation. You've been planning for significant change and you're just about all set to go. Before you do so, it's a good idea to check that everything's in place. And to do that you need a checklist. That's all the Seven S framework does, it provides that checklist."

"Okay, Marie," I say, beginning to take more interest. "Show me how it works."

"Well Philip, taking strategy first. Do you have a clear and logical strategy to achieve competitive advantage?"

I nod in agreement. I'm impressed by the natural use of a phrase like competitive advantage, which you do not always expect from someone in the personnel function.

"And from what Alan has told me, you have a good, logical organisational structure, based on the organisational processes necessary to achieve that strategy. So that's two out of seven of the checklist ticked off."

"Make it three," I say, "because I have the staff, or at least I will have when I've appointed a new Personnel Director and new people in charge of quality and product development."

"Okay, Philip," she says, "you're getting the idea. By the way, personally I don't like the word staff – I'd rather talk about people – and I have to admit that McKinseys probably used that word to make it fit into the S framework."

"I thought that human resources was the buzz phrase now," I suggest.

"Only for pretentious prats," she says, with a sudden show of strong feeling. The choice of word surprises me but somehow it seems to fit her style of conviction and certainty. "We don't call dogs canine resources do we?" she says. "It's devised by those who use complex words to describe simple ideas and give themselves status.

"Okay," she says looking round at the flipchart, "where were we?"

"I suspect you were about to ask me whether Weetflakes' style, systems and skills are all in place to implement the new strategy," I say.

"Oh yes, of course. Yes Philip, you're dead right. And also to ask whether you believe that there are consistent shared values among all the key players."

I wonder how far I ought to pursue this line at this stage. I'm enjoying the discussion and I'm sure there would be value in it continuing. But this is supposed to be an interview, I have plenty of other things to do and I would like to be home early. Also I've seen enough of Marie Goodhart to know that I want to take her on. The thought of her joining me at Weetflakes as the person from outside, the free thinker, the one who will always to prepared to challenge me, is irresistible. She hasn't the poise or the looks of her half-sister, but I believe she has an even sharper mind.

I've always been one to make up my mind quickly, particularly about people. I've made mistakes but they've usually been on the negative side, because I've written off people without giving them time to do things right. My record on the positive side – assessing people whom I can work with and who will deliver results – is pretty good.

"Marie," I say, "I want to terminate this interview as I feel we're wasting each other's time." I wonder how she'll take that one.

At last I see her confidence falter. She swallows hard and her voice is unsteady as she replies. I see Alan Angus looking at me, trying to signal his concern, even his anger.

"Well, if that's how you feel," her voice croaks, its confident tone disappearing rapidly, "I'll go now. The last thing I want to do is waste your time Mr Moorley. I'm sorry if I've bored you."

She stands up to go and I decide that it's time to stop playing games. I may already have gone too far, but somehow I couldn't resist it.

"You haven't bored me at all, Marie. I'm looking forward to continuing this debate when we have more time. You've given me food for thought about those other four Ss and I'd like you to help me talk it through."

"What do you mean, Philip?" says Alan Angus, "I think you ought to be more fair with Marie. She's come a long way and has other job offers which she could take."

I go towards her and shake her by the hand. She looks at me in puzzlement.

"Marie," I say, "please turn the other offers down. I need you at Weetflakes and I'd like you to start as soon as possible, so I can save on these ridiculous consultancy fees which Alan here charges and have the benefit of those eyes and ears which you talked about. And I'm sorry I teased you but I guess you'll have plenty of chances to have your revenge."

That friendly smile comes back and I know I've won her over. She tells me that she wants at least £50,000 a year and I tell her no problem. She says she can start a week on Monday if Weetflakes can arrange and pay for accommodation. I agree to this too. She has a very businesslike way of dealing with these kinds of issues. She knows precisely what she wants and somehow manages to ask for them without appearing mercenary.

Half an hour later I'm walking away form Weetflakes, looking forward to going back to my new home. I'm also looking forward to tomorrow when I'm hoping that Arthur will confirm his support and that the new organisation structure will be received with enthusiasm at the management meeting in the afternoon. I want to use this same meeting as the launching pad for the new direction in which I want to take Weetflakes.

I enter my front door to find a freezing cold house in total chaos, with two workmen in the kitchen and a wife in tears. My buoyant mood is instantly deflated. Managing change may be going well at Weetflakes but it's not going too well at Fairfield Farm House. As Jean makes a weepy comment about my leaving her to cope with everything, I long for the comfort of the Grimsby Moat House.

And four hours later, when we go to bed for the second night in our new home, there is an iciness between us that doesn't come from the lack of heating and which reminds me of the worst days before our divorce. I'm not sure how the blame is shared, but I do know that it's the last thing I need on my mind if I am to succeed at Weetflakes.

Chapter 14

Eleven days later, Marie Goodhart enters my office to start her first day at Weetflakes. I asked her to arrive at 10 am and, when reception rang to tell me she was here about five minutes ago, I was just finishing a meeting on sales strategy with Martin and Willis. I asked the two of them to stay on and meet her.

I guess I'm going to become used to the initial impact she has on people. The glamorous sounding name and the brief description of her career I sent round have built up expectations of a stereotype career girl, straight from an American soap opera. Instead Martin and Willis see this small, dumpy, unglamorous person, and their reaction is hesitant, to say the least.

But then she speaks, taking on her most confident and assertive manner, behaving as if it's they who are the new kids on the block. I suspect that, by now, she actually enjoys the impact she has and has learnt how to use it to her advantage.

"Good to meet you, Martin," she says, "I've heard so much praise about Weetflakes' customer relationships from Philip and others I've spoken to. I'm sure that we can work together to make them even better."

"And Willis Stocks," she continues, giving him a long look which combines admiration and approval, "it's excellent to have family traditions in a business and to see the values passed on from generation to generation. My previous employers in France had similar advantages."

How does she get away with such bullshit, I think to myself as she continues to flatter and charm them. In anyone else it would be transparent and patronising, but she makes it sound so convincing as she looks up at Willis with a sincere and confident gaze into his eyes. I'm impressed that she's done her homework and has used this first opportunity to win over two important people.

I've allocated the morning to helping her settle in and, once Willis and Martin have left, I bring her up to date on what is happening at Weetflakes. I told her a good deal during her previous visit and Alan Angus had also briefed her quite comprehensively, but a fair amount has happened during the last ten days.

Arthur accepted the arrangement I offered him and will move to his part-time position in about a month's time. I say to Marie that I would like her to become close to Arthur and to use his experience of the Weetflakes culture to accelerate her learning curve. I want her to act as my sounding board before I implement change, and both of us should draw on Arthur's unique knowledge of what is achievable.

I also describe the success of the meetings at which I announced the new vision and the proposed organisation structure to the management team. Rarely have I encountered such a positive and enthusiastic response and, this week, I have started the preparation of the detailed business plan with great optimism. I realise that converting the key influencers – Freddie, Willis, Martin – was the crucial step and I now feel that I'm making great strides. I make this rather complacent claim to Marie and she looks at me with a slightly pitying expression, something like the way her sister used to look when I failed to understand a basic financial concept.

"Philip," she says, helping herself to her third cup of coffee. "I hope you don't mind my saying this but, for someone of your age and experience, you are wonderfully innocent at times. You think that people saying the right things at meetings and agreeing with the Chief Executive's new strategy is so meaningful. I wouldn't mind betting that your predecessors had similar warm feelings at certain stages of their time with Weetflakes. But it's what people actually do that matters and what you want will only happen if the culture is compatible with the strategy. And that's where I can help you."

"With your Seven Ss, I suppose?" I ask rather disapprovingly, wanting to punish her for being so critical of my naivety even though, deep down, I suspect she could be right.

I notice the strength of her interpersonal skills, as she doesn't let our verbal duels become too serious. She smiles sweetly and says, "How did you guess?"

"Actually, Marie," I say, "since we last met I have thought further about your Seven Ss and I do find it an interesting framework. But then. . ."

I pause and open my drawer, pulling out a scruffy, folded flipchart.

"I thought back to when I first met your friend Alan Angus and I've dug out the flipchart he drew for me that day."

I hold it up for her to see. It says:

HOW ORGANISATIONAL CULTURE CAN BE CHANGED

1) By changing people
2) By changing positions
3) By changing beliefs and attitudes
   ● role models
   ● communications – videos, magazines, etc.
   ● group discussions, team briefings
   ● one-to-one counselling
   ● training courses
4) By changing (improving) skills and knowledge
5) By changing structures and systems

I'm rather disappointed that she doesn't respond, except to say, "So?"

"So the people who develop these sorts of frameworks for managing change – consultants, business schools, people like you and Alan – all seem to be saying the same thing, in a slightly different way. Alan says people, you say staff. He says positions, you say structure. He says beliefs and attitudes, you say shared values. You both say skills and systems, presumably because they both begin with S?"

She waits for me to finish and then repeats, "So?"

"So . . . well . . . we seem to be going over the same ground, discussing the same ideas but using different words."

"Think back, Philip," she says, fixing me with a penetrating look which I find rather unnerving. I'm not sure I like being given the third degree by a new employee in my own office. "Why did Alan give you those five ways of changing a culture?"

"Because he wanted to stop me from rushing too quickly into hiring and firing people as the only solution?'

"And was that framework helpful?"

"Yes, I guess so. Yes, it definitely was."

"And can you recall why I suggested that we could use the Seven Ss?"

"I'm not sure, let me think. Yes, I think you wanted to use it as a sort of checklist to make certain that everything is covered before we move to implementation."

"And could that be helpful to us, particularly as I'm trying to counter-balance your optimism after these meetings?"

"I guess so," I say begrudgingly, knowing that she's winning this argument game, set and match. I decide there and then that there'll be many other arguments with Marie and I'll make sure I win my share. And I know that I'm going to enjoy every minute. She looks at me, and we exchange a smile which shows that she knows just what I'm thinking.

"One up to you," I say, "and, to prove it, tell me which of your Seven Ss is likely to prove the weak link."

"I'm not sure yet, Phil. I need to do much more work, but there will be four areas I'll look at as first priority. How long before you want to start implementation?"

"I've got to write the business plan and that means a great deal of consultation – say about a month. What were these things you want to look at, Marie?"

She moves to the whiteboard on my wall and writes in rather wild, spidery letters:

- Shared values
- Style
- Systems
- Skills

"I'd like to talk to all your team and see if there are real shared values or whether they are just paying lip-service to your new ideas. In other words, have you won their hearts and minds?"

"And style?"

"Yes Phil, very important. How is your personal style fitting in to the Weetflakes culture? And mine too. And how compatible are the styles of the others in the top team? You seem to have a fairly relaxed style and you like to empower others, at least that's what Alan and Christine told me. How will that fit with Weetflakes' new strategy and with the styles which Arthur, Willis and Freddie have established over the years? I'm not saying we can or should change everyone's personal styles, but we can be aware of the problems which differences can cause."

"And systems?" I say. "Our information systems are fairly sound and I have a good guy to look after them."

"It isn't just information systems, Philip. It's reward systems, the performance management system and feedback mechanisms which I'm concerned with. How does appraisal take place, for instance?"

I feel extremely guilty that, despite assuring Alan Angus that I would ask about it, I still don't know the answer to that question. I remember Freddie once saying that he appraised his people twice a year, but I've not heard of a formal system. With Amanda Slade in charge of Personnel, I guess it would have been left to individuals to decide and I've found that, in that situation, most people tend not to do it.

I realise just how much I need a Personnel Director. A co-ordinated appraisal system wil be vital to link the objectives of individuals to the goals of the business plan.

Marie then moves on to talk about the skills required, how in her role as Personnel Director she needs to analyse the competences of management and staff to see how far they are compatible with the strategy. In particular, what new skills will need to be developed? She asks me for examples and, initially, I can't think of any. She makes me feel stupid by giving an obvious example.

"What about your sales force, Phil? With the move to own label, won't they need new skills? Like the skills of developing longer-term relationships with customers rather than doing one-off deals?"

"And they'll need to understand the principles of product costing," I add, realising how many other examples I could quote if we had a brainstorming session with Martin and his team.

"Okay, Marie," I say, "you've convinced me that the Seven Ss are helpful and that there are many things I've taken for granted. Remind me to include a section on training in the business plan and we must work on it with each of the management team."

I move on to tell Marie more about the strategy and the business logic behind it. She is surprisingly knowledgeable about business issues compared to most other personnel people I've met. She's obviously done her homework on the UK retailing scene and offers some useful insights from her French experience.

It is almost noon and I ask her what she wants to do about lunch. I've already got rid of the special senior management dining room which was so daunting on my first day, and I now rotate between sandwiches in the office, using the main canteen and going to the pub.

Without hesitation Marie opts for the pub and I ask Julie to ring round the management team to see who is available to join us. I hope that the informal atmosphere will help Marie to get to know people early on. Within ten minutes there are eight people assembled in my office – Willis, Freddie, Martin, Stephen Young, Peter Thackray, Gavin Simmonds and the two of us. As the only woman Marie seems to be dominated by the sheer weight of masculine numbers and by her tiny size compared to everyone else. And out of shyness most of the men talk to each other as they first come in, rather than to her.

I'm considering if I should intervene to help her when suddenly I hear a bang on the table and that confident voice rings out, "Gentlemen," she says, "I'd just like to say something to all of you before we go to knock a few back at the pub. You're probably thinking that I don't look much like a Personnel Director and I guess I don't. But being less than five feet tall and no oil painting makes you rather determined to make an impact. And that's what I hope to do at Weetflakes. But I want to make an impact which supports all of you in achieving your objectives and drawing the most out of your people. I don't think you've really seen what an effective personnel function can do for you, so I'm grateful to be working in a place with so much potential. So where's this pub, Philip?"

In anyone else it would have been outrageous, over the top, presumptuous, and I would have written him or her off at that point. But her obvious sincerity, her confident manner and the unique chemistry of her personality make it a virtuoso performance. Ten seconds after she's finished speaking, three or four of the guys are around her and they are still chatting animatedly as we all walk out to the car park. Fifteen minutes later she's sitting at the bar with a pint of bitter in her hand holding forth to Gavin, Peter, Martin and Stephen about her experiences with a French manager who apparently advanced his career by seducing all the directors' wives. I retire to an empty table with my orange juice and Freddie comes to join me.

"What do you think, Freddie?" I ask.

"I think that life is not going to be dull with that little lass around, Philip," he says. "I just hope you can control her."

I look up again at the bar where everyone is collapsing into helpless laughter and wonder if I'm taking an awful risk.

Five hours later I'm back in my office, feeling pleased to have just completed the introduction section of my business plan. I look at my watch and think that it will make a pleasant change to get home before six and forestall Jean's all too regular comments about the hours I've been working at Weetflakes.

Julie comes in to say goodnight and adds, "Miss Goodhart just rang to ask if she can see you before you go home."

I think of going home anyway but then remember that's it's her first day. I'm also quite curious to see if she's still standing up after her performance at the bar over lunch. Whenever I saw her she seemed to have another full pint in her hand and I was just amazed how she put it all away into her tiny frame.

She comes in looking very composed and I start by pulling her leg about her drinking exploits. There's something about Marie which makes you want to joke with her all the time and she responds so well.

"Oh yes, Philip, I can really knock it back, didn't you notice?"

I decide to be serious for a moment and wonder how she'll take it. "I think it was fine for the first day, Marie, and you really seemed to hit it off with everyone. But. . . well. . . it's not really. . ."

I suddenly find it difficult to tell her what I want to say, that she should be careful not to drink too much during the daytime. That standards here are very different from those in France.

She sits down opposite my desk and laughs out loud, obviously amused by my discomfiture.

"Philip," she says, "please trust me. I know how different things are in the UK. But it's obvious that going to the pub at lunchtime is part of the culture at Weetflakes and I thought that I should comply on my first day. I can assure you that I have a rooted dislike of pubs and the male-dominated atmosphere they typify. And do you know why I always had a full pint in my hand?"

I take it as a rhetorical question and just say, "No?"

"Because I hardly drank anything. Beer tastes like medicine to me. But it was what I thought I had to do to win over your male chauvinist managers and make them notice me early on. I promise I'll stick to Perrier from now on."

It's now my turn to laugh out loud and I realise how much I have underestimated Marie. This is a formidable operator who understands people and is prepared to adapt her behaviour with amazing insight and flexibility.

I then ask her about her afternoon and she tells me how she's been around the factory, meeting as many people as possible, trying to obtain a feel for the culture. She's already fixed meetings with the rest of the top team later this week.

"Just to familiarise yourself with their work?" I ask.

"No Phil, much more than that. As we discussed this morning, I need to move quickly during the next month, before you start to implement the changes in your business plan."

"But I'm still not sure why you need to move so quickly. I know you want to introduce some new systems and some management training, and I said I would incorporate those into my final version of the plan. But we could easily leave that to be finished a few months later."

"But remember, Phil, we also talked this morning about style and shared values. I thought I'd convinced you that these have to be right before we move to the implementation stage, and I don't think you are in a position to know that yet. I have a month to find out and I mean to do so. It would be disastrous for you to proceed if we don't have everyone's commitment and, whatever you may think, there's still likely to be a great deal of concern about what's happening."

I begin to feel defensive, always a fault with my rather insecure personality. "But Marie," I say, "much as I value your views, you've only been here one day."

"I have also talked to Alan Angus quite extensively, Philip, and, in any case, I don't need to talk to anyone. I just know you have a problem."

"What do you mean?" I say, finding it hard to conceal my irritation.

"Okay, Phil," she says, "I'd better come clean about the extent of my concern. I didn't want to go too far on my first day but there isn't much time. Have you got a copy of Alan's change cycle framework?"

I retrieve it from my desk drawer and give it to her. She looks at it with a worried expression.

"Despite what I said at my interview, I accept that this framework was useful to you and Alan in the early stages and we may well refer back to it. But I have even more reservations about it after chatting to a couple of people today. I think it misses out some important issues, and in a way, is negative rather than positive."

She passes it back and I see the familiar framework in front of me:

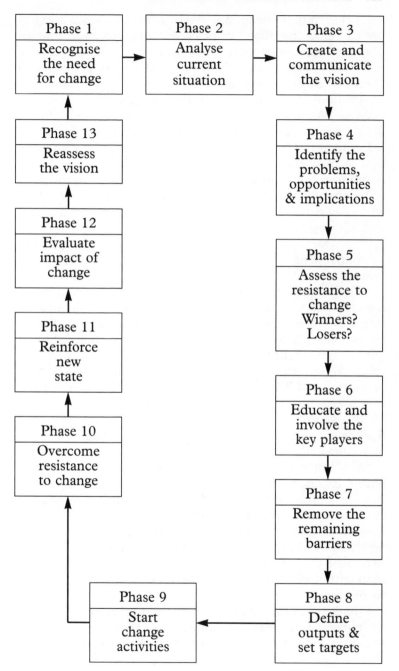

I feel even more irritation, maybe because it's late and I'm tired. I remember that I've paid Alan Angus a large amount of money and spent a great deal of time on this framework and now Marie, Alan's recommendation for Personnel Director, keeps running it down.

My body language obviously indicates my irritation because Marie says, "I can see that you're tired, Philip. Would you rather we talked about this tomorrow?"

I'm tempted by the thought of home but remember that I have a busy day of appointments tomorrow. I also feel a desire to resolve any conflict with Marie. I don't want there to be any outstanding acrimony after her first day. And, as with Alan Angus, there's something about her that makes me seek her approval.

"No Marie," I say, "tell me about your concerns. You personnel people remind me of economists, every one has a different view."

"That's quite a good parallel actually," she says. "You mustn't think that managing change is like finance or statistics where there's a right or wrong answer. Different people have different views, different ways of approaching it and all approaches have their strengths and weaknesses. I value some parts of the structured approach which Alan advocates, but I have my reservations too. He knows what they are and we've argued about it many times."

"But you've told me your reservations already, Marie, at the interview if you remember. That it was too structured and inflexible."

"Yes, but it goes further than that," she replies. "I also have this concern that it emphasises the negatives too much. It talks about removing barriers, overcoming resistance, emphasising the resistors rather than the drivers of change. I'd like to spend some time with you, examining the forces *for* change rather than just looking at the resistors. We need to be sure that there is enough drive to achieve the necessary momentum. Without that you won't move from one phase to another."

I think about this carefully. How valid is her point? One of the barriers to change we removed was the old organisation structure which was not compatible with the vision. But that could equally be expressed as a positive – we created an organisation structure which will support implementation. I mention this point to her.

"Okay, Phil, I'm not running it down completely remember, just pointing out a danger. But, in fact, the question of organisation structure reminds me of a further concern I have about your general approach."

"What's that?"

"Because, though I can see the logic of structure supporting strategy, there is also another factor to be taken into account, a key ingredient of effective change management."

"And what's that?"

She walks over to the whiteboard on the wall and picks up the pen. She writes in big letters:

CERTAINTY

"However well you think your announcement about the new organisation may have gone down, and however supportive it may be of your strategy, there will be many people who are concerned about how it will work. About the power and influence they will be able to wield, the way they will relate to others, new tensions which will arise."

"So would you have left it as it was?"

"I'd have wanted to talk through with you the extent to which it was likely to be a fundamental barrier which you couldn't overcome any other way. If there was another way, involving less uncertainty, I'd have taken it and then carried out a more fundamental re-organisation as part of Phase 11."

I look at the paper in front of me.

"To reinforce the new state?"

"Yes Phil, which it can do very well, particularly as it's based on the real business processes which you and Alan analysed."

I look at my watch and see that it's 7 o'clock. I must be going home, particularly as I haven't rung Jean. I said I would ring if I was likely to be home after 7.

"I have to go, Marie. But, before I do, tell me where this

leaves us, because it's too late to change the decision about the organisation. It's been announced and is already happening."

"I know, Phil, but it means that my meetings with your team over the next month will explore this issue of uncertainty as a key factor. It will be added to my list of questions – not only shared values, systems, style and skills but also certainty."

"If only certainty began with an S," I say and we laugh together. It's a warm moment to end her first day and we stand up to go. I walk towards my coat at the far end of the room when the phone rings. Marie is passing by the phone and picks it up.

"Marie Goodhart," she says.

She then looks up at me and says, "It's for you. Your wife, I think."

"Hello," I say.

"Who was that?" asks the voice I know so well. There's a sinking feeling in my stomach as I realise that I haven't told Jean that my new Personnel Director is Christine Goodhart's sister.

"It was my new Personnel Director," I say.

"Marie *Goodhart*?", says Jean. "A relation of Christine's, I presume?"

"Well actually yes, her sister," I say.

"Don't bother coming home," is the reply and I hear the phone go dead.

Chapter 15

It's now Friday afternoon of the same week and I wish I could say I was looking forward to the weekend. This week has been like all my nightmares coming back, all because of my stupidity in not telling Jean about Marie. It's happened before and it's always caused problems – I've held back from telling her something and then she found out anyway. I never seem to learn.

The lowest point of the week was when I returned home on Monday evening to find all the doors bolted from the inside. Even in our worst times before the divorce, that had not happened. I could hear raised voices inside and assumed that the children were trying to persuade her to open the doors. But I know from bitter experience how stubborn she can be when she's made up her mind about something. This is the woman who didn't speak to me for three years after our divorce and used to leave the children outside my flat at weekends without even a glance at me.

What hurts me most of all is the impact it is having on the children. After all they went through when we originally split up, they don't deserve this and I must try to get back on speaking terms with Jean over the weekend.

I decided to stay at the Grimsby Moat House on Monday night – you can't just stay outside your own house banging on the door. The neighbours may be quite a distance away by many standards, but not far enough for that to go unnoticed. And, knowing how Weetflakes dominates the village, rumours would be all round the site the next day. I went home early on Tuesday afternoon and saw Mark at his bedroom window as I drove up to the house. I signalled and, to my relief, he let me in.

Three days later Jean and I are still sleeping in separate bedrooms and I haven't found an opportunity to talk to her. All our contact has been with the children present and she's avoided all my attempts to speak to her on her own. I have the impression that the children are on my side but I'm reluctant to raise it openly with them. The last thing I want is them having to choose between us.

I'm still not clear what I'm going to say to Jean anyway. She just doesn't trust me where other women are concerned and now probably believes that I've been consistently unfaithful, even though Christine has been my only slip since we re-married. And how can I tell her that Marie isn't that type – that she's dynamic, exciting, confident and gregarious but totally lacking in sex appeal, at least to me? Jean would laugh in my face and probably be even more convinced that I'm sleeping with her. Only if she meets Marie will she be convinced, and I'm not sure how I can organise that.

Just as I'm thinking about this, Marie walks through the door of my office to keep our 3 o'clock appointment. We are to review her first week and she is to give me her early feedback on the extent to which I have won over the 'hearts and minds', as she likes to call it.

She tells me that she deliberately started with the middle ranking players whose commitment is so important to bringing about real and lasting change. She's seen Gavin Simmonds, Peter Thackray and Joe McEvoy individually and has been impressed by their lack of uncertainty and by the fact that they appear to have accepted the strategy. I feel pathetically proud when she tells me that this is largely to do with their respect for me and my track record. Apparently the US experience makes them think that I'm some kind of world-beater – if only they knew how much more of a challenge the task is at Weetflakes, compared to the predictability of US corporate life at Chapmans and ABT.

She also says that they respect my sincerity and regard me as fair-minded. I'm just revelling in the glow of this positive feedback when she spoils it by saying, "But I'm somehow uneasy, Phil. Though I'm not surprised at this feedback because I happen to agree with it, I think it possible that they are not being entirely frank with me. I have the feeling that there is still fear around and people are saying what they think others want to hear, not what they truly believe. Once a culture encourages that kind of behaviour, it can take years to restore the openness and trust which you need to find out what people really think."

"So where does that leave us?" I ask, a little impatiently.

"It leaves me concerned, Philip, particularly when I combine it with some anxiety I had on my first day. That, pleasant though your managers are, with the possible exception of Freddie if he's well motivated, they are not the driven types who really get things done, who can overcome all the potential resistance."

"Well I'm quite driven, Marie, even though I may not always show it, and I think you are too. We'll make up for the rest."

"If I thought we could on our own, Phil, I wouldn't be so concerned. But your style is to empower and to delegate and you need everyone to push in your direction. I just have this feeling that there could be too many resistors at present."

"Resistors?"

"Yes Phil, didn't Alan Angus talk to you about Force Field Analysis?"

"No, should he have done?"

"It's not for me to say, Phil. I have the greatest respect for Alan and we all have different ways of approaching these things, but I have found Force Field Analysis to be very powerful as a way of assessing the potential for change and finding ways of overcoming problems. Would you like me to show you how it works?"

"I've a feeling you're going to," I say with a smile which she returns.

"I'm sure it can help us to think matters through and assess whether my concerns have any validity. But it may mean that I don't have the time to report on the detail of all the meetings I've had because I have to be off by 4.30 – I need to meet someone about a personal matter. Is that okay?"

I nod in agreement. It seems rather odd that she's got to resolve a personal matter when she's only been here for a week and is, I know, living in lodgings in the next village. But it seems rude to enquire so I say nothing and wait for her to tell me more about Force Field Analysis.

She goes to the flipchart behind the chair on the other side of my desk. She writes up FORCE FIELD ANALYSIS and underneath she writes DRIVERS on the left and RESISTORS on the right.

"Now Phil," she says, "let's try to think from the point of view of the organisation as a whole, not just from your or my perspective, but also those of people at the sharp end like Gavin and Peter. What are the forces which are driving change and what are those which are resisting it?"

I find it difficult to think of anything very useful at first but, with Marie's help, I start to grasp the idea. After half an hour of combining our thoughts, we have on the flipchart:

FORCE FIELD ANALYSIS

DRIVERS

- Need to improve profitability

- Big competitors putting pressure on branded products

- Employees' desire for survival

- New management recruits coming in from outside

- Customers becoming even more demanding

- Phil, Marie and Freddie's drive for change

RESISTORS

- Managers uncertain what's in it for them

- Desire to protect Weetflakes brand

- Fear of moving from Claydon

- Potential inertia of middle managers

- Day to day matters preventing implementation

The issue of day to day matters impeding change arose from Marie's discussions this week. It was not something I had previously considered, as I have personally found it easy to avoid being encumbered by routine. But the fresh perspective which Marie has brought in, and the use of the Force Field framework to get us talking, have made me aware of it for the first time.

I admit to Marie that I should have seen this as a barrier before.

"It's very common for people like you, who've been in a Chief Executive role for some time, to forget what it's like down at the sharp end."

"And it's your job to remind me?"

"Yes, Phil. Part of my job certainly. Because I'm going to spend much of my time, particularly during my early days and while these changes are taking place, just talking to people. I think I'm quite good at that and at persuading people to talk to me. Though I'm not sure I know why."

I'm not sure if she's fishing for compliments and I wonder if I should tell her that it's because she oozes concern and interest in everyone she talks to. But I'm aware of the time and I want to talk more about some of the issues raised by the Force Field Analysis.

The very process of carrying out this analysis has been helpful because it enables us to discuss a number of issues which I hadn't thought about before or whose significance I hadn't appreciated. For instance, Marie is particularly concerned that the managers have no financial incentive and will not share in the spoils of success if it is achieved. I say that they will keep their jobs and she gives me a reproachful look.

"I know we're up in the North Phil," she says, "but there's no need to sound like a nineteenth-century mill owner. The younger ones are all good enough to take other jobs and they know it. I'd like you to think about ways in which they can share in the success."

"What do you mean – a bonus scheme or a share option?'

"Yes Phil, maybe. There are tax benefits from some schemes too. I'll let you have more information if you like."

"Okay," I say, "I'll think about it and maybe we could prepare a joint paper for the next Board meeting."

We also discuss the need to put more drive into the management team. Marie suggests that this could be addressed to some extent in the recruitment of new people. Though there will be many other factors to take into account, we will particularly favour candidates who are proactive, energetic and driving.

We discuss the ways in which we can release the necessary time for key managers to focus on change issues. I suggest the possibilities of appointing deputies and also creating a project steering committee, under my chairmanship, which they have to attend as a first priority.

"I agree that there may be a case for a formal monitoring process, once we are under way Phil, because the Board meetings will not be a sufficient forum on their own. But that's another issue. You are always looking for structural solutions but they're never enough on their own. I believe that, if people don't have the necessary drive and are only paying lip-service to change, they will find a hundred perfectly valid ways to let day to day priorities hold them back."

"So what do we do to prevent this?"

"We bring in new drivers, Phil. We don't have enough to overcome the resistors yet."

"But the new recruits and payment by results will be new drivers, won't they?"

"Yes Phil, and that means we must start moving on these quickly. And announce them quickly too. But I feel that we need something else, something I can't quite put my finger on. I think I need to give it some thought. And I'd like you to."

"If I knew what you were driving at, Marie, I might be able to help."

"We need something new, something high profile, something which makes people realise that this time we mean it, this time the change is actually going to be driven through."

Suddenly it hits me and I can't understand why I didn't see it before. Or Marie, for that matter, because the solution is very much up her street.

"We need training Marie, don't we? I've realised over these last few months that managing change is much more complex than I ever believed and that there are concepts, frameworks, ideas which can help you to manage it better. And the more you talk about the issues together, the clearer they become and the more committed you are to implementing change."

Marie looks at me with a rather irritated expression on her face. I'm relieved to find that she's irritated with herself and not with me.

"Of course," she says. "Though it may not be conventional training. We need some kind of process which enables us to work through issues together, using, as you say, some of the frameworks we've found helpful. And I think we'll need an external facilitator to help."

"Can't you do it?"

"It's not really my strength. You want someone who is skilled at facilitating this kind of process. People often assume that training is easy and it's not. And, in any case, I'm too close to it."

I'm just about to suggest that we involve Alan Angus when I hesitate. There are a number of reasons why it might not be a good idea. His connection with Marie, through Christine, is likely to make it a difficult relationship for Marie to handle. And it could bring me into contact with Christine again, something which I'm not sure my marriage will stand. Yet Alan Angus is highly skilled and he has invaluable knowledge of Weetflakes which it would be silly to waste.

Just as I'm debating whether to suggest this to Marie, she looks at her watch and says, "It's nearly 4.30, Phil, I really must be off. I'll have a think about the training need over the weekend – I'm sure it could provide the extra drive we need and remove much of the uncertainty too. And you might like to think whether you would be prepared to use Alan's firm. He's the best by a mile, but I'm not sure of his commitments right now."

After she's gone I spend a few minutes with Julie and then return a couple of telephone calls. It's about 5 pm and I decide to spend half an hour working on my business plan preparation. It's now coming together well and I aim to have it in place and ready for action within two weeks from now.

At about 5.30 pm I pause, knowing that I ought to go home but wanting to delay it as long as possible. I hate not looking forward to the weekend and it's somehow worse because I know it's my own fault. It's almost a relief when the phone rings.

"Hello, Philip Moorley," I say.

"Hi Phil," says an all too familiar voice. My heart pounds as I realise who it is.

"Christine," I say, "how lovely to hear from you. How are you?"

"Just fine, Phil. Just fine. I just thought it was time I gave you a call. What with Alan's involvement at Weetflakes, and now Marie of course. How are you coping with her?"

"I think it's her that's coping with me, Chris. She's doing real well" – I can't lose those Americanisms – "and in many ways she's like you."

"Like me? No one's ever said that before."

"Not physically, Chris. But in the way she challenges me and stops me thinking too narrowly. By the way, please thank Alan for recommending her."

"I will, Phil, but it's really me you have to thank. Alan told me of your situation and I just knew she'd be right."

We chat for a while and it's all very warm and friendly. I always wished I could have been friends with her and kept it like that, but it never seemed possible.

She asks me how things are going at Weetflakes and I'm amazed how much she has obviously been kept informed by Alan. Rather unfairly I think it must be part of their pillow talk.

While I'm speaking to her, I decide to enquire about Alan's availability to help with training if we do go for that option.

"He's very committed at present. Nothing for at least three months. But then you could use one of our other trainers, even me if you were really desperate."

"But I thought you worked on the financial side?"

"I did, Phil, and I still do. But I can work in other areas too and Alan's trained me particularly to handle training in managing chage.

I contemplate whether this is the real purpose of the phone call. Alan being busy, Christine being available and both of them knowing how easily I can succumb to her charms. I hope not but, in my heart, I think I'm being used.

I decide to terminate the call by saying that Jean's coming to pick me up. It always was the perfect excuse for ending our surreptitious conversations in the past and it gives me a strange satisfaction to use the ploy again.

I'm feeling quite depressed as I walk home, beginning to wish that I'd never become involved with Alan Angus and the Goodhart sisters. The concern and uncertainty I feel after Christine's call is more than it should be and I'm not sure of the reason.

All this is soon forgoten as I walk into our front garden and see Jean waiting by the door. I'm astounded to see that she's smiling.

"Hi darling," she says, coming forward to give me a hug.

"Hi," I say, "this is a bit of a surprise, love. What's happened?"

"Come inside," she says, "there's someone I'd like you to meet. There's an extra guest for dinner."

I follow her into the hall and hear shrieks of laughter coming from the lounge. Jean opens the door and there I see Angela, Mark and Marie Goodhart looking at the photographs from our first wedding.

Marie looks up at me as I enter.

"Hi Phil," she says, "sorry to do this behind your back. But the grapevine told me you needed a bit of help."

"The grapevine?" I say, worried that my personal affairs have been all round the Weetflakes site.

"No Phil, not really. I had a young visitor to my office yesterday. That's how I knew."

I look at Angela and she shakes her head. I look at Mark and he avoids my eyes sheepishly. I look at Marie and she nods.

I turn to Jean and she smiles back at me in the way that only she can.

I realise thankfully that I have won back my wife's love. And my son has definitely won back his father's.

Chapter 16

"Do you remember the last time we ran a course together, Phil?" asks Christine Goodhart, while checking that the overhead projector is working.

"I certainly do, Chris," I reply, "it was in our training room at Chapmans. Not as plush as this place, I must say."

"Marie tells me that it's all part of her strategy to mark this training down as something new, something away from their routine day to day involvement."

I know this already because I had to approve the use of this impressive training venue on the outskirts of Harrogate. Marie convinced me that we had to bring people away from Claydon for our managing change training to be effective. It would be false economy to try to reduce costs by doing it internally and we are giving a very clear message that this is something different. Never before has an internal course been held at such a venue.

I'm finding it hard to go along with Christine's attempt to be so casual about our meeting again. It's the first time we've seen each other for over four years and the first thing she does is remind me of the course we ran together just before she came back to England. How could she forget that on the same day she told me she was marrying someone else and leaving Chapmans? I guess it signifies that I now mean nothing more to her than some useful turnover for her new business.

I have this feeling that I made a terrible mistake in

allowing Marie to deal with Alan and Christine's business. Yet, if I'm honest, I didn't try very hard to dissuade her and, when I found that Christine was to do the training, it was too late to do much about it. My comment that Christine is an accountant was met with derision by Marie.

"You do stereotype people, Philip," she said. "Managing change is a topic which anyone with good training skills and knowledge of the key issues can carry out. Chris left her other partners to break away from financial training because she knew she could do well in other areas."

In the last few weeks, I've become more and more confident in Marie and her judgement. I will be eternally grateful to her for responding to Mark's plea for her to go to see Jean that Friday afternoon nearly two months ago, and the atmosphere in the family has now greatly improved. Marie is a frequent visitor to Fairfield Farm House and the children love her being around, particularly her zany sense of humour which is even more evident when she's outside work. She even managed to tell Jean of Christine's involvement in the training without it creating an incident. I've decided that there must be no more secrets.

I'm here at the beginning of the course because we agreed that the vision statement and the new business plan would be an ideal starting point, giving people a sense of direction and defining the targets we are aiming for. I plan to cover this in an hour or so, then stay for the rest of the morning, sitting in while Christine begins her early inputs.

There is a good cross-section of Weetflakes managers on this first course, with three similar groups following during August and September. As discussions about the training have taken place over the last couple of months, I've realised how crucial it will be and how wrong it would have been to proceed without it. I had had my own personal training from Alan Angus and Marie, yet I was expecting others to manage their part of the change process without it.

Marie is there to introduce the course and I'm surprised to find that she's not at all good as a presenter. All the dynamism and bubbliness of her nature seem to disappear when she stands in front of a group. She appears quite formal and stilted. As she hands over to me, I can feel that interest has already been lost. I am relieved that the starting point of my presentation has been designed specifically to grab people's attention and to involve them in discussion.

"How many of you know what Weetflakes' turnover was last year?" I say.

A few hands go up, including that of Freddie Stocks, who is representing top management on this course. I ask what it was and someone shouts out £200 million.

"Near enough right," I say, "actually it was £201.6m. And how much profit did we make before tax?"

There's a silence, even though I know that Stephen Young and Freddie both know the answer. I'm pleased that they are holding back from saying too much at this early stage.

I ask one of Joe McEvoy's production supervisors to guess and he says, "£10m?"

"Not quite, Brian, but not far off. In fact it was £9.3m. Do you think that was enough?"

There's another silence.

"Well, what if I tell you that the capital invested in this business is £130m – to buy the plant, equipment, vehicles and stocks, etc. which allow the business to run. Can anyone tell me what £9.3m is as a percentage of £130m?"

Someone tells me it's 7 per cent and I ask them what return they would like from their money if they were to invest it in a risky business like Weetflakes, rather than in a building society. The enlightenment on the faces of those present indicates that they have got the message and I notice Christine and Marie looking on approvingly. Chris will no doubt be pleased by the financial orientation of my opening.

I decide not to pull any punches.

"This is the reason why change is not an option, it's a necessity. We need to change to keep our company in existence and to keep our jobs. So you shouldn't be worried about the uncertainty of change because it's no longer uncertain. It's for real. You would be justified in worrying if we weren't going to change, because we cannot survive for long on 7 per cent return on capital. Let me show you where we'll be in five years' time."

I produce the transparency I've worked on the previous week, an extract from the business plan.

	Now	5 years' time
Sales	£201.6m	£320m
Profits	£9.3m	£32m
Profit margin	£4.6%	10%
Assets employed	£130.2m	£160m
Return on capital	7.1%	20%
Employees	1,947	2,000
Sales per employee	£103,543	£160,000
Profits per employee	£4,776	£16,000

"This will be a story of effort, success and shared reward," I say, "because you're all going to work hard and deliver greater productivity. Sales per employee – the amount each one of us will play a part in delivering – will go up by 50 per cent and profits per employee will go up by even more. And the Board have agreed a profit sharing scheme which will enable you to receive a proper reward for your efforts. So coming along on this journey with me, with Marie, with Freddie, with all the members of the Board, will not only ensure job security but will also make you better off. So, if you have any doubts, if you think that it's just another MD who's talking a good game, forget it. You might as well leave the bus now. I only want motivated, committed people on this journey and, knowing the sort of people you are, I'm confident we'll all get there together."

This introduction was agreed by Marie and me at a meeting last week. Marie has always insisted on the need to drive change through in a vigorous way and to create maximum possible certainty. I can tell by the smile on her face that she thinks I've done so and I have the feeling from the atmosphere in the room that she's right. I decide to press on with other aspects of the vision and the detail behind the business plan.

It takes me about 45 minutes and there are a few questions. As previously agreed we have a break for coffee, followed by some group work, allowing them to prepare questions of clarification. This is all part of our plan, through the course design, to remove all possible uncertainties.

It's nearly 11.30 am before Christine has the chance to take the floor. The questions went on longer than we thought, but that is a good sign. Freddie was particularly supportive when difficult questions were asked about the role and attitude of the Stocks family. We were open about the need for some employees to move from Claydon and gave reassurances about there being no compulsion and about removal costs being covered. We were surprised that no one appeared to have concerns about the move to own label products, as long as the Weetflakes brand was retained to some extent. They showed themselves to be well aware how impossible it is to compete directly with the Kelloggs of this world – we were perhaps guilty of underestimating their understanding of the market and their realism about Weetflakes' power.

As Christine begins her input, I am reminded how competent she is in this role. Relaxed, yet in control, confident but not patronising. She starts by stressing the importance of the manager's role in change, how it has to cascade down the organisation, how just one broken link in the chain can wreck everything.

"I'm going to start by showing all of you what we regard as the ten commandments of change. They represent principles which Philip has been working to since my organisation first became involved and which Marie has reinforced since she joined us."

I'm a little surprised at this because I haven't seen these ten commandments before, but I soon realise that it's just a useful packaging of the principles which Alan Angus and Marie have been putting over to me. As I look at them, I realise how necessary it is to pass these principles right down the line, and not just leave them at top level.

Christine takes the group through the principles and invites questions after each one.

1) Be clear and open about the reasons for the proposed change.
2) Prepare a clear action plan and communicate it to all those affected.
3) Make sure you have all the information you need to explain things and clear uncertainty.
4) Identify those whose support you need and the risks and

opportunities for them.

5) Identify those who might resist change and decide how you will overcome it.

6) Assess your relationships, in terms of power and trust, with those who will support and those who will resist.

7) Develop different, tailored approaches to deal with those whose support is required.

8) Timetable your change plan carefully and update it regularly.

9) Prepare contingency alternatives in case your plan for change goes off the rails.

10) Communicate, communicate and keep communicating.

I can see why Alan Angus didn't give me this list early on. It would have been too structured and too prescriptive for someone as sceptical as me. But he said all these things to me at some time, with the exception of the contingency alternative. I haven't really thought about what would happen if the business plan goes off the rails through factors which might be out of my control. I resolve to give this some consideration. I also resolve never to forget the tenth commandment and never to let anyone else do so.

I notice how cleverly Christine takes questions and uses them as an opportunity to reinforce the points and make new ones. I was totally wrong in my doubts about her as a trainer in this area and I'm sure that I'm the only one, apart from Marie, who would dream that she had once been my Financial Director.

I begin to take notes of the points she makes which are new to me and which I feel a need to retain. There is a particularly interesting discussion on resistance to change and I note down these points:

* Resistance to change is usually to the *how* (the process of change), not the *what* (the content of change).
* Resistance can take the form of fight or flight behaviours – they may oppose you or they may walk away. It is too late when they've walked away, so you must anticipate resistance early on.
* Caring for people and respecting the impact of change

on them is the key to successful change management.

I find these points particularly helpful because I believe that things at Weetflakes are going almost too well at present. Everyone has told me that resistance is sure to come sooner or later and I want to be fully prepared for it. I look at the programme and note that resistance is covered in more depth on the third and final morning, so I decide to try to come back here in time to sit in. Already I've agreed to return for a final open forum that afternoon.

As the course breaks for lunch, I tell Marie that I'd like to leave so I can be at a meeting with Willis and Gavin early in the afternoon. She thanks me for coming and I agree to meet her at Claydon tomorrow – she's staying at Harrogate for the rest of today. As I walk to the door I hear that familiar warm voice which once I knew so intimately, "Phil," says Christine, "can I walk to the car park with you?"

I can't say much else but yes and, in any case, what else would I want to say? She looks older now, more mature, with a slightly fuller figure, but more attractive than ever.

She says nothing as we walk towards my car and it feels embarrassing. Why did she want to walk out with with me if she's not going to say anything?

I get to my car and turn round to face her. I go weak at the knees as I look her in the eyes and remember how close we once were. How much I once loved her, maybe still do.

She seems uncertain what to say and how to say it. Eventually she speaks out and what she comes out with bowls me over.

"Phil, I'd like you to know that I've always regretted letting you down and rejecting you to marry Steve. I made the wrong choice and it has screwed up my life, I'm really sorry."

Her voice falters and she looks down, avoiding my eyes. She says "I'll see you on the final day" and runs back to the building.

I drive back to Claydon, asking myself if my life is going to be turned upside down once again.

Chapter 17

Two days later I'm having breakfast at home with the family before beginning my journey to Harrogate. It's a beautiful warm July morning and I really ought to feel as happy as any man could be.

But I don't. Ever since Christine dropped her bombshell in the car park, I've been moody, restless, on edge. I'm hoping that the children can't see it, but I know Jean can. She always notices the slightest change of mood and last night she asked me what was wrong. I said it was nothing and I know she didn't believe me. Fortunately she doesn't seem to have any suspicions about Christine, having been assured by Marie that using her was not my decision.

I feel very mixed up inside. Half of me is grateful for my family security and hates the idea of doing anything to break it up. The other half is fantasising about going away with Christine, maybe back to the USA where I first had an affair with her.

As I drive to Harrogate, I ponder over and over again why she decided to say what she did. If it had been at the time when her marriage was breaking up I could understand it, but she's now living with Alan Angus, after he left his wife and children.

The course is having a coffee break as I arrive and I see Christine talking to a group of participants who are gathered around her. I can tell that Freddie, always one for the ladies according to office gossip, is entranced. Christine sees me and comes to greet me, looking confident and unconcerned.

"Hi Phil," she says, "you've come at just the right time, we're going back into the main room now. Have a good journey?"

In this public location I can do no more than respond to her chatty approach and I join the course as we file into the conference room. I resolve that somehow before the end of today I'm going to have a private chat with her and try to clear the air. It's driving me crazy, not knowing where I stand.

For a while my mind wanders back to the days in the USA when we were having our affair – wonderful times, probably the most exciting of my life. I was successful at Chapmans, had a lovely wife and family, with a beautiful mistress as well. I really thought I had it all.

I try to bring my attention back to Christine giving the course some feedback on their presentations which I should have been listening to. I decide that I must concentrate more, particularly as she may bring me into the discussion.

"There are just a few points I'd like to pick up before we move on to resistance," she says. "They summarise many of the issues you've brought out in your group work. I was pleased how much you focused on the human dimensions of change – you showed real sensitivity in the way you dealt with the impact on other people. Let's try to bring this together."

She picks up an overhead projector slide and shows it on the screen. It says:

THE HUMAN DIMENSIONS OF CHANGE

- CATHARSIS
- LETTING GO
- COMMITMENT
- EMPOWERMENT

As I listen to Christine expanding on these headings, I'm once again bowled over by her confidence and authority in such a difficult and new area for her. I'm also bowled over by her sexuality, as I always have been. If only I wasn't so weak and vulnerable where she is concerned.

"Catharsis is a very important process whch those affected by change must be allowed to go through," she says. "You've rightly stressed in your presentations that we shouldn't shut this out, shouldn't prevent people from talking things through. It's natural for people to want to show their feelings and express their opinions about the problems of change and the impact it has on their lives. That's what the catharsis stage is concerned with – encouraging everything to come to the surface. It's far better for you to hear it than for it to be bottled up inside."

Stephen Young interrupts in a natural way which tells me that this kind of dialogue has been going on throughout the course.

"Christine," he says, "that's all very well, but if you can't do anything to help them, aren't you just wasting your time? There are several people in my department who are having to change their whole approach to their jobs. They're having to move from being negative bean counters to becoming management accountants who need to provide a service to their customers. And they don't like it, they keep telling me so all the time. But I can't do much about it because they do have to change and I can't make it go away."

"Don't think that listening and understanding is doing nothing, Stephen," says Christine. "My point is that it can be helpful for them to speak their mind and you must not try to stifle it."

"But I mustn't give them any indications that they will be able to avoid change. Is that right?"

"Yes Stephen. That's crucial. You must be consistent, open and honest throughout and you must also stress the positive aspects, based on your own experience. Show that you understand, you identify with them and are willing to support them. Try to make them see the benefits of change, without underestimating the disruption it may cause to their lives."

A few more people join in with their own change issues and I'm impressed by the level of the debate. It all seems very natural, they don't seem affected by my presence and Freddie is joining in like everyone else. I'm convinced that this course will prove to be a good investment and will provide the necessary drive to support our culture change.

Christine has been using a mask to cover and then gradually reveal the headings on the screen. She moves the discussion on:

- CATHARSIS
- LETTING GO

"You have to guide people carefully through the letting go process," she says. "You have to be sure that they let go but also allow them to experience a sadness and sense of loss. Remember that change may be part of your life and you become used to it. But those without your vision and your experience find change much harder, particularly when they weren't involved in the original decision. So taking your example, Stephen, when they let go of their comfortable roles as bean counters, processing invoices or adding up columns, help them to cope with that loss, allow them to experience sadness and don't play it down."

"That applies even more to our sales people," says Peter Cullen, one of Martin Moss's National Account Controllers. "We're having to stop them calling on small customers and ask them to spend more time in the office, dealing by telephone and analysing financial information. They're hating it and I've tried so far to stop them whingeing about it. But you're saying this is wrong, Chris, we should acknowledge what they've lost, even encourage them to whinge?"

"Yes Peter, precisely that."

I feel like intervening with one or two other examples but hold back, wanting the debate to continue without me. I need not have worried because others add their own ideas and Christine copes with them superbly. The discussion makes me realise how much I underestimated the impact which the new strategy has on everyone in every function at every level, and how much our managers are benefiting from being trained to manage it.

Christine moves on to discuss:

- COMMITMENT

"This is a critical phase because you're having to turn

people from the negative into the positive. You have to persuade them to commit themselves to the vision which you are providing for them and work with them to establish the standards which they will work to. Do any of you feel that you've achieved this yet?"

The discussion which follows delights me, first because everyone takes part and secondly because it confirms how much progress managers are already making in preparing their people for change, even though the detailed business plan has only just been agreed. It looks as if the vision which I gave them has been accepted and, even more importantly, passed down the line to others. It is particularly encouraging to hear Peter Cullen and another of his sales colleagues saying that, despite all the protesting and the nostalgia for the way things were, they are really buying into the idea of Weetflakes as a partner to the major retailers.

Most of those present admit that they haven't got too far in establishing new standards of work, and I intervene to tell Christine that I had requested people to wait until the business plan was published before setting new objectives for their people. Then, I reasoned, we will achieve a match between business and personal objectives.

"Okay, thanks Phil," says Christine. "We must move on as time is limited. Let's look at the final and most difficult part of managing the human dimensions of change."

She reveals the full slide again.

THE HUMAN DIMENSIONS OF CHANGE

- CATHARSIS
- LETTING GO
- COMMITMENT
- EMPOWERMENT

My initial reaction to seeing 'empowerment' up there is to think "yet another buzz word", a fancy label which is just common sense. But, as I listen to Christine explain it in the context of managing change and relate it to what I am trying to do at Weetflakes, I become less cynical. And I look around the room to see that my managers seem to be accepting it.

"Empowerment is the final stage of persuading people to buy into change," she says, "and to achieve it, you have to be prepared to give people responsibility, to let them set their own standards, to allow them to be accountable for their results without having to refer every decision to you. It may not come easy to many of you but, believe me, it's a crucial step in managing change and making it stick. Otherwise you're going to have to be checking up constantly to ensure that people aren't reverting to old ways."

I can see that Freddie is beginning to look unhappy. I now know him well enough to anticipate when he's going to disagree. Usually it's with me, now it's with Christine.

"Now come on Christine, I've gone along with most of what you've given us and it's been useful. But all this stuff about empowerment, or delegation as we used to call it, depends on having good people, people who will do things when you tell them to. What if you don't have that?"

I'm not surprised that Freddie mentions this because, despite a slight improvement recently, he's still very critical of the people who are working for him. I'm worried about the frankness of his remarks because there are a number of people in the room who work for him or for someone who reports to him. Fortunately Christine deals with the question tactfully and impressively.

"You've raised a number of points there, Freddie, and I'd like to build on them. First of all, empowerment is not the same as delegation, particularly if you regard delegation as telling people to do things. Empowerment involves giving people as much control as possible over their work environment, agreeing with them the results which can reasonably be achieved and then letting them get on with it. I'm not saying that you should adopt this style Freddie – you're much too experienced for me to tell you what is right for you. But I can give you my view, and quote substantial research evidence which says that people will be more likely to accept change if they are empowered in this way."

"Okay Christine," replies Freddie. I'm pleased to see that his tone remains friendly. "But you've cleverly avoided answering my main point. What if the people you have aren't up to the job?"

"I think you know the answer to that better than I do, Freddie. It's no good for anyone to be in a job which they can't cope with. But all I can say is that people are usually capable of doing far more than you would ever believe, once they are empowered. And the time when significant change is taking place is often the time when they are able to prove it, as long as management is prepared to put faith in them."

I decide to intervene. I say, "And prepared to let go of detailed control, Freddie, which means taking a few risks with people, something I want you all to be ready to do. And you'll have my backing, even if it goes wrong a few times. But I don't think it will too often, because we have some excellent people. As Christine says, the key is to persuade them to buy into the vision we have for Weetflakes and empower them to implement it. Then we won't have to use detailed control."

This is all rather spontaneous from me – I hadn't planned to say it and it has never been so clearly implanted in my mind as a philosophy before. But others have often told me how I tend to empower people in the way Christine described and it usually seems to work quite well. Marie has constantly stressed that the new vision of Weetflakes must be supported by a consistent management style which matches my own. I just hope that Freddie got the message.

We now have a short break before Christine moves on to cover resistance to change, and I'm frustrated that I'm still not able to talk to her on my own. As the course gathers back in the room again, I try hard to concentrate on her imput on resistance to change which was, after all, supposed to be my reason for coming here early.

"Resistance to change is natural and is to be expected, even where it's been managed well," she says. "Be surprised if it doesn't happen, not if it does. Let's have a look at the causes and what we can do to cope with it." She's prepared a slide on this too and she reveals it all this time.

CAUSES OF RESISTANCE TO CHANGE

- FEARS AND THREATS
- LACK OF SKILLS AND RESOURCES

- LACK OF INFORMATION
- LACK OF TRUST

"It's most important for us to focus on the causes of the resistance, rather than the symptoms," she says, "because, for one thing, the symptoms are often well disguised and difficult to pin down. It's often inertia rather than open resistance which impedes change."

I'm on the point of interrupting to say how relevant this point is to Weetflakes. How my predecessors as MDs found that to be their biggest problem – there was no apparent open resistance but things just didn't happen. But I stop myself, realising that, with this kind of mixed level group, it could be difficult to talk about this issue.

"So you look for the circumstances which might make your people fearful or threatened and by doing so you will cope with resistance, with luck before it's gone too far. What sort of fear do you think people might have when faced with significant change in their lives?"

I'm pleased how many people respond to this question and also with the calibre of the answers.

Stephen Young suggests fear of the unknown, no doubt thinking again of his accounts staff who are being asked to become management accountants. A discussion about this problem leads to one of Stephen's managers suggesting that it is more fear of failure than fear of the unknown for this group. They know what is wanted but are afraid that they cannot deliver.

One of the distribution managers suggests that, with his people, there is a fear of looking stupid and inferior, particularly when faced with new ideas. Weetflakes people have always tended to keep their heads down and let others try anything new.

Freddie, with typical forthrightness, says that the biggest fear is of losing jobs and we should never forget it. And we should also be clear that, in some cases, this fear may be justified.

This leads to a fascinating debate, to which I am tempted to contribute but decide that I shouldn't. There is a good range of views expressed and I am pleased to see that they appear to have forgotten about my being there.

The debate is about whether it is ever justified to reduce fear by hiding facts – for instance, to conceal possible future job losses. I am impressed by Christine's way of bringing the discussion to an end in a balanced way.

"You must all decide on your own personal position about telling the truth to people and I'm sure you would all be reluctant to tell outright lies. But I accept that there are occasions when you have to take a view about whether sometimes it is best to delay bad news, even when you know it is eventually going to happen. Good timing of announcements is critical and you often have to keep everything confidential until then. But remember that we talked earlier about fear of the unknown and this can often be an even stronger negative factor than the fear of losing jobs. If you tell people nothing they will make their own assumptions, which may be even worse than the real situation. If you tell them the truth about their chances as early as possible, they will usually respond better."

Stephen Young, who seems to be participating very actively and obviously has great concerns about the changes his people are going through, comes in with some more examples of their fears.

"I notice that you bracketed fears and threats in your earlier list, Christine, and the main problem of my people is that they feel threatened. This creates their fears – the fear of losing . . ."

"Losing, Stephen?" encourages Christine, "losing what?"

"Well, it's the fear of losing status. One of my people told me last week that her core skills – bookkeeping, clerical work and accounts preparation – are no longer valued. Everyone is looking for analytical skills which they don't feel they possess."

As he is saying this I think of the parallel situation at a more senior level. Ernie Taylor must be feeling just the same fear and threat, yet I have done nothing to reassure him. And as he still retains the key functions of treasurer and company secretary, he would find it easy to obstruct implementation of many changes required by the new strategy.

I lose the thread of the discussion as my mind wanders

away to consider what I need to do about Ernie. Christine just said that you shouldn't wait for resistance to occur, you should identify then eliminate the causes as far as possible. This makes sense to me and I resolve to ring Julie today and arrange to see Ernie when I return. I tune back into the discussion and the point being made by Christine, which she summarises on the flipchart, confirms more than ever how much I need to deal with Ernie. The flipchart reads:

FEARS AND THREATS

- Fear of the unknown
- Fear of looking stupid
- Fear of failure
- Fear of losing job

- Threat to value of core skills
- Threat to status
- Threat to power

Christine has obviously added the last entry while I was not concentrating. She develops it further by saying, "And don't think of threats to power in just a formal way. It's often the power to influence events in an informal way – to receive information, to be able to discuss issues with those in positions of influence, to be present at meetings where decisions are made."

I realise with some guilt and concern that these all apply to Ernie over the last few months. My desire to develop Stephen has caused me to leave Ernie out of the picture – including attendance at Board meetings.

As Christine moves on to the other causes of resistance to change on her list – lack of skills and resources, lack of information, lack of trust – I try to relate it to what is now going on at Weetflakes. Am I guilty of other neglect which might trigger resistance, in the same way as with Ernie?

I can't think of any obvious example where we have failed to provide necessary skills or resources, but I'm put on the spot by Gordon Jones, one of the Distribution Managers. "We're expected to improve our distribution service, to provide more flexibility to customers," he says, "and we're still running crappy old vans which are just not reliable."

I feel guilty as I recall that it was I who delayed the capital expenditure request at that first Board meeting.

"The sales people in the field are expected to develop longer-term partnerships with customers – or so we're told," says Peter Cullen, "and we've been given no training in negotiating or business awareness."

I'm feeling increasingly uncomfortable because I feel that, to some extent, these comments are being directed at me. Yet I'm still glad to be here. I wish Marie was here too – she's supposed to arrive at about lunchtime – and I must ask her to start moving quickly on the training of sales people. We have already discussed it several times but, with so much else going on, it has fallen behind in the queue of priorities.

As Christine confidently asks the group for examples of cases where lack of information and trust could cause resistance at Weetflakes, I once again marvel at her confidence and composure. One would never dream that she was, still is, an accountant – you would believe that she has been a specialist in managing change from way back.

But as she recounts an anecdote from our days at Chapmans when lack of information caused her accounts team to resist change to reporting systems, I realise that she has really been a manager of change for many years. She has much experience of managing people, she always was a skilled communicator and she is now linking these attributes to the training expertise and conceptual frameworks provided by Alan Angus.

"Lack of trust is the final cause of resistance," says Christine, "and, as we're coming up to lunch, I'd just like to leave that one with you to think about and maybe to discuss as we eat together. All I will say is this. Trust starts with the example which is set at the top. One or two of you have told me how the MDs who came in from outside before Philip came along, did not win your trust. You believed that they were not being fully open and this caused you and others in Weetflakes to resist."

As I listen to this, I realise the benefit of having someone from outside like Christine to run a course away from the normal work environment and to encourage people to talk freely. In all the time I've been at Weetflakes, I've never been able to obtain reliable information on the problems of my predecessors. Now apparently Christine has encouraged them to open up and declare lack of trust as a key issue. But I'm not quite prepared for what follows.

"But you've also told me that this doesn't apply to your present MD, who has come to join us this morning. And I can tell you, as someone who has worked for him twice" – I can feel the surprise in the room and wonder why she has decided to say this – "that you are right, Philip Moorley will be fair and earn your trust as long as you do the same in return. But remember the implications of this for you and your people too. If they trust you, they will not be so likely to resist the change which you try to carry out. So ask yourself if you are displaying the same fairness and openness as Philip does, when dealing with your people."

As always with Christine, I allow my feelings for her to overcome any other, more rational view. I ought to be questioning whether it was a good idea for her to bring up our previous working relationship and embarrass me with her public statement that I am worthy of their trust. Instead I am rather pathetically basking in her approval, pleased that she still seems to have this respect for me which has stood the test of time. Thinking back to two days ago I wonder if her feelings go beyond that and I know that I have to find out. I decide to wait while the others go out to lunch and speak to her in private.

She's putting away papers and turning over the flipchart as I walk towards her from the back of the room to the front. She turns to face me and I have to use all my willpower to refrain from grabbing hold of her.

"Christine," I say, "what did you mean when you told me that you made a mistake, marrying Steve?"

"Phil, is it a good time for this?"

"I need to know, Christine. Did you mean that you still feel for me?"

"What do you think, Phil? I know you've always lacked confidence where I'm concerned, but do I have to spell it out?"

"But what about Alan?"

"What about your family?"

"You know that I'd have given them up before and I'd do it again. I just didn't believe that you would ever want me."

"Well I do, Phil, I really do."

I'm just on the point of leaning forward to kiss her when I realise that there's someone else in the room. Chris and I pull back at the same time as we see Marie standing by the door.

At first I wonder how much she has heard, but I have no doubt when I see the expression on her face, as black as thunder.

"They just told me out there that you'd been talking about the importance of trust and how you, Christine, told everyone to trust Philip. I think I'm going to be sick."

Chapter 18

The next morning I'm in my office early as usual. I see an envelope on my desk and my name is written on the front. I recognise it as Marie's handwriting.

As I open the envelope I have a feeling of foreboding which adds to the depression I've been feeling since the embarrassing encounter at Harrogate yesterday.

There are two pieces of paper inside. One is typed and says:

"I hereby tender my resignation as Personnel Director of Weetflakes. I will, if necessary, serve out my 3 months' notice period, though I would prefer to leave at the end of the month.

Yours sincerely,

Marie Goodhart

The other paper is in Marie's handwriting and says:

Dear Philip,

If anyone asks me why I'm leaving, I will say it is for personal reasons and ask them to see you for an explanation.

If you start your affair with Christine again, I swear I will tell Jean. If you don't I will say nothing.

I'm genuinely sorry to be leaving because I respect you

and have enjoyed working with you. But I also enjoyed being with your family and cannot condone what you seem prepared to do.

Sincerely,

Marie

The pile of papers on my desk suddenly seems irrelevant. I feel a chill in the pit of my stomach as I realise what a mess I'm in. But, despite the threat of my conversation with Christine being revealed to Jean, the children and everyone at Weetflakes, I'm still haunted by Christine's words yesterday. She seems prepared to leave Alan for me, so why shouldn't I take my chance? Why should I allow Marie to stop me with what amounts to blackmail?

I try to think of a favourable scenario which would allow me to stay at Weetflakes, maybe live in a flat with Christine in Grimsby or Scunthorpe and keep in touch with the family most days. But would Christine be prepared to live out here in the sticks?

And this scenario now involves my losing the best Personnel Director I'm ever likely to have. I decide that I must try to talk her round and persuade her to keep her personal feelings separate from her responsibilities to Weetflakes. I convince myself that she is being unprofessional by mixing the two up. I even begin to blame her for the whole mess, reasoning that it was her fault for bringing in Christine to do the training. How blind one can be when trying to rationalise an action which is not rational.

I ring Julie and ten minutes later Marie is sitting opposite my desk, looking very different from normal – not cheerful, not bouncy, not friendly. Quite the reverse.

I start by asking her to stay, telling her how much I value her and need her, asking her to keep the personal and business issues apart, implying that this should have been the principle we worked to when selecting someone to do the training. She suddenly gets up and makes to leave the office.

"I don't think I want to hear any more of this, Philip. You have just convinced me more than ever that I need to leave.

I can see you've kidded yourself that it's all my fault."

"Marie," I say, "it's not anybody's fault. You couldn't have known about the effect Christine has on me. And it's so much easier to know what we should have done with hindsight."

Still standing up and close to the door, she turns round to me, looking up with a fierce expression on her small round face. Her voice falters with emotion.

"But I did know, Philip, I did know about the impact Chris has on you. Because it's not unlike the impact she has on most of the men she becomes involved with. I just thought that you, with Jean and Mark and Angela and Susie and that lovely home, would not be prepared to throw it all away. But I suppose I underestimated the lengths my lovely half-sister will go to wreck everyone else's life."

"Now there's no need to be unpleasant about Christine, please Marie," I say.

"Why not?" she shouts. "Why bloody not?" I begin to worry that Julie and the next door offices will hear and wonder what is going on.

"It's about time you heard a few home truths about that woman, Philip, and I'm going to tell you whether you like it or not."

My own temper is raised now and I ask myself whether I should order her out of the office, but that would cause even more embarrassment. Word would be around Weetflakes in no time. And why shouldn't I hear what she has to say about Christine? It won't make any difference to the way I feel, infatuated as I am. Marie is obviously jealous of someone who is so much more attractive and successful than she is. I ask Marie to sit down and I pour her some coffee. She then begins to tell a story which completely takes the wind out of my sails.

"I don't know whether you know, Philip, but Christine has another younger sister, Philippa, who is about a year younger. They were six and seven when our father left them and came to France to marry my mother. I suppose you can't really blame them for the way it made them become what they are. Apparently they were impossible in their early teens – Father often used to have to rush across the Channel to sort out the problems they caused."

"What do you mean, 'what they are', Marie? Many teenagers are rebellious but they get over it."

"Well those two never did, Phil. Of course, they no longer cause trouble as they did as teenagers, but they are fiercely competitive, determined achievers and quite prepared to walk over anything and anybody to get what they want."

My desire to defend Christine and say that she couldn't possibly be like that is overcome by my curiosity about the rest of the story. I ask her what career Philippa is in.

"She's a Marketing Director with an ice cream company – brilliantly successful like Christine was on the finance side. Even more ruthless, so I hear."

"Now come on, Marie," I say. "I know Christine quite well and ruthless is not a word I think you can fairly apply to her."

"Okay Philip, it was perhaps not a good word to use. Maybe the best way of describing both Philippa and Christine is that they're determined to have anything which comes along, anything which anyone else has, anything which meets the immediate need. And then they'll discard it in favour of the latest interest."

"Which is me?" I say.

"Which is you, Phil. Which was Alan Angus. Which was Steve, her husband who adored her, was so good to her and tried desperately to keep her. Which was you once before in the USA, wasn't it? Years ago she even got herself pregnant to trap someone who wouldn't leave his family to marry her. I love her, Phil, but I'm not blind to her faults. She will do anything she can to get what she wants. Anything to have more than her sister. More money, more success, more men."

My mind goes back nearly ten years, to when I saw Christine off at Heathrow, when she was going to Harvard and I had just been reconciled with Jean after our first separation. She told me then that she had once become pregnant and that the father was married. I remember feeling sorry for her, assuming that it was she who was being used.

I wouldn't be believing any of this if it wasn't coming from

Marie. Despite the short time I've known her, I trust her implicitly and cannot accept that she would say these things out of bitchiness or jealousy. I have to be wrong about one of them and something inside tells me that it must be Christine. I've been a fool all along and have allowed her to pick me up and drop me whenever she wanted.

I suddenly realise what I now have to do. I must do everything I can to keep my family together and make a success of this job. And there is no doubt in my mind that persuading Marie to stay is critical to my success at Weetflakes. I've learnt to become dependent upon her, upon her realism, her practical approach, her tendency to challenge and question my more reactionary attitudes. Also her ability to see clearly what needs to happen and then to achieve it, quickly and effectively.

As all this goes through my mind Marie sits there patiently, putting no pressure on me to say anything. I suspect she knows what I'm thinking.

Suddenly there's a knock on the door and Julie comes in, looking unusually hesitant. I have no doubt that she heard the raised voices and is wondering what is going on.

"Ernie Taylor's here to see you," she says.

With all the trauma I had forgotten that I rang Julie on my car phone yesterday evening and asked her to arrange for me to see Ernie, following my concerns about his likely resistance to change.

As Julie goes out to fetch him, I ask Marie if she will reconsider her decision and come to see me again before we go home tonight.

"I don't blame you at all for resigning, Marie – I deserve it. But what you've just told me has changed things. It's over now, I promise. And Weetflakes needs you, as much as it needs me."

"I'll think about it, Phil, but no promises. Give me a call around 5 o'clock."

As Marie strides out of my office, Ernie Taylor steps back to let her pass, then nervously shuffles forward towards my desk. I realise what a sad character he has become and how he seems to have lost the dapperness and confidence he had when I first joined. I also realise how little I have thought about him, all my efforts going into developing Stephen Young on the management accounting side.

I remember what Christine said on the course yesterday – that it is fear of loss of power and status which leads to resistance. I try desperately to put my personal problems out of my mind and think about Ernie as a person who, despite his loss of influence, is still very important in the organisation. He deals with matters which are critical to smooth operations and which no one else can deal with – such as pensions, insurance, legal matters, car administration – and he has vast experience which we should not risk losing.

"Ernie," I say, "I feel guilty that I haven't spent enough time with you during these last few months, so I thought it would be good for us to talk things over. In particular how the changes are affecting you."

"Thanks, Mr Moorley," says Ernie. I think of asking him to call me Phil but remember how many times I've asked him before. There are some things you can't change. "I'm glad you've asked me because there is a great deal I want to talk to you about. I am concerned about the way things are going."

For 45 minutes I sit and listen. As I do so I remember what Christine told my managers about catharsis and letting go, and this stops me from intervening. Otherwise I would have challenged him when he became emotional about the preference being given to Stephen Young. And I would have tried to stop him whingeing about his loss of status and yearning for the days when the Stocks family was fully in control. But I remember that this is a necessary process, something which will help Ernie eventually to accept the new situation.

As I listen to him, I become more convinced than ever that, if resistance is not coming from Ernie now, it is only a matter of time. His feelings are emotional and bitter, so much so that, once he starts pouring his heart out, there is no stopping him. Somehow I have to remove the fears and the threats which he is feeling. I decide that the best way is to listen and then give him reassurance, about his value, about his job security, about the continued importance of his role.

But to do this, I have to be able to interject and Ernie is difficult to stop once he's under way. As I try to put on my best listening manner, my eyes stray past his shoulder to the noticeboard on the far wall. There I've put up the typed version of the ten commandments which I picked up when I attended the first day of the course. I had already put up the change cycle which Alan Angus gave me, what seems like years but was only months ago.

I realise how easy it is to fail at implementation because you become selective about the people you are communicating to. I look at commandment (1) – be clear and open about the reasons for the proposed changes. I've been clear and open with Stephen Young and Gavin Simmonds because they are young, attractive people whose company I enjoy. I've communicated the vision to everyone in some way, but it's not been at all consistent. Ernie would have attended one of the meetings and received a paper on it, but I've never given him any time for real communication.

I've never tried to inspire him or sell the benefits for him. I ask myself how many others I've neglected in this way and whose resistance I can expect. My eyes fix on commandments (5), (6) and (7):

5) Identify those who might resist change and decide how you will overcome it.
6) Assess your relationship, in terms of power and trust, with those who will support and those who will resist.
7) Develop different, tailored approaches to deal with those whose support is required.

Just three days ago, I sat there while Christine went through this list, congratulating myself on how I'd done everything right. How complacent I have been.

I move my eyes to glance at the change cycle and see Phase 8 – define outputs and set targets. What have I set for Ernie, even though he still reports to me? Answer – not a thing.

I move my attention back to Ernie, feeling guilty that I haven't been listening to him for the last few minutes. Now I resolve to do so, not just now but in the future. And not just him, all the others whom I might have been ignoring in the same way.

"And frankly, Mr Moorley, I wonder whether I'd be better taking early retirement and looking after my garden. At least I know the wife appreciates what I do in there."

I realise that he's stopped and pause for a while, uncertain how to start. This seems to unnerve him. He displays a worried expression and says, "I'm sorry if I've spoken out of turn, Mr Moorley, but I needed to get it off my chest. It's been a very sad time for me. I feel as if I'm grieving for Weetflakes as I know it."

I think back to the discussion on the course yesterday. Ernie is 'letting go' and he needs to talk about the sadness which change has brought to him. I know what my response has to be.

"No need to be sorry, Ernie, you've got nothing to be sorry about. It's me that should be apologising."

"Oh, I don't know about that, Mr Moorley."

"I do know, Ernie. It's not in the old culture of Weetflakes for the bosses to admit they make mistakes, but that's yet another change you'll need to get used to. Shall I tell you why I am the one who should be feeling sorry?"

He nods – I guess there isn't much else he can do.

"Because I've been guilty of not thinking about you, Ernie, about the things that are important to you. And there's no excuse because I've been receiving all sorts of excellent advice about how to manage change and I've tried very hard to apply it. How to sell the new vision, how to think about the implications for everyone who is important, how to give them all the reassurance they need to take away their fears, how to make them committed and empowered. You name it Ernie, I've tried to do it. But I'm ashamed to admit that you and your department have been forgotten. I've put my attention elsewhere and because you're doing work which is important but low profile, and because I've been engaged on other matters which are closer to my immediate interests, you've been left out. But this is going to change in a big way."

I can tell that Ernie is lost for words. He's not used to a Chief Executive who is so open about the mistakes that he's made. The paternalistic style of Arthur, and before him Wilfred, is what Ernie grew up on. And that meant a belief in the infallibility of those at the top. Now I have to persuade Ernie that those who work for me should be open, about both successes and failures.

"Ernie," I say, "I feel guilty for not knowing, but how many management people are there in your section, people whose commitment is important to the smooth running of your department?"

"About four – or maybe five or six."

"Okay. I want you to arrange a meeting with them, you and me, so that I can make up for what I've failed to do. In the meantime I have a few issues I need to make clear to you personally."

I find it hard to keep my mind on what I'm doing, as the events of earlier in the morning keep coming back to me. But I discipline myself to concentrate and generally I manage to keep my mind on Ernie and his needs. I try first of all to obtain his commitment by explaining the vision and why it needs to happen. I tell him how important the information and controls which his department provides are going to be. I try to give him security and certainty by reassuring him that his job is safe. I tell him how much I appreciate people who can be self-contained, who are prepared to commit themselves within a framework of empowerment and autonomy. How I will sit down with him to agree objectives and a process for monitoring them.

I find myself using this discussion with Ernie as an opportunity to practise all the principles which Alan, Marie and Christine have taught me. I feel as if I'm going round the change cycle and practising all the ten commandments at once. It makes me realise that, with all the frameworks in the world, the key is to think of the person who is experiencing change, to try to feel what he or she is feeling. And it's highly rewarding to see the impact on Ernie. It's as if he's become ten years younger and he seems much more like the quiet and confident man I met on my first day at Weetflakes. I realise just how much power I have to influence motivation and I find it rather frightening.

I decide that I'll also use this opportunity to remind Ernie of the danger of resistance.

"But there's something I want to make clear to you Ernie, and to your people. Once I've done what I should have done before, once I've communicated the vision and agreed objectives, I will expect changes to happen. I will rely on the members of your department to commit themselves to the new Weetflakes and to support all your colleagues. Are you prepared to accept that, Ernie? Because the one result I will find it hard to accept is any resistance to change."

"I think that before today, Mr Moorley, we were already resisting in small ways. We've been putting off taking action connected with the new strategy, like the office moves which Sales and Marketing requested, for instance."

I'd forgotten that. A month ago I asked Martin, Willis and Gavin to move offices so that all three of them and their people could be closer together. It hasn't happened because Ernie's department organises office moves. I consider how many other problems like this have been happening and could still happen.

"But resistance to change is over now, Ernie, at least as far as you are concerned?"

"Yes, Mr Moorley."

"But there must be one further change if I'm to believe it, Ernie."

"Yes, Mr Moorley."

"That you call me Phil. It's a condition of the new deal, Ernie."

"Okay, okay . . . er . . . Phil."

I can see the effort which this takes for him but I will make sure it happens. It will somehow be a symbol, for him and for me, that I have convinced him of the benefits of change.

After Ernie has gone, I spend a short time with Julie, catching up on messages and dealing with the paperwork which can be moved quickly. I find, however, that my mind is not on what I'm doing and I keep drifting back to what Marie said. After Julie has gone I sit in the easy chair in the corner of my office and think back to the time I've known Christine. Certainly, if I'm honest with myself, her behaviour while we were together in the USA fits Marie's description. She saw the move to Chapmans as a step forward in her career and realised that an affair with me would ensure that I reported favourably on her performance. And then she dropped me for Steve as soon as the time was right for her to make a career move.

I realise that I won't be able to concentrate on my work at all today so I decide to walk round the factory. Before I do so I have a look at the new organisation chart and consider if there are any other departments feeling like Ernie's people, left out and therefore likely to resist. I find it hard to know and decide to arrange a meeting with Arthur so that I can obtain his advice. I've been pleased that Marie has been having regular meetings with Arthur and they are getting on well. But I've not kept up the monthly meetings we planned and this is an occasion when I can benefit from his understanding of the people involved. I'm sure he could have warned me of the problems with Ernie if I had bothered to ask him.

I decide that I'll visit the Distribution Department because George Plant has been keeping his head down recently and I wonder how far Freddie has been involving him in the change process. Freddie does not generally speak well of George who, despite his impressive outside experience, seems diffident and lacking confidence when Freddie's around. I wonder how far Freddie and George between them have communicated the vision to those below them.

After four hours with George and his people, including lunch with the loading supervisors on their special table in the canteen, I realise how much more you learn when you leave your desk. It reminds me of a notice which I once read that Louis Gerstner of IBM has on his office wall – 'a desk is a dangerous place from which to see the world.'

Generally I was pleased with the response from most of the people in the department. George had done a good job of telling people about the changes and the impact on them, which will be quite dramatic in many cases. Yet the positive aspects of the vision weren't always communicated as well as I would have liked and, with George's support, I was able to tell them about some of the benefits, including the likelihood of continued job security, even if this must involve a move of location for some. I was able to bring home the message that doing nothing to change Weetflakes would be the riskiest strategy for all of them in the long term.

As I walk back to my office I decide three things. First that I will spend much more of my time with people in their workplaces in future. Secondly that managing change effectively involves constant checking that the right message is filtering through to everyone who has a part to play in that change. Thirdly that I must do nothing to harm my career at Weetflakes, because I'm growing very attached to the place and the people. And that means persuading Marie to stay and avoiding the loss of credibility which would result from the story about Christine and me becoming known.

As I get back to my office I ask Julie to ring Marie. It's now close to 5 o'clock and I feel that I can't wait any longer to know if I can change her mind.

She enters my office looking calm and composed.

"Marie," I say, "I can only repeat what I said this morning. I've been a complete idiot and you were right to resign. But it's all over with Christine now, it truly is, and you and I are both needed here at Weetflakes. What can I say or do to persuade you to say?"

"Just one thing, Philip. On Monday Christine is coming here to discuss the training we've carried out so far. You can tell her that it's all over while I'm here and you can also tell her why. And we can both tell her that there'll be no more training courses unless she stops pestering you. It's about time Christine found out that you, at least, have seen through that charming façade."

The thought of this encounter appals me and I try to think of something I can say to change her mind.

"Take it or leave it, Phil. In the meantime my letter of resignation stays on the table."

Chapter 19

Next Monday we're sitting in the Weetflakes training room, just the three of us, Marie, Christine and me. By agreement Marie and I decided to enter together, thus removing any possibility of one of us speaking to Christine on her own.

All weekend I've been worried about this encounter and have paid less attention to the family than I should have done. Recently I have felt increasingly guilty that I have not been spending enough time with the children, in particular Mark. I hoped that his action in going to see Marie would be the spark which brought our relationship back to the good times in the USA, but after a few rather artificial attempts at activities together, we've returned to distance and silence. I know it's because my mind is always on Weetflakes, far more than any other job I've ever had, and I wonder if it's because we are living in the same village as the factory site.

It does not do my male ego any good to be so much under Marie's dominance, but I know it's my own fault. Apart from deciding that we had to enter the room together, she has also told me that we will raise the personal issue at the end of the meeting, after we have discussed the feedback from the first training programme. I obediently agree to this, cursing myself for allowing this to happen and wondering if I will ever recover the right balance in my working relationship with Marie. It cannot be wise for an MD to be completely under the thumb of his Personnel Director, but there's not a great deal I can do about it right now.

Christine gives me a hesitant and rather concerned smile as we enter. I know she must be wondering why I haven't rung her as I promised after the embarrassing encounter with Marie last week. Possibly she senses that I'm having second thoughts.

Marie takes control of the meeting, though this is no more than she probably would have done anyway. She has been the dominant force in developing the training courses and she was the one who arranged this meeting, to review the first course before running three more.

She makes an introduction which confirms the role of the courses as a driving force of change. I'm not surprised to hear her once again refer to the 'Seven S' framework which she has been using quite frequently at management meetings where the change process is discussed.

"If you remember, Phil, our Force Field Analysis indicated that we needed a driving force for change, and that's the context in which I think we should review this course. In fact it was our primary course objective – 'to provide the driving force to launch the change process in Weetflakes'. But there are other objectives too and these are the ones I gave to Alan and Christine to work with, after our various discussions around the Seven S framework."

I can see that Marie is enjoying this – being centre stage, showing Christine her position of power, confirming to her how closely Marie and I have worked together. I consider for a fleeting moment whether I could be wrong, whether Marie has deceived me about Christine, whether she is the one who is using me. But it's too late to do anything about it now.

"You will recall, Phil, that on my first day at Weetflakes I said that the key question I would ask in my first few months would be whether four of the Ss – skills, style, systems and shared values – were well enough in place for the change process to work effectively. I think I convinced you that they weren't and that's why we're going to introduce various other initiatives over the next few months. In particular I want us to carry out appraisal training, linked to a more formal system of performance review."

This is something which Marie and I have discussed several times over the last few weeks and I'm not sure why she's repeating it here. Or maybe I am sure – it's purely to impress Christine and perhaps even to whet her appetite for the future potential of work at Weetflakes. I have no doubt that appraisal training is within the scope of Angus O'Rourke's activities.

"The need for more work on style, skills, systems and shared values was also built into the subsidiary course objectives, to ensure that the overall objective had some focus. I'm not sure if you've seen these, Phil – Christine certainly has."

She shows a transparency on the overhead projector.

Managing Change Programme – Specific Objectives

As a result of this course, participants will:

- improve their personal skills so that they can more effectively manage others through the change process
- better understand their own leadership style and its fit within the Weetflakes culture
- be more able to develop and operate systems which monitor performance through periods of change
- be more informed and willing to accept the new vision and shared values of Weetflakes

I'm impressed by what Marie has done here and it's typical of her ability to use a conceptual framework in a practical way. She has tied down the training suppliers to deliver results which are relevant to our new strategy, and it makes this kind of review session so meaningful. Successful though the course may have seemed last week, has it in fact delivered against these objectives?

I decide to pose this question to Christine and see how she responds. She is looking lovely this morning, her blonde hair now quite short in the latest fashion, her face as beautiful as ever, the lines which are beginning to develop around her eyes somehow making her seem even more desirable. She no longer wears the smart, power dressing clothes that she favoured in the USA, now preferring a more feminine style. This morning she's wearing a long, flowered dress, cut below the knees but bringing out the curves of her figure, which are still very much in the right places. I try to recall how old she is now – maybe 35 or 36. She is so much more mature, and so much more desirable than the anxious-to-please management accountant who first came into my life about ten years ago when my career and my personal life were at such a low ebb.

How can this desirable woman fancy me and be prepared to risk her career for me, I ask myself, not for the first time. I then remind myself that Marie has given me an answer which is not so flattering – she is just easily bored. I think about how Alan Angus would feel if he knew. He went into a business partnership with her, then left his wife and family to live with her – now she is prepared to cast him aside after only a few months.

Christine begins to respond to my question in a way which makes me think of one possible explanation of her readiness to risk splitting up the business. She is very good at this, just as good as Alan Angus, so she would be likely to achieve great success on her own.

"I'm more than pleased to answer that question, Philip, and thank you Marie for putting this feedback into such a helpful context. It is unusual and gratifying to have course objectives which are so closely linked to a change strategy. The problem is – and I suppose this applies to almost all management training of any complexity – it is difficult to measure in the short term. I believe that we have improved their skills – we did some very effective role playing on the second day. We also discussed leadership styles after that session. I gave them information and guidance on performance management systems which will link very nicely into the appraisal training which you mentioned, Marie. And I'm sure that neither of you will be surprised to hear that we would love to help you with that next step."

Marie again displays her enjoyment at being in the power position by saying, "I'm not surprised at all, Christine, but that's another issue and we may have other suppliers in mind."

"Of course Marie, I quite understand. And with regard to the fourth objective, I strongly believe that those who attended will be more likely to accept the new vision and share the values which it represents. I even have course feedback questionnaires to prove it. But we won't know for a few months until they have had a chance to convert these objectives into a series of new behaviours. And, without wanting to opt out of any responsibility, that depends on you two as well as me."

Marie's tone becomes sharp, even aggressive, and I feel an atmosphere of competition and confrontation developing between them.

"What precisely do you mean by that, Christine?" snaps Marie.

"I think I can best explain by coming back to a framework which Alan introduced you to, Philip. He asked me to be sure to remind you of its value."

As she puts the change cycle onto the OHP screen, I sense Marie's irritation. I'm not surprised to hear her say, "Oh, not that old stuff again. I've told Alan time after time that it's too procedural and inflexible to be applied in practice. It may have been helpful at the beginning to give Phil some structure, but we're way past that stage now."

Christine looks at me for support and I'm tempted to take the easy way out, to let Marie have her own way again. But I decide to give Christine some help. First because I genuinely do want to see where the course and our present position fit into the change cycle, secondly because I think Marie is going too far in trying to dominate the meeting.

Indeed, from what I've seen so far, I realise that Marie is also very much part of the sibling rivalry of the Goodhart family. I suspect that, knowing she can't compete with the physical attractiveness of Philippa and Christine, she looks for every opportunity to score points off them in other ways. And, in this case, she's doing it through a position of personal power which she has created for herself. Have I been wrong about Marie? Was I too naive in assuming that I could trust her? Should I allow the embarrassing confrontation which Marie has lined up for later?

With difficulty I put this to one side for a moment and say, "Now hang on, Marie. Let Christine carry on. I've agreed with you that, in some ways, the change cycle simplifies life by dealing with things stage by stage. But it was useful and I'd quite like to see how it fits now."

Marie gives me a furious look and I am reminded that she could still carry out her threat to resign with all the problems that revelation of the reasons would bring me. But there are limits to how far I can let her walk over me.

I look at Alan Angus's version of the change cycle again (see opposite).

I remember how helpful it was in the early stages, as a way of disciplining me to create a vision, think about its implications and then work on the key players. Okay, maybe it was difficult to ensure that you completed Phases 4 and 5 before you became involved in 6, but it was a useful way of ensuring that I went through the right thought processes. Recalling the resistance problems with Ernie Taylor, perhaps one weakness is that it tempts you to put too much emphasis on one or two key players like Freddie and Willis, while forgetting those who are less prominent but still important. I suspect that Phase 10 is the time to cope with this – I remember Alan telling me that, however well you prepare, there is always some unexpected resistance.

"Where do you think we are on the change cycle now, Philip?" asks Christine.

"No problem, Chris. I'd say we're just past 9 and certainly involved in 10. In fact I need to tell you both about some experiences last week which make me believe that we need to address resistance in a more systematic way."

"Okay Phil, let's pick that up later because I have some data from the course that confirms possible resistance, particularly at lower levels. I agree with you about the phase you're at. Phase 9 began when your business plan went live a month ago and, from what I hear, the sales side in particular is moving fast already. I heard that one big contract is just about in the bag, isn't it Phil?"

With all the personal trauma last week, I tended to forget the good and significant news – that Martin Moss, closely supported by Willis, has agreed a letter of intent for Weetflakes to supply own brand multipacks to Pathway Supermarkets, one of the top five in the UK. It delivers the first of our strategic milestones – a large new contract with

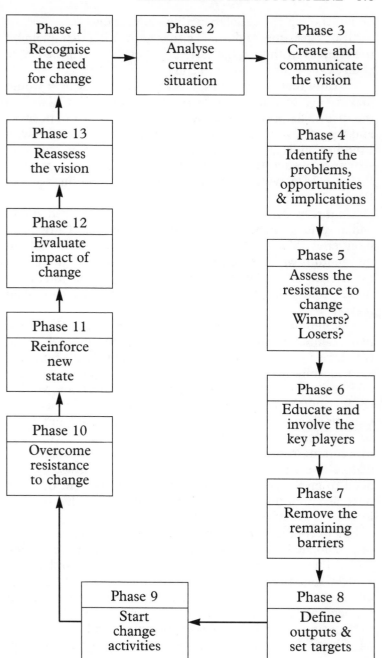

one of the top five retailers within six months.

"It is, Christine, and much else is happening to implement the plan, even though it's early days yet. Now tell me where you see the training course fitting in."

"I admit that it doesn't fit in tidily, because ideally I would like to have seen it earlier, as part of Phase 6. But Alan told me that he felt it was too early, you were only just in position and the critical need was for individual communication with Freddie, Willis and Arthur. He also felt that the organisation structure needed to be settled first. So I see it as extending Phase 6 to a wider audience, but also supporting you in Phases 10 and 11."

"And to provide the driving force which was needed and which your framework just doesn't cater for, Christine," intervenes Marie. "It assumes that there is an inbuilt momentum which takes everyone from phase to phase. My experience is that inertia will often mean that you never move from one phase to another, indeed you can often regress."

This intervention from Marie confirms to me that these two talented young women are locked in competition to convince me of the rightness of their particular approach. And, despite my loss of faith in Christine after what Marie told me about her and my very high respect for Marie's ability and integrity, I find myself more convinced by Christine's argument. The change cycle has been helpful and still is. I can see that, last week, I was very much involved in overcoming resistance and, if I am to retain the support of people like Ernie and the distribution supervisors, we will need to give a great deal of positive reinforcement over the next few months. Which is presumably what happens in Phase 11 – reinforce new state.

I'm worried that the conversation is becoming too much of a dialogue between Christine and me, with Marie making the odd negative intervention. I try to open it up and also to achieve something positive from the meeting. Ever since my day in the distribution department, I've been convinced that we need better communication channels to lower levels.

"I'm sure that the course is supporting us in Phases 10 and 11, Chris," I say, "and we'll look at the feedback in a minute, but I'd like all three of us to consider what else needs to be done. How many courses are we planning? A further three, isn't it? Well, that's about 60 people and it's not enough. I'm not saying that we need the same course, or indeed any course at lower levels, but we have to have some processes to ensure that resistance is overcome and the new behaviours reinforced."

Christine replies quickly. I suspect that she's very happy with the way the conversation is going, with Marie on the sidelines.

"That was my whole point when I said that the objectives could not be achieved by a course alone, Philip," she says. "Even those who attended the course will need reinforcement, particularly about the new values. They buy into them at the intellectual level – they certainly fully understand the reasons why Weetflakes has to change and why new values are necessary – but I saw some evidence that they could easily regress. And, as you say, there are many more at lower levels who won't attend the course and we're relying on others to pass the values down to them."

Marie now intervenes but in a less aggressive way, presumably realising that she must not let her personal feelings obstruct a valuable debate.

"But surely, Christine, we've got to rely on them. That's what we're basing our plan on, the idea of empowerment and autonomy for the key managers. If we have to intervene and do their communication for them, we take away their authority and their motivation."

I find this debate fascinating, particularly when I relate it back to my visit to the distribution department last week. I can see Marie's point and it's very much in line with my own views on empowerment – you can't be interfering every time you suspect that people are not communicating as you would like them to. Yet you cannot stand by while the message is weakened, distorted or not communicated at all. My recollections of last week are that both Ernie and George wanted me to communicate directly with their people to fill gaps which they could not do themselves. I tell Marie and Christine about my experience in the distribution department and decide to throw a specific suggestion into the debate.

"I'm with you 100 per cent there, Marie, and the last thing I want to do is remove people's authority to communicate. And I can see that I took a risk last week. Some of the stronger characters like Freddie or Martin might have resented my interference. And I was certainly very careful to speak to George Plant first. But I'm sure that he wanted my help and would probably like to have it again, because communication of a vision is not something he finds easy."

Marie and Christine both nod their agreement and I feel that I may have found some common ground. At last they seem to have stopped competing and to be looking for a solution which is right for Weetflakes.

"So, if we are going to achieve the most out of these courses and deliver your Phases 10 and 11 of the change cycle, Chris – what was it, overcoming resistance and reinforcing new state? – I think we need to have some more formal structure of communications."

"You mean team briefings?" asks Marie, sounding as though she doesn't approve.

"Not necessarily," I say. "I've heard of team briefings and believe that they can perform a useful purpose in some organisations, but they are rather too top down and inflexible in their approach for me. I had in mind something much more flexible, tailored to the needs of each department and each manager. The only requirement we need from them is the assurance that regular communication has taken place and that reinforcement of the new behaviours is given. We will judge each manager on the outputs – whether resistance is happening and whether new behaviours are being retained. Our job is to monitor this on a regular basis by meeting the managers concerned for progress reports."

"But I thought you wanted to become more directly involved yourself," intervenes Christine. "Indeed I was hoping that was the case, because the strong message from last week was that many of the managers would like to see you personally involved in communication. You are associated so strongly with the new strategy and have built up a very positive image – I think it needs you personally."

I try to put aside the possibility that Christine might be

flattering my ego. Obviously Marie suspects this because she rolls her eyes at me as if to say "she's bullshitting you". I suddenly feel very irritated that such an important debate is being dragged down by rivalry between these two women who each have so much to offer. I wish for a moment that I had followed my initial instincts and never allowed either of them to be involved at Weetflakes.

"It's good of you to say so, Chris, and I'm sure you will appreciate that it's difficult for me to be objective about that. But I want to be involved where it is helpful and where the managers appreciate my support. So let's arrange to see each of the key managers and discuss how they are going to handle the communication process to the next two levels down. I can offer help if they want it by attending or leading the meetings, with the manager present, assuming he or she wants to be. And, so that we are sure they are objective, you can make the offer to them, Marie."

"And I can mention it on the course if you like, saying that Marie will be approaching them," adds Christine. I look at Marie about this one and she nods her agreement. Marie also adds a powerful and complementary suggestion.

"I think we should include more on the course about the skills of positive feedback, Christine. That's what people need to reinforce the new behaviours. Weetflakes has traditionally had a culture of what I call 'bollocking and blame' and, though I love the Stockses in many ways, Freddie and Willis are the worst of all. It's regarded as wimpish to tell people they're doing it right. So I think that our role, and particularly yours Phil, is to work on Freddie, Willis and some of the others who are copying that behaviour. Where we can't change it easily, you have to be involved, Phil, though I see this as much less formal than what you suggested earlier. I think you must be seen walking the job much more than before. Not interfering and impeding the managers, but just showing interest and giving positive feedback."

"You mean management by walking about, as Tom Peters called it?" I ask.

"Yes Phil," says Marie. "MBWA was the label which Peters gave it. But it's not so much the label which is important or even the fact that you do it. It's the why and the how. Here we have a specific objective which makes it more than the MD just wanting to be seen looking interested. You are there to reinforce the new behaviours, to give the positive feedback which Weetflakes managers find hard to give."

"You're not suggesting this as an alternative to my involvement in the communication processes we discussed earlier, are you Marie?" I require.

"No Phil, I see this as complementary and probably most useful in cases where you have not been closely involved," she replies.

"Perhaps I could spend some time with Phil, on an individual basis, helping him with feedback skills, if that's helpful," suggests Christine, and I can feel the atmosphere become tense. I suspect that Marie will not be able to let this one pass and I am not mistaken. She seizes the opportunity to talk to Christine in the way that I've been dreading all weekend.

"Christine," she says, "before we respond to that suggestion, we've got to give you some feedback. Philip and I have been most concerned about what happened last week and there are some issues which we need to make clear."

In the next five minutes Marie Goodhart helps me – no, makes me – destroy the one remaining chance I had to fulfil the dream of a lifetime. And, despite the dreadful feeling of loss, I can't help being relieved that it's finally over.

Chapter 20

It's Spring again, nine months after that meeting with Christine, and we are just celebrating a year at Fairfield Farm House. Jean and I will be having a dinner at home this evening – the children will both be out at one of the many social activities which they now seem to be involved in.

As I walk to the office on such a beautiful sunny morning, I think to myself that I'm finally getting myself and my life organised. What I must do is try harder to give more time to Jean and the children, now that Weetflakes is on the road to success. I have been working very long hours and becoming very absorbed in the fascinating process of managing change. Now that we seem well on the way to achieving our strategy, I must relax more.

This morning I have a meeting with Martin Egerton, the first one-to-one encounter I've had with him since he came to see me in Richmond soon after I joined. I guess he must be pretty pleased with the way the business is going, judging from his positive responses at Board Meetings. Today's meeting is at his request and I'm not sure of the reason. Maybe a chance for a detailed update on the implementation of strategy, which is just not possible at Board meetings. Certainly I'll enjoy telling him what we've done and how we've done it, in particular how we overcame the resistance problems encountered by my failed predecessors.

I will not be afraid to admit that much of the credit must go to Marie, a dynamo of a Personnel Director. I will be forever glad that I persuaded her to stay, whatever the cost to my personal life and my self-respect. The memory of that embarrassing confrontation with Christine still haunts me. I still don't know whether or not to believe her apparent sincerity. Or was she just saying what she needed to extract herself from trouble?

"I'm really sorry, Philip and Marie. I have no excuse for the way I behaved and I will quite understand if you ask me not to work with you again. But – well, Marie, you may not believe me but Philip knows. We have something between us that won't go away and fate seems to keep drawing us together again. I just acted instinctively and it was highly unprofessional."

Marie later said that it was one of her more impressive performances and should have been awarded an Oscar. I said nothing but preferred quietly to believe that she was sincere. If it's true for me, how could I blame her for feeling the same way! And it would explain the lack of logic behind her actions.

Anyway, the outcome was that Christine, later supported by Alan Angus as he became more able to find dates in his diary, ran a series of highly varied and successful programmes for us – extending into appraisal skills and business awareness for sales people.

Then came the news which surprised me but was met with cynical acceptance by Marie – Christine left Alan Angus in both a personal and business sense to go back to the USA. She was apparently offered a research scholarship at Harvard by one of the professors she met when doing her MBA. Just the latest flavour of the month according to Marie and to hell with everyone else. I didn't know if she would come to see me to say goodbye – I had only run into her a few times in the months after the ultimatum in the training room and that was when I was giving imputs on the courses she was running. But I was relieved when she didn't come to see me – I feel that it's finally over now.

Martin Egerton is not due to arrive until 11 am and we have a meeting fixed before then to assess progress against the business plan. Marie initiated these meetings every month and we invite those who report direct to me –

Freddie, Willis, Martin, Stephen, Marie and Ernie – as well as anyone who has a particular contribution to offer. Alan Angus voiced his approval about this process, saying that they were 'Phase 12' meetings, putting the final touches to the change cycle by constantly evaluating the impact of change. They certainly do that and I always look forward to them very much, not something I am always able to say about meetings at Weetflakes.

Alan Angus's remarks about them being 'Phase 12' meetings stimulated me to use the following month's meeting to raise the issue of how far we need to move to Phase 13 – to reassess the vision in the light of other changes taking place outside Weetflakes. Ernie Taylor, who has been a revelation since we finally persuaded him to accept the new vision, offered to bring together an analysis of key changes taking place in the environment, drawing on the knowledge and experience of everyone in the company. Ernie effectively acts as secretary at these meetings, bringing skills of administration and co-ordination which no one else can offer.

As usual, Willis and Freddie dominate the discussion at the meeting. This is partly because of the central nature of their roles in innovation and supply chain management respectively, but also because of them, their personalities and their history with the company. While I thank my lucky stars that I didn't follow my initial instincts and replace one or both of them, I still worry constantly about their impact on the people reporting to them. While Martin Moss has managed to bring out the best in the people below him – particularly Gavin Simmonds who thrived once he was freed from Willis's control – Willis and Freddie have not fully entered into the new spirit of empowerment. It is particularly worrying that, of the two new people recruited to report to Willis for Quality and New Product Development, one has left already and the other is showing signs of unrest. There have also been rumours that Peter Thackray, a young man of immense promise in the crucial role of buying, is looking for another job because of the problems of working under Freddie's style of management. "All drive and no sensitivity", as Marie put it a week or so ago.

This is still my biggest challenge – it hasn't seriously

affected implementation of the strategy yet, but it is bound to do so in the future. If I don't do something, I will be left with no management succession in the key areas under Willis and Freddie's control. As I watch Willis reject a perfectly sound idea from Stephen Young, I decide that I should take this issue up with Arthur at one of the monthly meetings which Marie and I now attend together. The idea of our using Arthur as a sounding board has worked well and he and Marie seem to have a good relationship. He has helped us to gain a real understanding of North of England social patterns and the Weetflakes culture. Without this advice, Marie's transition from the French environment would have been much more slow and difficult. But I think that the issue of Willis and Freddie's management style is still likely to be highly sensitive – Arthur is open and supportive but still concerned about the future, particularly where his son and nephew are concerned.

After the meeting breaks up just after 11 am Martin Egerton comes into my office, smiling greetings at everyone as they leave. He has some friendly banter with Freddie about Grimsby's football team before he sits down to join me on the new easy chairs which I've recently bought to replace the ancient ones I inherited.

"Freddie's a new man these days, Philip, and to think we were discussing replacing him around this time last year. What made you change your mind?"

"It was a guy called Alan Angus. Remember I told you that I was using someone to advise me on managing change? He convinced me that I was taking the easy way out. I think you also made me think again because, though you said you would back me, you made it clear that it would be only as a last resort."

"Yes, I was very concerned, Phil. I could see you going the same way as your predecessors who just wanted the Stockses out as quickly as possible. I suppose we should be grateful to your Mr Angus."

"Yes Martin, we should. But, to me, it just confirms the value of someone from outside to advise and challenge at every stage of the change process."

"Is Angus still involved, Philip, because I suspect you

might need him again?"

"He's still involved in some training but it's coming to an end now. I need his help less now that I have Marie. Why do you say I might need him again?"

"Because there's going to be even more change, Philip, or at least there could be. Remember we talked last year about the possibility of floating Weetflakes on the Stock Exchange?"

I feel a twinge of excitement as I realise what he's going to say.

"Well, that was only a distant possibility a year ago, but now that we have a new strategy under way and already a substantial improvement to the bottom line, Hill Benson sees no reason to wait. There is at least enough of the Stocks family in favour to push us over the 50 per cent mark, and those who are not in favour can hold on to their shares."

"So when do you plan this?"

"It depends on you to some extent Phil. When do you think you can cope with it? Because the impact on the man at the top is very significant. You'll have to give a large amount of your time and be sure that you have managers below you who can cope. There is also the issue of timing from the Stock Exchange point of view. I'm going to see our flotation specialists tomorrow morning for their advice. We want to float at a time when the market is on a high. Leaving that aside, though, how quickly do you think you could move to flotation?"

I think for a moment. As usual I have mixed emotions. Only this morning I was looking forward to a quieter period, with more time to spend with the family. But now there's a new challenge, something I've always wanted to do, something which will almost certainly make me rich beyond my wildest dreams. Martin hasn't mentioned share options but they are bound to be on the agenda, particularly if I push for them. I'm in a very strong position – my experience with a US public company and my record of success so far mean that, without me, the flotation would be nowhere near so credible. Yet I am aware that there are problems which need to be resolved.

"Do you have some doubts, Philip?" asks Martin, seeing

my hesitation.

I decide not to mention my personal doubts, about the impact on my family. Instead I mention the other doubts, about the lack of management strength, particularly if I am to be less able to be involved in day to day matters.

"We discussed the part Freddie and Willis have played in this transformation, Martin, and they have been marvellous. But there are still weaknesses below them, partly because of their controlling management styles and the aura which the Stocks family still has here. I have to give time and effort to solving this problem, by trying to change them or, if not, by changing the organisation structure to give others more autonomy. I'm worried about what will happen if I have to spend more time away from day to day routine. The last thing we want is poor results in the period leading up to flotation. And then there's the problem of the calibre of people in the finance function. Stephen Young and Ernie Taylor are great in their roles here, but both would be out of their depth as Financial Director of a plc."

"I realise that Phil, and I should have mentioned the need to recruit a new Financial Director. You don't know anybody from your previous companies, do you?"

I ask myself if he knows something and is pulling my leg. But he seems perfectly serious.

"No," I say, "I can honestly say that I don't know of anyone who would be suitable."

I feel as if a load is off my mind, not just because I said it but because I meant it. Now I know that I will not see Christine again.

Martin stays for lunch and seems pleased and surprised when I ask him to join me in the Weetflakes cafeteria, which we have now upgraded to a higher standard, available equally to everyone. Marie and Stephen Young join us and, as usual, Marie soon has everyone laughing. I see two of the factory supervisors passing with their trays and ask them to join us. I am pleased how relaxed and open they are, even with Martin and me present. I think how far we have come in a year and how much this is due to the managing change courses and the communication meetings which followed them. The factory supervisors are used to seeing me because

Joe McEvoy, for once ignoring Freddie's wishes, asked me to attend several of their communication meetings, or 'change process briefings' as Marie has labelled them within Weetflakes.

As Martin leaves, I walk with him to the car park.

"What you have achieved here in twelve months is amazing, Philip, quite amazing. I'm more keen on a flotation then ever. I'll call you tomorrow and we can discuss the date further."

As I walk home to Fairfield Farm House for my celebration dinner with Jean, I feel quite pleased with myself. There is a new challenge, a new vision, another chance to manage change in Weetflakes. With the experience of the last year, I should do even better this time. All in all, life is rather good.

Chapter 21

I pour the remains of the bottle of wine into our glasses as Jean goes to put on the coffee. I notice that Jean's glass is empty whereas mine is still half full – it's unusual for her to drink more quickly than me. The wine was okay, not what I would have chosen myself in the days when I had time to think about such things, but quite palatable.

We haven't talked much during the meal but that's what's good about being married to someone for so long, I tell myself – there is no need to make polite conversation just for the sake of it. It's pleasant to have a meal without the children – much as I love them all, it is often hard to cope with their frenetic conversation after a demanding day at the office.

As Jean comes back to the table I notice how lovely she looks and it seems impossible to believe that she's nearly 50. Having little Susie so late in life seems to have made her look and act even younger. I now find it incomprehensible to think that, less than a year ago, I would have been prepared to leave her, this home and the children because of my obsession with Christine, or my "blonde Achilles' heel" as Marie has been calling her.

Jean is carrying a piece of paper in her hand and she starts to study it as she sits down.

"What's that, love?" I ask, thinking that I ought to show some interest.

"I found it on your desk," she says, "something called the

change cycle."

She shows it to me across the table. "I thought it looked interesting."

It's not often that I talk to Jean about Weetflakes – it just somehow never seems appropriate. Indeed she told me only last week that she learns more about what I do from Marie's regular visits than from talking to me. I decide that her interest is a good chance for me to tell her what I've been doing these last twelve months – maybe understanding the size of the task I took on will make her more tolerant of the commitment I've had to give.

"Would you like me to explain how I've used it, love?" I ask, and she nods. I take a sip of my coffee and think about where to begin.

"The idea of the change cycle is that, for any project involving significant change, whether it's a small project involving part of the business or, as in this case, a culture change for the whole company, you need a systematic, stage-by-stage process. Marie had some doubts about this – saying that life is never simple enough to work stage by stage – but in the end we agreed that the value of the cycle is as a checklist, a discipline to ensure that you do everything you need to in a logical order. It's important to accept that a number of stages may happen simultaneously and you will have to loop back on many occasions."

Jean is sitting there listening intently, but something about the look on her face gives me a warning sign that there may be trouble to come this evening. I can best describe it as a look of cynical amusement, as if she's enjoying some hidden joke at my expense. But I plough on regardless.

"You start with a vision, which represents how you want things to be, the desired new state. And you have to create and then communicate this vision to everyone whose commitment you need to implement the change. The vision needs to be capable of attracting people emotionally, yet it must be specific and achievable. You also have to convince people that it is necessary, that the dangers of not changing are as great as or greater than those of change."

"And, in Weetflakes case, you had to convince everyone that just carrying on with the old ways would have meant disaster?"

"Yes, love, that's right." I feel pleased that Jean seems to understand so well, yet I'm still slightly uneasy about her manner.

"Haven't you really missed something out here, Phil?" she says, looking at the paper. "You've moved on to Phase 3 and left out Phases 1 and 2. 'Recognise the need for change' and 'analyse current situation'. Aren't they critical because, without them, you may never see the need to change?"

"Yes love, you're right." I try hard not to sound patronising as I add, "You've obviously got a real feel for these things."

"Oh I have Phil, I have. Anyway, you carry on and explain the rest to me."

I spend the next five or ten minutes telling her how we've used the change cycle at Weetflakes, how I had to identify the winners and losers, how I realised that the key to success was understanding the motivation of the central players, in the early stages and also when resistance came along. How this understanding has also been important in the nine or ten months since implementation started. How Marie and I have constantly monitored progress and done everything possible to reinforce the new behaviours that we need to encourage. How communication of the vision and the new values of Weetflakes has been a continuing, not a one-off task.

I pause when I have the feeling that Jean has stopped listening.

"Am I boring you, love? I'm sorry if I've gone on too much."

"Oh no, Phil. It's fascinating – I wish you'd told me about the change cycle before."

"Why's that, love?"

She says nothing and looks down at the paper in her hand again. She looks at me directly and I can suddenly feel the force of her emotion coming across the table.

"Philip," she says. "Do you have a vision for the future of our marriage?"

I knew that when she called me Phil I was in trouble. But, when she calls me Philip it's really bad. We don't use first names when things between us are good.

I'm not sure how to reply. If I say yes, she'll ask me what

it is. If I say no, I'm admitting the truth, that I've never really thought about it. I decide that a neutral response is best – to reply with another question and let her talk about what's bothering her. I think I know what's coming and that I deserve it too.

"Why do you ask, love?"

"Because I fucking well know you haven't, that's why Philip Moorley." The use of that word is so out of character that it makes me sit up and think. This is not a routine whinge, this is serious. She carries on, her voice rising, her face becoming increasingly emotional.

"You're so bloody systematic about changing things at Weetflakes, but you don't even get to Phase 1 at home. You don't recognise the need to change, you haven't even thought about the current situation of your family, never mind analysed it. And if you do have a vision of what our life is going to be, you've certainly not communicated it to me."

I decide that the best tactic is not to argue but to let her say everything she wants to, without being defensive. Mainly because I have no defence. The comparison of my attitudes to work and home is powerful and devastating.

"What is your vision, love?" I ask. "I know I should have one, but I'd like to hear yours."

"I have two visions, Phil. One is what I'd like it to be. In ten years' time, I'd like you to be moving into retirement, sharing some interests with me, I'd like us to be close and loving, as we have been before. As when we were first married, as when we were in the US. When you used to notice me and the children, talk to us, spend time with us, not always be preoccupied with other matters."

I shuffle in my chair uncomfortably, uncertain how I'm going to answer all this when the tirade stops. But it shows no sign of doing so. She's in full swing now.

"And I'd like to think that the children will have left home, maybe got married, maybe given us grandchildren, but will always want to come back, always feel that they have a relationship with the two of us. Always feel that, though we've had our problems in the past, they can feel secure in the closeness of their parents' relationship."

"But that's a vision that I want too, love, really I do."

"Well you're doing bugger all to achieve it, Phil, that's my point. The second vision is the one we're heading for."

"And what's the second vision?"

"The family splitting up again Phil, because I can't stand the idea of a relationship without love and without care. Or, perhaps even worse, we carry on as we are, with you living here but not really being here. Do you know how long it is since we made love?"

I think back and mumble something about it being two weeks ago.

"No Phil. That was having sex. I mean making love. I can tell you, it was quite soon after we moved in here. After I over-reacted to you not telling me about Marie and then we made up. Then something seemed to happen, you just seemed to freeze. I thought at first that you were starting again with that blonde, but Marie assured me that her involvement with Weetflakes was entirely business and I trust Marie."

I feel I ought to argue at the idea of her trusting Marie more than me, but I'm on poor ground there. I decide to let it pass and, instead, try to defend myself more generally.

"I accept what you say, love, I have been much too preoccupied and that will change, I promise. I'm sorry it's been so tough for you. I hope it hasn't been too obvious to the children."

Her eyes look directly into mine with even more intensity.

"Of course it's been obvious to them, at least to the two older ones. It's not only that they notice how far away from each other we are, and believe me they do, they also see how little notice you take of them. Look what Mark did for you when I was so stupid about Marie. Okay, you may have thanked him and talked about playing basketball with him for a few weekends, but then it was back to where you were before. No real communication, just paying lip-service. And over the last twelve months Angela has done brilliantly at her new school and is heading for straight As in her A levels, and I don't think you've even noticed, you certainly haven't asked."

At that moment, I hear a door bang and the two children enter the dining room. Angela, looking stunningly attractive, dark hair down to her shoulders, with her mother's lovely blue eyes and prominent cheekbones. Mark, now taller than Angela, light brown hair about the same length but these days tied in a neat pony tail. I know that girls find him attractive, though I've often puzzled why – perhaps it's the vulnerable look in his eyes.

"Oh sorry, are we interrupting something?" says Angela.

"No, children, in fact your timing is perfect. Your father and I are about to tell you about a new vision which we're going to achieve together. Your father is an expert at managing change and this time he's going to do it for us. Come on darling, all the key players are here for you to influence. But the difference from Weetflakes is that there's not going to be too much resistance to change from us, Philip, you're the one who's going to have to change."

"Okay Jean, okay," I say. "Sit down you two and have some coffee. I need a whisky, anyone else want one?" To my surprise Mark says yes and I get up to pour one for us both.

For the next half hour I get the hardest feedback I've ever had in my life, certainly harder than anything I've ever had at work. Any idea I may have had that this was Jean being over-sensitive or showing menopausal symptoms is blown away by the forthrightness of the children's comments. They are so clear and so consistent that I even wonder if they've been rehearsed.

They all add up to one thing – I'm not the parent I was in the USA. After the family was reunited after the divorce, I was an interested and caring father. Now I'm more like the father they remember as small children before Jean left me – distant, apparently uncaring, not showing any obvious affection. The conversation makes me highly depressed, realising just how low I have sunk. As always happens with me, the more success I have in business, the more I fail in my home life. But I am also determined that this has to change and I suddenly think of a way to show my commitment to doing so, both to them and to myself.

"Look you three, there's nothing I can do about the past except to say I'm sorry. It has been a particularly absorbing time at Weetflakes and I do find it difficult to switch off when I come home. Until today I would have said that times are easier now and that I would be able to spend more time with you, show more interest in my family. But then I learnt that Hill Benson, our merchant bankers, want to float Weetflakes on the Stock Exchange, which will require yet more of my time and a number of new, demanding challenges."

"So you're not going to be able to change?" asks Jean.

"Yes love, I am. Because tomorrow I'm going to ring Martin Egerton and tell him that the flotation needs to be postponed for at least twelve months. I may not tell him the full reason, but it will be so I can put everything right here. That's my bottom line."

"I'm pleased it is, Philip," says Jean, "because it's our bottom line too."

"Now," I say, "let me get out that champagne we didn't drink at Easter, so that we can toast our family."

One hour later, Jean and I go to bed to make love, really make love, for the first time for a long while.

Next morning I telephone Martin Egerton first thing, only to find that he's already in a meeting. I ask him to call me back urgently. I try again an hour later but he's still in his meeting. I suspect that he's already talking to his flotation specialists.

About 11.30 he calls me back and, before I can say anything, he says, "Phil, great news. The flotation guys say we're on but they say it must be this Autumn, after which they expect a market downturn. So there's no time to lose."

"Martin," I say, "I tried to call you earlier. I've been thinking it over and I'd rather leave it for twelve months. I just don't think I'm able to give the necessary time right now, without it having adverse implications elsewhere."

"Nonsense, Phil. Autumn has to be the deadline. That's the bottom line. And I've already talked to Hill Benson's chairman about the way to solve the problem of your time and commitment."

"How's that?" I ask, feeling a sense of defeat and foreboding.

"Well, he's agreed for me to be seconded three days a week to Weetflakes. Thus I can work with you closely, taking some of the load off your shoulders. You'll need to give a great deal of time but I'll be there by your side. And I can promise you a share option scheme that will make you a millionaire this time next year. You're not going to say no to that, are you Phil?"

I pause for a moment, feeling that I'm making a choice that will determine the direction of the rest of my life.

"No, of course I'm not, Martin," I say, "an Autumn flotation will be my bottom line too."

I spend the rest of the day, amid rising excitement, breaking the news to my team and preparing them for another managing change project. I can feel them all being turned on by the tremendous new vision which it provides for Weetflakes.

As I drive home that evening and park my car in front of the home of which I expected so much, I keep telling myself that surely Jean and the children will understand. But deep down I know they won't. I've made my choice, recognised my personal bottom line, and I'll have to live the rest of my life with the consequences.

Commentary

Within the format of a novel it is not always possible

1) to include every possible view and argument about key issues;
2) to stress those learning points which are of higher priority than others and therefore need reinforcement;
3) to challenge the actions and thought processes of the leading characters.

This Commentary is therefore intended to supplement the main content with chapter notes which fill these gaps. It has been prepared by the author in consultation with behavioural tutors and managing change specialists Mark Ryan and Bryn Jones, who are his colleagues at the Management Training Partnership (MTP). Many of the frameworks and learning points in the book itself also come from the work of Mark, Bryn and the rest of the behavioural team at MTP.

Where there are no comments about a particular chapter, this is because there is no need to expand on the text or because the content is primarily storyline.

Chapter 4

- The style of the novel means that we are privy to the thought processes of Philip Moorley (PM) in a way that is never possible in real life. Thus we will try not to be judgemental about what he thinks (how many of us would seem similarly insecure if people knew what we were thinking?) and focus on what he says and does. However, we can reinforce some key learning points which arise from his thought processes. This chapter shows clearly how he was thinking of bringing in new people to Weetflakes even before he entered the gates, and the underlying reason is his own insecurity. It is not good practice to have such a preconceived view when approaching a challenging managing change project such as this one.

● Some people in Andrew Kent's 'headhunting' role might question whether his briefing on the journey up to Claydon was too prejudiced and would be likely to distort PM's views before the interview. It might even have contributed to PM's desire to bring in outsiders to support him. Would it have been better to leave PM to make up his own mind? On the other hand, it must have been helpful for him to be aware of the power structure beforehand. Perhaps this could have been achieved with a slightly less judgemental stance about the individuals involved.

Chapter 5

● Though it is not part of the objectives of this book to cover interviewing, it is worth highlighting the poor, one-way technique of Arthur Stocks at the beginning of this chapter. It is tempting for people like Arthur to see the interview as an opportunity to talk to a captive audience, rather than to ask open-ended questions and listen.

● This interview is the first mention of a key issue which recurs many times in later parts of the book – the need to take into account the exisiting culture when managing change. Particularly revealing is the information from Martin and Arthur that the previous MDs failed to take this into account when deciding on the speed and style of change. They underestimated the inbuilt resistance to change at Weetflakes and made the mistake of using language and methods which were inappropriate, e.g. "memos", "full of jargon". Also evident is Arthur's passive attitude and the fact that he distanced himself from the previous MDs. PM should be noting these points for the future, realising that Arthur's support could be a critical success factor.

Chapter 6

- It was helpful that PM was able to read the strategic plan before he started at Weetflakes. It enabled him to see that the plan itself was based on sound logic and an analysis of distinctive competencies. It was however 'counter culture', challenging many of the company's traditional strengths such as the strong brand and the Claydon location. It should have helped him to see that the problems were in the processes of implementing strategy, not the strategy itself.

- If Alan Angus (AA) had been assisting at this point in the story he might have pointed out to PM the difference between rational and emotional responses to change. Seeing the need to change at a rational level is a relatively easy process; coping with it at an emotional level is much more difficult. And when people are put under pressure, it is the emotional response which prevails. No doubt the previous MDs were logical, rational people, and perhaps they found it difficult to appreciate the emotional reactions of others at Weetflakes. Unless the people involved buy into change, it is unlikely to happen. Thus the emotional responses have to be overcome.

Chapter 7

- AA is quick to seize upon the issue which Christine Goodhart had probably warned him about after the telephone conversation between her and PM – PM's tendency to see replacing people as the easy answer to the problem of managing change. His way of persuading PM away from this easy temptation is sound – encouraging PM to see change as a total process with many possible approaches to achieving success.

- The issue raised early in the chapter, about whether managing change is no more than a cliché, needs to be explored further. It is true that all management, to some extent, involves the management of change. The argument for making it into a separate topic which, for instance, justifies special treatment in this book, is the very considerable benefit which comes from seeing it as a total process. This is already coming through as AA warns PM not to rush into hasty, isolated action at a point where the process has hardly begun. This benefit is not confined to total company culture changes such as the one faced by PM, it also applies to smaller-scale projects carried out by operational managers.

- The definition of culture – "the way we do things around here" – comes from Roger Plant's book *Managing Change and Making it Stick*. It's a helpful way of expressing what culture means in an organisation – it defines the limits of what is acceptable behaviour, based on norms and values which may go back generations. If someone, however senior, goes outside the norms of acceptable behaviour, there will be problems. Cultures can, of course, be changed, but it is usually a longer and more difficult process than is expected by the outsider.

- AA's introduction of the BA story was sensible and particularly appropriate for someone like PM – senior, practical, cynical – for whom an example from a company with such a good reputation is worth much more than theoretical frameworks. Angus could perhaps have made even more of the relevance of BA to the task facing PM – how the top management of BA saw that the existing culture was the key barrier to their achieving competitive advantage from improved customer service. They did not try to cut the process short but managed change in a planned, realistic way, making sure the internal culture was right before trying to change behaviour towards customers.

- Those who are familiar with McKinseys' Seven S framework will note its similarity to AA's five ways of changing culture and will perhaps question why that wasn't introduced at this stage. The Seven S framework does appear in subsequent chapters (first in Chapter 13) and is used by a later character as a checklist to ensure that all the various elements of change have been addressed.

- The brief mention of PM's successful move of a personnel man into a sales management role refers to an incident from *Beyond the Bottom Line* when PM was based in the USA. This kind of move can be a powerful stimulus to a particular type of change which is becoming increasingly essential in many companies – moving people out of their functional 'silos' so that they can think cross-functionally. It is also true, of course, that, if such a move proves unsuccessful, it can become a barrier to future changes of this kind.

- The point made by AA in relation to the autocratic style of people like Robert Maxwell should be reinforced. People who copy the behaviour of a role model who relies on unique personality characteristics to carry off his or her leadership style, are likely to fail. This applies particularly to autocratic and charismatic leaders – they can be admired if they are effective but cannot necessarily be copied.

- AA introduces Tom Peters' work as a way of warning PM about the dangers of easy, instant solutions to complex issues of change. This is a valid point. It is, however, perhaps a little unfair to Peters (and Waterman) who, for all the weaknesses of their approach, did help to put more focus on the 'softer' issues involved in strategy and change. The enormous success of *In Search of Excellence* ensured that these issues – particularly the importance of culture and values – were opened up to a large audience.

- It is not always appreciated how important the first few weeks are in a new job, particularly at this level, and it is good that PM has the chance to discuss his intentions with someone who knows the pitfalls. The problem lies in achieving the right balance between doing too little and doing too much, keeping all options open while not appearing to be too easily persuaded. Later chapters give examples of PM's problems in achieving this balance.

- There is a fairly brief reference near the end of this chapter to the role of various methods of communication in changing beliefs and attitudes. The important message here is that there is no one method which is likely to be effective on its own. The vital need is to plan a mix of methods and media which suits the people and the culture. Later chapters cover the use of training courses, something which, it could be argued, Weetflakes introduced rather late in its change process. Most specialists in this area would agree with PM and AA that one-way communication methods are unlikely to be effective on their own. It is highly dangerous to assume that the company newsletter, video or briefing document will be absorbed by everyone. As the BA example shows most powerfully, the personal presence and visible commitment of top management should support communication methods if they are to be effective.

- AA is giving PM sound advice throughout this chapter and he rounds it off with perhaps the best advice of all – don't try to impose styles and solutions which have worked sucessfully before. Each culture is different and styles need to be adapted, not adopted. The history of business is littered with casualties who forgot this simple but important rule.

- The importance of vision is mentioned as AA's final point in this chapter and it will be developed later in more detail. This concept of vision is probably familiar to many at the company or business unit level, but is perhaps less commonly thought of as a requirement for managing change on a project or departmental basis. Yet, even at this lower level of operation, it is just as necessary to have a vision to inspire and drive change.

Chapter 8
- Here we see attempts by PM to apply the advice given by AA, to achieve the right balance between holding back and asserting himself. Generally he seems to achieve this fairly well, perhaps overdoing the assertiveness towards the end of the chapter and jeopardising the important relationship with Freddie Stocks (FS). Yet it is easy to understand and sympathise with his desire not to be controlled by the Stockses.

- The 'TAGG' manager is an interesting concept,

developed in real life by a large chemical company which was concerned at the apparent success of that type of individual. How many organisations reward and promote on the strength of what is said rather than what is done?

- PM's tendency to make quick, sometimes unfair judgements about people is shown in this chapter, particularly in relation to Freddie, Willis and Amanda. In his favour is the fact that he often expresses guilt about these judgements and, in later chapters, admits that he was wrong, particularly about FS.

Chapter 9
- This chapter highlights that, despite all the good advice he has received, PM has rushed into hasty conclusions about the problems and solutions. Perhaps this shows how difficult it can be to change the naturally impetuous tendencies of someone with a large amount of experience.
- It is tempting to be critical of Martin Egerton's confidential visit to see PM, because it is outside the normal channels and behind the backs of the Stockses. Since the company has lost three MDs, it is perhaps understandable and would probably be appreciated by anyone in PM's position, particularly if there were early problems. This is perhaps a case of pragmatism overcoming business ethics.
- On a number of occasions during this book, there are discussions about the value of the change cycle and the extent to which it is practical to apply in real life situations. The position can best be summarised as follows:
  a. It is intended to give structure to the change process, particularly for people like PM who tend to rush into instant solutions.
  b. It does not always happen in a sequential, stage by stage progression because life is not like that. Over the period of time when change is implemented, the status quo is constantly changing.
  c. Thus, while retaining the vision as a constant, there

will be a regular need to re-evaluate the current
situation in the light of changes to the status quo.

d. The main value of the change cycle is as a discipline
and a checklist to ensure that stages are not
overlooked.

e. The 13-stage change cycle is a composite version
used for this book in order to cover all aspects of
change. There are shorter, simpler versions which
capture the essential elements and convey the
general principles.

f. It is not a replacement for other approaches to
change, merely an overall framework which should
be capable of incorporating others. For instance, it is
pointed out in Chapter 15 that driving forces are
needed to move the process from one stage to
another. Therefore Force Field Analysis can help to
assess the balance of drivers against resistors and see
whether more drivers are required.

- AA's point about the common failure of top people to
communicate their vision may be a little sweeping but is
nevertheless valid. In our training work we frequently
come across companies where we know the vision and
the strategy but the managers who are being trained do
not.

- PM's argument that there are limits to how far you can
change people is sound. This is only one example of how
well AA and PM balance each other. Like many
specialists in behaviour and change, AA perhaps believes
that change in behaviour should always be possible,
given skilful management of the person concerned. This
is a rather idealistic view which it is right to challenge.
The danger of PM's view is that you give up too early
and adopt his preferred easy option of bringing in new
people.

- AA's encouragement to look at the positive
characteristics of the Stocks brothers is a good example
of the benefit of an outside consultant who can
encourage more balanced thinking by the use of
facilitation and questioning skills. This is particularly
powerful with someone like PM who often seems to see

negatives rather than positives when meeting new people. He has also shown a tendency in the previous two books to become quite polarised about people, classifying colleagues as 'goodies' or 'baddies' and allowing his judgements to become self-perpetuating.

● 'Requirements of a vision statement' could perhaps be improved by a reference to measurability, which is in fact added in the next chapter.

Chapter 10

● PM's frustration with the Board meeting agenda is understandable. Management of meetings is not part of the content of this book, but it is worth mentioning how poor it can often be, particularly by those at high level. Yet frequently the weakness is overlooked or accepted by those who suffer from it.

● PM should clearly have had an individual meeting with FS earlier. Discussions in public, particularly at meetings with a number of people present, often fail to reflect the true person and the true relationship.

● PM is quick to spot FS's tendency to be over-critical of others; he is, perhaps, not always so good at spotting it in himself.

● PM illustrates his own weakness by his negative dismissal of Ernie Taylor – "one of the worst performers of all". In later chapters we will see how this weakness adversely affects the process of managing change.

● There is an interesting contrast between the Stocks brothers' reactions to the encounters with PM. FS seems to value the opportunity to have a more informal discussion; WS feels threatened by it, perhaps preferring the more superficial contact of public encounters. This should give PM some insight into the underlying insecurity felt by WS, despite his confident behaviour in public.

● The meetings with Freddie, Willis and Arthur reveal how essential it is, in a family business, to know as much as possible about the relationships and underlying tensions. AA's advice to find out more about the winners and losers of change has enabled PM to manage the change process with much more insight into the motivation of the key players.

- The first draft vision statement seems to meet the criteria in AA's briefing. It could be criticised as being rather short, but it is better to be that than too long. It does lack quantified measures against which performance can be assessed, but PM later accepts the need to set specific goals on profitability and customer satisfaction. The latter is obviously more difficult than the former, but there are now many examples of companies which have introduced regular customer feedback processes to monitor performance in the areas which are important to success. In this case Weetflakes needs to introduce systems which measure its customers' perceptions of its innovation, flexibility, co-operation and value for money.

Chapter 11

- PM's judgement in confiding to FS about Julian and Amanda could be questioned. That kind of discovery creates a dilemma which it is usually very difficult to resolve satifactorily, and we do not offer PM's actions as examples of correct or incorrect behaviour in such circumstances.

- Our behavioural specialists at MTP have some doubts about AA's wisdom in suggesting a change of organisation structure this early. Though it obviously helps to have a structure which relates to organisational processes, there is no obvious evidence that the present structure is ineffective or would provide a significant obstacle to change. The argument for keeping the present structure is that it provides an element of stability; changing it could add to the general uncertainty and insecurity. There will be new interpersonal relationships to become used to and this may distract people from the vision. Even if the outcome may be better in the long term, in the short term it could create uncertainty and slow down the change process. A better time for reorganisation could be after most of the implementation has taken place, as part of the reinforcement of the new state. Perhaps AA is being too ambitious too early, particularly as he admits that the emphasis on processes is a relatively new approach to organisation design.

● The process model developed by AA builds on the 'value chain' work of Harvard's Michael Porter and is very close to the models actually developed by a number of UK FMCG companies. If any readers would like further information, it may be possible to arrange contact with a company which has applied this model in practice – contact (0) 1296 23474, Alan Warner.

● AA refers briefly to another benefit of analysing processes which is outside the scope of this book – its potential for increasing efficiency and reducing cost. The three companies quoted (and many more) are increasingly using BPR (Business Process Re-engineering) to analyse and then rationalise their business processes. Again, telephone the above number if you require more information.

● As a former business school tutor who moved into consultancy, the author is perhaps not fully objective when discussing the value of academic research into management topics. It is, nevertheless, an interesting issue which is rarely debated – do business schools lead or follow in the quest for new ideas? The author's view is that they tend to follow more than is widely believed; they research, conceptualise and package what the best companies are already doing. This is not to deny the value of this service, merely to put it into context. It does therefore follow that training consultants who are in touch with 'best in class' companies can provide a short cut to the process by transferring knowledge from one organisation to another.

● PM is right to challenge and overrule AA's desire to be rigid about the link between processes and organisation structure. The people issues also need to be considered, and PM is entitled to act on his belief that Martin Moss needs an increase in status which reporting to FS would not achieve. All organisation structures have ultimately to be a compromise between rational and emotional factors, between processes and people.

- The decision to make those responsible for day to day brand management report to the sales/customer management side has already been taken in real life by a number of companies in the FMCG sector. It reflects the reality of marketing via retail outlets – that all promotional and pricing decisions have to be taken in close liaison with major customers.
- It is arguable whether 'quality' should be a separate function. The argument against this is that quality should be an essential part of the management of every function, and to set it aside as someone's specific responsibility is to give the opposite message. PM seems to understand this argument as he says, "for the time being, until quality has been made an integral part of supply chain management, quality control needs to be powerful and independent." The aim should be that, eventually, the quality function will become unnecessary as supply chain managers are trained to follow the principles of quality management.
- PM seems to be following his 'black and white' tendency towards people by writing off Julian Weatherall. Perhaps AA could have encouraged him to think more positively about his strengths, as he did with FS and WS earlier.
- There is a danger that PM and AA are putting too much emphasis on the formal structure in their planning. They should bear in mind that informal relationships also matter in organisations and that the new structure will not necessarily change these. This could be another argument for delaying formal organisational change – people have a habit of working out the necessary communication channels, whatever the formal structure.

Chapter 12
- Again PM experiences the benefit of seeing the key influencers on an individual basis. This is perhaps even more beneficial when operating in a new culture, where the game playing and political undertones which affect behaviour at meetings are not known to the newcomer.
- PM's judgement in leaving WS to resolve the problem with his father could be questioned. Showing trust and

empowering people are to be welcomed, but the complex dynamics of a father/son relationship are likely to make this a high risk strategy. PM should have used his good relationship with Arthur to maximum effect and made the offer himself (though, as AA correctly points out, the offer was always going to be rejected because it did not meet Arthur's needs).

- Though it is easy to appreciate PM's reasons for wanting Julian Weatherall off the premises quickly, this kind of instant dismissal can have a negative effect on an organisation's morale, even more so than allowing the dissident to work out his or her notice. While it is right for PM to move quickly and to plan the timing of the announcements carefully, there is a strong case for seeing Julian first, in order to assess his mood and find out his preferences.

Chapter 13

- Marie Goodhart (MG) introduces some of the reservations about the change cycle which were discussed in the notes to Chapter 9. There is no need to repeat the points made there, except to say that if it has helped PM and others in his situation to manage change, it must be a valid framework. MG is perhaps guilty of unnecessary polarisation in her desire to make an impression – it need not be the change cycle *or* the Seven S framework, there is room for both.
- The Seven S framework can be more than a post hoc checklist for change management, it can provide a total structure for the planning of culture change. Then the interesting issue arises of where to start. Are 'shared values' the starting point from which the strategy should follow? Or should the strategy determine the shared values which then need to be communicated and internalised? There are no easy answers – all depends on the priorities of the stakeholders and top managers – but this framework encourages such a debate to take place.
- MG's reference to PM's life being "uncluttered" is a valid comment on the way the story has concentrated only on the change issues. In real life the manager of

change has many more variables to cope with, particularly when he or she is operating at a lower level. In those circumstances the actions of others at a higher level are likely to make the change process even more unpredictable and difficult to manage on a stage-by-stage basis.

- As McKinseys – an actual firm – is quoted in Marie's dialogue, it is important to qualify what is said. McKinseys would perhaps argue that they develop their approaches to change management in line with company needs and changes in the business environment, rather than "as one fad wears off and another comes along".

Chapter 14

- PM's discovery that AA's 'five ways of changing culture' and MG's 'Seven S' model are very similar reinforces what has been said earlier. Frameworks may overlap but, if they are helpful to managers at any stage of the change process, they are valid. Arguments about which one is 'best' are unlikely to be fruitful.
- MG is right to question whether only lip-service is paid to shared values. PM is probably unlikely to glean valid information from meetings with staff whose careers are dependent upon him. This is a good illustration of the sort of task which a Personnel Director can carry out for a Chief Executive – an example of how well MG understands her role.
- Another example is MG's commitment to introducing performance management systems. PM's feeling that people will shy away from appraisals if there is no formalised system is true of many managers. If MG can introduce a system which is conplementary to the culture and ensure that the performance objectives link to the business plan, she will have made an enormous contribution to the implementation of the new strategy.
- It is yet another benefit of the 'Seven S' framework in this chapter that it effectively becomes a checklist for the development of immediate priorities for the new Personnel Director. The practice of relating required skills to the new strategy is a particularly powerful

example of its use.

● MG's behaviour on her first day is perhaps excessive and contrasts with suggestions in earlier chapters that it is best to adopt a low profile in the first few weeks. But this appears to be a case of a unique personality who can, and probably has to, break all the rules and get away with it.

● MG's emphasis on certainty reinforces the doubts raised about changing the organisation structure in the notes to Chapter 11. How far this should overrule the desire to reorganise in line with processes is a matter of judgement. AA should perhaps have raised the danger of uncertainty before PM agreed to reorganise.

Chapter 15

● It is typical of his sort of insecure personality that PM is surprised how well he is regarded by those underneath him. It would be interesting, but probably impossible, to know how many Chief Executives are unaware of the respect (or disrespect?) which others have for them. 'Seeing yourself as others see you' is not a quality often met at top level.

● MG is right to point out how cultures such as that at Weetflakes do not become open overnight. Management of people and organisations should never be based on what is said, but on expectations of what people will do. By checking on this first, MG is playing a valuable part in managing the change process.

● MG's point about empowerment requiring managers with drive is one which is easily overlooked. This is valid to some extent in all circumstances, but particularly in cases such as this where significant change is required.

● MG makes a fairly brief reference to Force Field Analysis, so it is important to stress its wider potential as an aid to managing change. First it helps to identify the obstacles to change which need to be removed, as well as encouraging the development of new drivers. Secondly it can become an analytical framework which is used to monitor progress at several stages along the change cycle. How far have the new drivers been effective; have resistors been lessened or removed?

One difficulty of using Force Field Analysis is in applying valid weightings to the various drivers and resistors. Some of those who use the framework try to apply such weightings and display them by the length of a line from the centre. Such quantifications can, however, become spurious and can turn people away from what is otherwise a helpful framework. The use of the Pareto (80/20) principle is a more effective way of agreeing priorities and providing focus on the key drivers and resistors.

- MG makes a powerful point when she challenges PM's tendency to look for structural solutions (hence his easy acceptance of AA's recommendation to change the organisation structure). Her view that "if people don't have the necessary drive and are only paying lip-service to change, they will find a hundred perfectly valid ways to let day to day priorities hold them back", is worth repeating and stands on its own. The secret is to obtain commitment and MG is right to point out the potential benefit of a profit sharing bonus in achieving this.

- Recruiting types who will fill gaps in the current personality profile of the management team is perfectly valid. If more driving personalities are needed, this should become a factor in the recruitment decision. The difficult issue is how far this should dominate the decision when so many other factors – technical skill, experience, other personality features – have to be taken into account. Again, this has to be a question of personal judgement.

- The failure of MG and PM to think before of training as a driver of change may seem a little unrealistic. But it is very common for HR executives to see training as something which is used only to reinforce change, not to support it while it is taking place. Another common fault is to see managing change and training as separate issues, rather than as two activities which support each other.

Chapter 16

- The importance of the right venue for high profile training is frequently underrated. Good training ideas can be spoilt or diluted by misguided attempts to save money or by lack of attention to detail in the selection process.

- PM's interactive style is a good way of starting this kind of event. Too often Chief Executives who 'open' a course feel that they have to talk at their people for an hour or two; they are then surprised when 'any questions?' is met with a stony silence.

- Some might question the financial orientation of the opening session, but if PM's objective is to convince his people of the need for change, and that *not* changing is the riskiest option of all, the concept of return on investment is a powerful and justified approach. Though it is not clear from the text exactly what follows the introduction, there would clearly need to be coverage of the qualitative aspects of the plan in order to create the right balance.

- The statement in the text that the opening session was intended to remove all possible uncertainties is a good example of effective linkage of course design to a clear training objective.

- The use of the phrase "ten commandments" could be challenged as contrary to the principles of flexibility and adaptation. Perhaps "guidelines" would be more appropriate, though not more attention catching. They are in the book as a summary and reinforcement of earlier content, with the added references to the need for updating and contingency planning.

- The reference to the potential of any manager in the chain to wreck everything is obvious but nevertheless fundamental. It confirms the need for comprehensive training and monitoring of the effectiveness of communication. There is further reference to the need for monitoring, and how PM deals with it, in Chapter 20.

Chapter 17

- There may be some who would argue that a course of this kind should not have a wide variation of management levels attending it, particularly in an organisation such as Weetflakes with its recent history of autocratic style and family traditions. How far are the less confident, lower level managers able to participate? Against that can be set the potential benefits of breaking down barriers and bringing in different perspectives. The key tests must be – will it inhibit, will it prevent openness, will it cause tension? If not, there must be a strong case for as wide a mix as possible.

- The interchanges on catharsis and letting go should stand on their own, but there is one piece of dialogue which is important enough to need repeating, that is, "Don't think that listening and understanding is doing nothing." One of the manager's roles in change is to be a sympathetic listener to those whose lives are affected by it. Far from doing nothing, this is actively contributing to the change process.

- Christine Goodhart (CG) was right to stress the importance of establishing standards of work which give meaning to the concept of commitment. PM's intervention that such standards must be linked to the business plan is also important and this is a factor which the control processes must monitor.

- This chapter places great emphasis on commitment, which should be the ultimate goal for the achievement of lasting change. Frequently, however, this has to be balanced against the time available. The option of compliance should not be excluded if it is felt that a long drawn out attempt to gain commitment could be seen as indecisiveness by those players who have already accepted the need for change.

- Recent interest in the concept of empowerment is perhaps likely to make cynics like PM and FS see it as nothing new – "another word for delegation" is a frequently heard criticism. CG's way of linking it to managing change and seeing it as "a crucial step in managing change and making it stick" is very powerful. If people are empowered, the change is more likely to last and there will eventually be less need for detailed control.

- The encounter between CG and FS on empowerment is

worth reinforcing. First it exposes Freddie's lack of understanding of empowerment; he wants "people who will do things when you tell them to", not people who are empowered to make their own decisions within an agreed framework. CG again relates empowerment to managing change by saying that it is not necessarily the right style of management for all people in all organisations. It is, however, a style that works very effectively when you require people to bring about fundamental change. FS is, of course, right to say that ultimately it depends on the quality of the people and the extent to which you can gain their commitment. The danger is that managers like FS never even give it a try. As CG says, people who are empowered will normally do more than their superiors previously expected.

- PM's intervention when he agrees to offer support for risk taking and occasional mistakes is most helpful. Empowering people requires courage and the penalty for occasional errors of judgement should not be too high.

- The emphasis on tackling the causes of resistance rather than the symptoms is correct for another reason. It helps one to take action early, rather than waiting for problems to arise.

- PM's open style did not extend to encouraging course discussion about his predecessors' problems, even though he knew that they had been discussed earlier in his absence. It is not clear what held him back, but he may have lost an opportunity here. There are obviously limits to his openness.

- PM's poor treatment of Ernie may have been merely because he didn't like him very much. He was perhaps bored by Ernie's role and was attracted to the more dynamic personality and function of Stephen Young. It's easier to say than to do, but, when managing the change process, you should not differentiate between those you like and those you don't. All managers should, from time to time, assess whether their treatment of individuals is distorted by personal like or dislike.

- CG's judgement may be affected by her own personal feelings, but it is questionable whether she should have been quite so supportive, even sycophantic, towards PM. It might cause her to be seen as less credible and objective as a tutor. It might also rebound by causing the more rebellious course members to reject her opinions.

Chapter 18

- There is further evidence in this chapter of how PM allowed his preference for the company of the 'younger turks' to let him forget about the needs of less attractive people such as Ernie Taylor. It is good that he is so open about this, both to himself and later to Ernie. The quiet types like Ernie are the easiest to neglect, yet they are often the ones who need the greatest attention in the process of managing change.

- Despite the signs of insecurity which he shows regularly in his thinking, it requires some confidence and courage to be as open as PM has chosen to be. He will have to be careful how much he uses that self-deprecating style in a culture where 'the bosses' have always been seen to be right. There is a danger that there could be a loss of faith and respect if he moves too far too quickly.

- PM hits on one of the key qualities of effective change management which he has clearly failed to apply to Ernie Taylor – the ability to "think of the person who is experiencing change, to try to feel what he or she is feeling". If that was achieved in every case, there would be far fewer problems in change management.

- PM might have taken a risk when deciding that using first names will be a symbol of his new relationship with Ernie. Such changes can be far more difficult to bring about than people think, particularly when it clashes with decades of tradition.

- PM is perhaps discovering rather belatedly the benefits of 'MBWA' – management by walking about. Maybe PM's problem is that he has seen the management of change as too much of a distant process, handled by plotting stages on a flipchart rather than by talking to people. It is encouraging that PM now accepts the benefits of direct contact and resolves to change. It is also encouraging that he sees how his failure to keep in contact with Arthur has caused him to miss valuable advice.

- The other important insight he gains from his visit to the sharp end is the need to check constantly that the message is getting through and not to assume that the vision and the strategy have been passed on. This is one of the factors which later encourages him to put in regular control and feedback processes (see Chapter 20).

Chapter 19

- It is impressive that the primary course objective has been so clearly defined and related to the change strategy. The same comment applies to the specific objectives which relate closely to the 'Seven S' framework. This is a clear and positive benefit of using such a framework – it helped the course objectives to have focus and ensured that they covered all the areas of change which were required. It also enabled MG and PM to see what other follow-up training is likely to be required, e.g. training in appraisal skills.

- Measuring the effectiveness of management training is always going to be difficult, whatever the type or level of training. CG is quite right to make the point that what people can do after a course depends on the culture to which they return. For effectiveness to be measured perfectly, one needs to know how participants would have behaved if they had not been trained, which is clearly impossible. It is, however, much easier to measure the effectiveness of this training in overall strategic terms than it would be in the case of a course which did not relate so clearly to stated objectives. At least PM can see an output which relates to the business plan – people who have the shared values, style and systems knowledge to achieve the new strategy. If not, he can clearly question the value of the training, even if it may be difficult to apportion responsibility between the providers of the course and those responsible for implementation.

- CG's point that the training could and probably should have taken place earlier in the change cycle has some validity. There is evidence from the story that AA, PM and MG were so involved in other aspects of the change process that they simply didn't think of it. AA may be guilty of post-rationalisation by saying that it would have been too early, that the individual discussions with Freddie, Willis and Arthur had to take place first. However, it would clearly have been dangerous to proceed with courses which people like Freddie were to attend, if the relationships and the commitment were not right.

- CG's emphasis that the course is only the beginning of the change process for those who attended could be seen as defensive and a failure to take responsibility. But the point is clearly valid. Participants can leave a course with a great deal of motivation and shared values, only to find that others do not share their enthusiasm. Thus there is a need for planned reinforcement of the new behaviours and follow-up training for all those who are in key positions to influence change.

- Team briefings constitute a systematic approach to passing information to the workforce. Regular meetings are organised for all the key teams in the organisation and the implications of the strategy are described. PM is right to reject such a formal, structured approach if he feels that he needs more flexibility. He also wants more than to ensure that information is passed down – he wants to be able to assess whether new behaviours are being retained. Thus his desire for the development of a two-way process, tailored to the needs of each group, makes sense.

- The skills of feedback would clearly be a useful addition to the course because, in cultures similar to that which Weetflakes has been in the past, such skills are not valued. It could be argued that feedback is so important that there should be separate training. There is a danger that this three-day course could be trying to do too much.

- MBWA was given an attractive label by Peters, but it has been a crucial ingredient of success for many entrepreneurs over the years. What is good here is that

PM has a specific objective in doing it – "to reinforce the new behaviours, to give the positive feedback which Weetflakes managers find hard to give". This is better than doing MBWA just because it's trendy.

Chapter 20

- Meetings, or some other process which monitors progress against the plan, are an important but often forgotten part of the change process. It is easy for behaviour to slip back into old ways and for inertia to set in; thus regular review is necessary.

- The problems being experienced with Willis and Freddie illustrate how difficult it is to change the management styles of people who have become set in their ways in a traditional, autocratic culture. It is encouraging that PM still sees this as his main challenge for the future and is not accepting their behaviour in the long term.

- The idea of an external consultant to help a Chief Executive through a significant change such as a public flotation or an acquisition has much to recommend it. Too often the top person is thrown into a new situation which he or she has not encountered before and is faced with internal and external specialists who have their own personal objectives. Someone with no axe to grind and who is capable of giving good, common-sense advice should more than justify their cost.

- Becoming a quoted public company imposes many extra burdens on those in certain roles, particularly the Chief Executive and the Financial Director. The person at the top of the company has to acquire skills of communication to the outside world, the person at the top of the finance function has to acquire greater knowledge of corporate finance and stock exchange practice. An issue which PM will now have to face is whether, in addition to acquiring a new FD, there is a need for a different Chairman who has experience of the City and who will be respected by analysts and fund managers. This will be difficult to achieve without upsetting Arthur Stocks and those over whom he has influence. Yet another challenge in the never-ending task of managing change!

Chapter 21
- There is a serious point behind PM's problems at home. Anyone who goes into management needs to achieve the right balance between home and business life, a balance which suits personal needs and lifestyle. The principles of managing change should be applied in personal life too, to ensure that the vision is achieved. The visions of personal and business life should be compatible – otherwise something has to give.
- Philip Moorley seems to have achieved his career vision at the expense of his family.

The Goal
Beating the Competition
Second Edition

Eliyahu M Goldratt and Jeff Cox

Written in a fast-paced thriller style, *The Goal* is the gripping
novel which is transforming management thinking throughout
the Western world.

Alex Rogo is a harried plant manager working ever more
desperately to try to improve performance. His factory is rapidly
heading for disaster. So is his marriage. He has ninety days to
save his plant – or it will be closed by corporate HQ, with
hundreds of job losses. It takes a chance meeting with a colleague
from student days – Jonah – to help him break out of
conventional ways of thinking to see what needs to be done.

The story of Alex's fight to save his plant is more than compulsive
reading. It contains a serious message for all managers in
industry and explains the ideas which underlie the Theory of
Constraints (TOC) developed by Eli Goldratt – the author
described by Fortune as 'a guru to industry' and by
Businessweek as a 'genius'.

As a result of the phenomenal and continuing success of *The
Goal*, there has been growing demand for a follow-up. Eliyahu
Goldratt has now written ten further chapters which continues
the story of Alex Rogo as he makes the transition from Plant
Manager to Divisional Manager. Having achieved the turnround
of his plant, Alex now attempts to apply all that Jonah has taught
him, not to crisis management, but to ongoing improvement.

These new chapters reinforce the thinking process utilised in
the first edition of *The Goal* and apply them to a wider
management context with the aim of stimulating readers into
using the technique in their own environment.

1993   352 pages   0 566 07417 6 Hardback   0 566 07418 4 Paperback

Gower

It's Not Luck

Eliyahu M Goldratt

Alex Rogo has had a great year, he was promoted to executive vice-president of UniCo with the responsibility for three recently acquired companies. His team of former and new associates is in place and the future looks secure and exciting. But then there is a shift of policy at the board level. Cash is needed and Alex's companies are to be put on the block. Alex faces a cruel dilemma. If he successfully completes the turnaround of his companies, they can be sold for the maximum return, but if he fails, the companies will be closed down. Either way, Alex and his team will be out of a job. It looks like a lose-lose situation. And as if he doesn't have enough to deal with, his two children have become teenagers!

As Alex grapples with problems at work and at home, we begin to understand the full scope of Eli Goldratt's powerful techniques, first presented in *The Goal*, the million copy bestseller that has already transformed management thinking throughout the Western world. *It's Not Luck* reveals more of the Thinking Processes, and moves beyond *The Goal* by showing how to apply them on a comprehensive scale.

This book will challenge you to change the way you think and prove to you that it's not luck that makes startling improvements achievable in your life.

1994   288 pages   0 566 07637 3

Gower

The Noah Project
The Secrets of Practical Project Management

Ralph L Kliem and Irwin S Ludin

'David Michaels sat behind his mahogany desk, elevated his feet upon it, and then placed his arms behind his head. Everything at the zoo was running like a fine tuned engine. No problems. None. He had everything under control ...'

Until, that is, the Executive Director of the zoo announces that the zoo is to be sold, and completely dismantled in exchange for employment with the new company. David finds himself the project manager, with over 3,000 animals, from cockatoos to kangaroos, to relocate; and deadlines and the threat of redundancy looming if he fails.

This is a novel about project management. Although the characters are fictitious, the techniques, tools, and circumstances described ring true for just about any project in any environment, from technical to financial. David encounters common pitfalls such as failure to achieve targets on time, budgetary restrictions, an already unreasonable schedule cut back even further, and of course the inevitable staff conflict. And does he succeed in the end? Well, this isn't real life, but it could be ... would you have made it?

1994   208 pages   0 566 07439 7 Hardback   0 566 07469 9 Paperback

Gower

Stand and Deliver
The Fine Art of Presentation
Ralph L Kliem and Irwin S Ludin

David Michaels is afraid. His palms sweat. His knees threaten to buckle. And his tongue, like his stomach, seems to be tied in knots. For David is due to give a series of presentations.

His objective is to win support for his project to save sick children in Amazonia. Fortunately, help is at hand in the unlikely shape of Demosthenes, the 4th century Greek orator. Under his tutelage David overcomes his fears and learns how to create a powerful presentation. What he learns, he realises, can be applied to any presentation, large or small.

By following David as he gradually masters the techniques involved you will learn how to:

- define the audience
- determine what to say
- organize the content
- control nervousness
- deliver in style
- use visual aids
- deal with questions.

The fictional treatment makes this an entertaining as well as an informative guide. As an additional aid to learning the key points are summarized in checklist form at the end of the book. *Stand and Deliver* will be valued by all managers faced with the need to give effective presentations.

1995   200 pages   0 566 07574 1

Gower

Why Your Corporate Culture Change Isn't Working...

And What To Do About It

Michael Ward

- More than 80% of change programmes fail: this book looks at the reasons, and at how to avoid adding to this alarming statistic.

In his preface, Michael Ward warns that: 'DIY culture change makes about as much sense as DIY brain surgery.' Change is often seen as threatening. In order to effect an organization change it is essential to first understand the importance of the culture, and the impact change can have on employees, owners, consumers and suppliers – and therefore on the organization itself.

Management in the 1990s is about the successful management of change. Many organizations face radical change, as markets expand and contract, technology revolutionizes whole industries, companies merge, are taken over, go public, or go back to being private. Most people learn best from experience, and Michael Ward's approach is to illustrate principles and errors throughout with examples, from organizations considering change (often the point at which the most damaging mistakes are made), to examples of implementation – highlighting some of the more common errors. Each example follows the same structure of subject heading, narrative, discussion of relevant issues, key points, and concluding principles.

1994   168 pages   0 566 07434 6

Gower